A Fighting Chance

The Chances
Book 1

Emily E K Murdoch

© Copyright 2024 by Emily E K Murdoch
Text by Emily E K Murdoch
Cover by Dar Albert

Dragonblade Publishing, Inc. is an imprint of Kathryn Le Veque Novels, Inc.
P.O. Box 23
Moreno Valley, CA 92556
ceo@dragonbladepublishing.com

Produced in the United States of America

First Edition July 2024
Print Edition

Reproduction of any kind except where it pertains to short quotes in relation to advertising or promotion is strictly prohibited.

All Rights Reserved.

The characters and events portrayed in this book are fictitious. Any similarity to real persons, living or dead, is purely coincidental and not intended by the author.

ARE YOU SIGNED UP FOR DRAGONBLADE'S BLOG?

You'll get the latest news and information on exclusive giveaways, exclusive excerpts, coming releases, sales, free books, cover reveals and more.

Check out our complete list of authors, too!

No spam, no junk. That's a promise!

Sign Up Here

www.dragonbladepublishing.com

Dearest Reader;

Thank you for your support of a small press. At Dragonblade Publishing, we strive to bring you the highest quality Historical Romance from some of the best authors in the business. Without your support, there is no 'us', so we sincerely hope you adore these stories and find some new favorite authors along the way.

Happy Reading!

CEO, Dragonblade Publishing

Additional Dragonblade books by
Author Emily E K Murdoch

The Chances Series
A Fighting Chance (Book 1)

Dukes in Danger Series
Don't Judge a Duke by His Cover (Book 1)
Strike While the Duke is Hot (Book 2)
The Duke is Mightier than the Sword (Book 3)
A Duke in Time Saves Nine (Book 4)
Every Duke Has His Price (Book 5)
Put Your Best Duke Forward (Book 6)
Where There's a Duke, There's a Way (Book 7)
Curiosity Killed the Duke (Book 8)
Play With Dukes, Get Burned (Book 9)
The Best Things in Life are Dukes (Book 10)
A Duke a Day Keeps the Doctor Away (Book 11)
All Good Dukes Come to an End (Book 12)

Twelve Days of Christmas
Twelve Drummers Drumming
Eleven Pipers Piping
Ten Lords a Leaping
Nine Ladies Dancing
Eight Maids a Milking
Seven Swans a Swimming
Six Geese a Laying
Five Gold Rings
Four Calling Birds
Three French Hens
Two Turtle Doves
A Partridge in a Pear Tree

The De Petras Saga
The Misplaced Husband (Book 1)

The Impoverished Dowry (Book 2)
The Contrary Debutante (Book 3)
The Determined Mistress (Book 4)
The Convenient Engagement (Book 5)

The Governess Bureau Series
A Governess of Great Talents (Book 1)
A Governess of Discretion (Book 2)
A Governess of Many Languages (Book 3)
A Governess of Prodigious Skill (Book 4)
A Governess of Unusual Experience (Book 5)
A Governess of Wise Years (Book 6)
A Governess of No Fear (Novella)

Never The Bride Series
Always the Bridesmaid (Book 1)
Always the Chaperone (Book 2)
Always the Courtesan (Book 3)
Always the Best Friend (Book 4)
Always the Wallflower (Book 5)
Always the Bluestocking (Book 6)
Always the Rival (Book 7)
Always the Matchmaker (Book 8)
Always the Widow (Book 9)
Always the Rebel (Book 10)
Always the Mistress (Book 11)
Always the Second Choice (Book 12)
Always the Mistletoe (Novella)
Always the Reverend (Novella)

The Lyon's Den Series
Always the Lyon Tamer

Pirates of Britannia Series
Always the High Seas

De Wolfe Pack: The Series
Whirlwind with a Wolfe

Noble titles throughout English history have, at times, been more fluid than one/you might think. Women have inherited, men have been gifted titles by family or gained them on through marriage, and royals frequently lavished titles or withdrew them as reward and punishment.

The Chance brothers in this series agreed to split the four titles in their family line, rather than the eldest holding all four. It is a decision that defines their brotherhood, and their very different personalities.

Get ready to meet a family that is more than happy to scandalize Society...

Chapter One

May 5, 1812

THE HONORABLE MISS Alice Fox-Edwards—as she had once been—was not going to cry. Most definitely. Probably.

It was this brisk early morning air, Alice told herself as she strode purposefully through Hyde Park, carefully examining every gentleman that passed. That was all.

Not him.

Not him.

Not that one was walking arm in arm with a woman. Not worth the risk.

Her pulse was hammering painfully and her fingers felt numb, but Alice had made the decision and there was no going back. Mr. Shenton had been very clear about the money required, and there was no other option. She had to get it back.

She would simply have to find a husband at the swiftest opportunity, and that was that.

The handle of her reticule dug into her palm as she walked, the bag swinging by her side and knocking into the elegant muslin gown she had chosen for that day's efforts. A light blue, perfectly suiting her pale coloring and the almost white-blonde hair her lady's maid had piled upon her head that morning.

A little pink for the cheeks, a smile that hid her panic, and she was ready.

Alice swallowed as she passed a gaggle of ladies. Try as she might, it was impossible not to lower her head, ever so slightly.

It had been so long ago. Surely no one would remember—

"Dear Lord—is that Miss Fox-Edwards?"

"Who?"

"Miss Alice Fox-Edwards—you remember, there was that hint of scandal, four years past. You must have heard . . ."

Whatever it was the woman assumed her friend would have heard, Alice could not tell. Her pace had quickened just enough to end the possibility of hearing. Her escape, however, did not prevent her cheeks from reddening and a most discomforting twist in her stomach.

Botheration!

Staying away from London these last years had been not choice but necessity. And Alice had presumed enough time had passed, enough other ladies had come out into Society, that some had to have made more impressive mistakes than she had.

But apparently not. Her name was still known, spoken in such terms—

The sight of a woman just a few yards away, strolling along Hyde Park with what appeared to be her husband, made Alice's heart soften.

Miss Marnion.

Not *the* Miss Marnion, of course. The elder sister was still unmarried and, according to the scandal sheets Alice had managed to get her hands on the prior evening, was causing a bit of a rumpus by attracting the attention of two gentlemen who had already threatened a duel.

But this was the younger—Alice's friend.

Pulse thumping wildly, relief soaring through her veins, Alice made for her. Henrietta Marnion would understand—they had been bosom friends for the first Season of their coming out.

She was saved.

Trying desperately not to think just how close she had come to ruin, Alice stepped into the path of the woman who had been Miss Marnion and the person who was presumably her husband, and she smiled.

"My dear," she said, with as much friendliness as possible. "It seems ridiculous I do not know how to address you, it has been so long. You must introduce me to—"

Alice's voice broke. It was not the only part of her to shatter.

Without meeting her eyes, without speaking to her or nodding her head, without giving any indication whatsoever that Alice was even there, the former Miss Marnion strode on by, arm in arm with the gentleman who looked bewilderedly back at Alice over his shoulder.

Alice halted, her torso ice, her feet stone.

The Cut Direct.

She had only ever heard about it. Her mother had been most attentive to her education and ensured that she was well versed in the most disgracing way to behave to another person in public.

"You completely ignore them," her mother had said in a whisper, as though guilt could be attached merely by speaking of the wretched move. "To ignore a person after they have so publicly addressed you . . . it is the end of good Society. A woman who receives the Cut Direct is a fallen woman indeed."

Hot, prickling tears throbbed at the corners of her eyes. Alice tried desperately to prevent them falling.

This was not happening. It could not be. No one knew the full truth of her disgrace—she had been very careful about that. Even the gossips at the time had not quite understood the full depth of her mistake.

And yet Miss Marnion—or whatever her name was now—evidently no longer wished to court the friendship of the Honorable Miss Alice Fox-Edwards.

There was a strange ringing in her ears, a painful pitch which did not disappear when Alice swallowed.

What was she going to do?

"Did you see that? The Cut Direct—"

"Never would have believed it! She must have done something

terrible—"

"Yes, the Miss Fox-Edwards, and she's back in London!"

Almost without thinking Alice raised a hand to her forehead, which was beading perspiration, but the early May day was hardly temperate enough for such a response. It was the shame, the burning shame within her that was sparking such fervor through her head. Such heat she could not think, could not consider what to do.

She was right in the middle of Hyde Park. No matter how she attempted to retreat, she would have to pass innumerable people. People who would surely have heard of the scandal, gossip moving faster than the light spring breeze rustling the budding trees.

Alice's head spun.

Oh, this was intolerable. What had she been thinking, returning to London?

And then the reason why, the reason she had burdened herself with the decision she had made last night, swam back into her mind. Resolve steadied her and her head stopped spinning.

She had to do this. There was no other choice, and it was not just she who was depending on her plan's success.

Holding her head high and plastering a smile across her lips that Alice hoped no one would examine too closely, she shifted the chain of her blue velvet reticule farther up her arm and turned in a random direction.

Keep moving, that was it, Alice told herself. She couldn't hear the disgraceful comments about her personage, her character, her reputation if she kept moving.

The thought was, sadly, most incorrect.

"Oh, my goodness, it's you!"

Alice halted. She had not intended to, but there is something about a shriek like that which will stop anyone in their tracks.

Turning, she saw a matronly woman approaching her with an astonished expression in her eyes.

Alice sighed. *Hungry for gossip, no doubt.* Well, she should have expected this. Her mother, God rest her soul, had attempted to connect her with every respectable mama in London when Alice had come out into Society just five years ago. It was impossible to hope they had all forgotten about her.

When the woman finally reached her, panting from exertion, Alice tried to incline her head pleasantly. "Mrs. Howarth. How agreeable to see you."

"I would suppose it is, you coming here to London without a friend in the world, I'll be bound!" said Mrs. Howarth with a raised eyebrow.

Alice's smile faltered only slightly before she regained control. "I must say I don't know what you mean."

She knew precisely what the woman meant. Of course she did. But there appeared to be no way to extricate herself. Although perhaps it was not such a bad idea, having a civilized conversation with a woman of Society.

The civility departed rapidly.

"You should not be back in polite Society, you know," said Mrs. Howarth, a beady eye sweeping up and down Alice's attire. "Did you not know your reputation was quite ruined?"

Alice swallowed.

Reputation ruined. Two words any young lady in Society trembled to even consider.

When she had been but twenty . . .

Well, it had been the sort of thing that happened to other young ladies. Silly young ladies. Young ladies who did not take care of their person, who made wild decisions with most unsuitable men, and had to pay the consequences.

The thought that it could happen to someone she knew . . . to her . . .

"I do not believe anyone has anything to accuse me of," Alice said, as though they were discussing a particularly interesting recital.

But Mrs. Howarth did not appear convinced. "You can attempt to smile at me, young lady, but it won't wash! I heard that you were . . . well"—her cheeks reddened—"taken up, you see. By . . . by a gentleman."

Alice's pulse skipped a beat. "Yet here I am, perfectly respectable, without a gentleman."

More's the pity.

Mrs. Howarth did not seem to agree either. "But the outrage! Miss Fox-Edwards, you must remember—"

"I recall nothing of note," Alice lied, highly conscious of the glances sweeping her way.

If Mrs. Howarth were not careful, she would soon be tied to a woman whose reputation was loose at best.

"But you left London so suddenly all those years ago," Mrs. Howarth persisted, apparently deciding the opportunity to obtain gossip was worth the risk to her own reputation by associating with such a woman as Miss Alice Fox-Edwards. "There was such talk, rushing away halfway through the Season, something must have—"

"I was forced to return to Brighton due to my father's ill health," said Alice smoothly, trotting out the lie which had been given out at the time. A most convenient lie, if convenient was the right word. Her father had died not three months later. "He left us that summer, if you recall."

If she had hoped Mrs. Howarth would be cowed by the reminder of her loss, Alice was sorely disappointed.

The older woman waved a hand, as though wafting away the inconvenient truth of a deceased father. "Yes, yes, but why so suddenly? The rumors that circulated afterward—"

"I do not think I can be held accountable for the tittle-tattle of others," Alice said, in her best attempt at sternness. "Really, Mrs. Howarth, indulging in such rumormongering!"

And she saw immediately that she had gone too far.

Mrs. Howarth raised herself up with a snort of derision and fixed Alice with the beady gaze she remembered all too well from the last time she was in London. "Mark my words, Miss Fox-Edwards, you will not make many new friends in London with that attitude—and I say *new* friends, for I believe you are sorely in want of them. No one else will own you, will they? No, for all your fine words, I know something happened that Season, and your fallen reputation is, in my opinion, well deserved!"

And with that she flounced away, bonnet wobbling with the effort of retreating as far from the offending young miss as possible.

Alice swallowed. *Well, that could have gone worse*, she supposed. Though she wasn't sure precisely how.

Perhaps she should not have returned to London without greater preparations. She should have found... oh, an ally. A friend. A protector, an elderly woman perhaps that she could be a companion to.

But no. Alice had considered that, and it simply would not work. Being a companion to an elderly lady was all very well, but she needed ready money now. Mr. Shenton had been most clear in his latest letter. His patience would not continue forever, and the small shillings she had sent were simply not enough.

Blackmail.

It was not a word Alice had managed to speak aloud, but that was it, was it not? Blackmail. Or bribery, she was not totally sure. He had the document, and he refused to give it to her until she paid.

She needed a protector who was going to live for many years, give her the respectability that she so craved, and most importantly, who had money. Money she could access. She needed someone who could adore her enough not to ask difficult questions about the past. Someone who was besotted enough to overlook any hint of scandal, any whispers of wrongdoing.

Alice blinked away the tears and focused hard on what she knew had to happen. She had to find one.

A husband.

Or a man, at any rate. A man who was alone, a man who looked as though he was fortunate enough to be able to afford a wife and children. A man who looked kind, who appeared to have a great deal of sympathy for—

Alice shook her head with a wry expression and settled on the end of a bench in the dappled shade of a large oak tree. The two ladies at the other end took one look, noticed how everyone else was staring, and promptly rose from the bench.

Oh, it was going to be like that, was it?

Keeping her head resolutely high, Alice slowed her breathing, hoping the thrum of her pulse was not audible to anyone else.

So. A husband. All she had to do was find one.

There were not actually, as she quickly discovered, that many gentlemen walking alone. Almost all of them were accompanying ladies, which made it rather difficult.

The gentle spring breeze rustled the hem of her skirt, but Alice did not bother attempting to adjust it. Her attention had become fixed on a gentleman of great height and severe look. He marched past Alice, a scowl darkening his features.

No. A man like that would surely be most unsuitable.

Another man caught her eye, mostly because of the bright bottle green of his greatcoat. He caught the eye of a great many ladies, as far as Alice could see, and could therefore be discounted. She did not wish to argue over a man like a ribbon in a haberdasher's.

What felt like hours later, Alice was almost ready to give up and return to the lodgings she had taken with what little funds she had left. This had been a ridiculous idea. Wander Hyde Park and find a husband, as though she were choosing to have a gown made to order at the modiste?

What had she been thinking?

It was because she was brushing her skirts in distraction, removing a few errant leaves and annoyed at the waste of the day, that she did not immediately spot them.

A trio of men.

True gentlemen. One only had to look at their comportment to see they were entirely respectable. All were wearing jackets of what appeared to be the latest fashion—Alice had only been in London a few days and was still acclimatizing to style's changes—and one was holding a cane which appeared to be topped by a sphere of marble.

They were brothers. Alice did not need to examine their calling cards to know that. The same dark brown hair appeared on all three of their heads, though one's brightened slightly in the sunlight. And they all had the same sharp jaws, the same glittering eyes.

Standing just far enough from her to be examined without reproach, and sadly too far for Alice to hear their conversation, she watched them through her eyelashes, pretending she was searching for something in her reticule.

They appeared to be arguing.

Well, that's what it looked like. One appeared to be remonstrating with the other two, neither of whom were taking his words seriously, as far as she could make out.

Alice's gaze drifted over the one trying to keep the others under control.

He was... handsome. Charming, even. There was something intriguing about the sparkling sky-blue eyes that were at such odds with his dark hair. He held himself well, though his shoulders were slumping with defeat as his two companions spoke over him.

Alice swallowed, trying her best to be as mercenary as possible.

He was wealthy. At least, he was wearing a twill jacket with an impressive gold silk waistcoat catching the sun. His cravat was tied in an impressive *Sentimentale* knot, so he must have a valet of skill and style.

And he seemed . . . caring.

Alice straightened up as the man she had been observing separated from the other two and started to stride along the path.

Handsome, wealthy, and caring. That was enough.

Trying not to make it too noticeable precisely what she was about, Alice started to follow him. Not too closely, obviously. It would never do for anyone to guess what she was doing. Not that anyone would be likely to guess at her intentions even if they did notice her. No one would be so foolish as to think one could just select a husband in Hyde Park.

He was walking sedately, thank goodness, so Alice was not forced into breathlessness to keep behind him. The trouble was, how to make the introduction? How, in short, to guarantee that he would have to marry her?

The gentleman took a turn to the left, making for a shortcut only gentlemen ever took through a small woodland to the Lancaster Gate.

Yes, that was it.

Falling back, she turned left also but quickened her pace. It was imperative she met with him within the wooded area itself. Yes, that would be perfect.

Her heart hammered as trickles of doubt started to seep into her mind.

Was this truly the only way she could rescue herself? Was she so desperate that she would forgo all manner of civility, and give up all hope of true happiness?

"You're being a fool, Alice Fox-Edwards," she muttered to herself.

Then immediately regretted it. It was all very well muttering to no one in particular when she had been living in her parents' old home. But debts had to be repaid, and Mr. Shenton had made it perfectly clear what he would do if she were not forthcoming. And now she was out in the world. She couldn't just talk to herself!

And that was precisely why she had to find a husband, wasn't it?

There was no more money—at least, precious little. When that ran out, she would not be the only one who was doomed.

Her resolve hardened. She would make an excellent wife for someone. All she had to do was find that someone.

She had to hope it was the gentleman she was following.

His footsteps were increasing in pace and Alice sturdied herself to do what must be done. It was hardly ladylike, but then, perhaps true ladies did not find themselves in this desperate position.

The shape of the gentleman started to grow clearer through the trees.

This was it.

Alice barreled forward, forcing her feet into a pace she knew she could not maintain, and managed to crash right into the unsuspecting gentleman.

"Oh!"

Her cry had not been planned, but it had been impossible to keep it inside the moment her body struck his.

And what a body it was. Alice had expected the gentleman's chest to give way, for her to sink into it, perhaps softening the blow of the collision.

She could not have been more wrong. As the gentleman's hands came around her to catch her, preventing her from falling to the ground, there was nothing but hard muscle under the jacket and waistcoat she had already espied.

And that wasn't all. A scent filled her lungs that was quite heady and most unexpected. Sandalwood, and the musk of a man driven to irritation, and a darkness of something else. Cinnamon, perhaps, or another spice. It made her head giddy and her heart flutter, and something wasn't quite working in her lungs. Every breath seemed to make her dizzier.

Alice could feel, could hear, the man's pulse thumping. Pressed up against him as she was, there was nothing she could do but feel him—

feel his touch, the warmth of his fingertips on her arms, the way her body quivered to be so close to that of a gentleman's.

Of a stranger.

Alice blinked up into the sky-blue eyes of a gentleman she would never, no matter what happened now, be able to forget.

"Dear God," said the man in a surprised voice.

She blinked again, then remembered precisely why she had concocted this charade in the first place.

"Dear me!" Alice cried loudly, desperately hoping someone would hear. "Now you'll have to marry me!"

Chapter Two

"Y͟o͟u͟ ͟a͟r͟e͟ ͟b͟e͟i͟n͟g͟ a complete idiot, purposefully obtuse, and if you are not careful I will—"

"What, tell on us?" grinned Aylesbury with a laugh. "We're not at Eton anymore, Cothrom!"

The intermingling laughter made William Chance, Duke of Cothrom's head hurt.

"That isn't the point," he said testily, wishing to goodness he had chosen a more private place to have this conversation. "The point is—"

"There is no point, you just talk on and on," interrupted Lindow with a snort. "You've always been like this, Cothrom, so I won't ask you to change—but I will ask you to please desist!"

He nudged Aylesbury who was still laughing.

William's icy expression stiffened.

Well, he shouldn't have expected anything different. Hadn't he known, for years, that his brothers were going to be entirely unmanageable? And his fourth brother . . .

The less said about Pernrith, the better.

It was these two brothers that he was attempting to deal with at the moment, though he wasn't having a particularly easy time of it.

The trouble was, neither of them had any real incentive to listen to him. Oh, William was the eldest, and in most families, that would be enough. He was the head of the family. A duke, no less.

But John Chance, Marquess of Aylesbury, and George Chance, Earl of Lindow, just simply . . . didn't care.

It was exasperating.

William took a deep breath and tried again. *If he could just get his brothers to under—*

"It's not like it's your reputation that we're ruining by having fun," Aylesbury pointed out, his focus meandering as a pretty woman passed them. "It's . . . it's . . ."

William waited for a few moments while the second-born Chance brother's eyes lost all focus.

Damn it, man, but couldn't he concentrate for more than five minutes together?

"Ahem," William said, clearing his throat loudly.

Aylesbury blinked, then turned back to him with a grin. "What were you saying?"

"You were the one talking!" William said, attempting not to explode with anger. It was most difficult. Every inch of him was trembling with irritation, and the temper he knew was always bubbling under the surface threatened to overspill.

But he wouldn't let it. He was William Chance, Duke of Cothrom. He had a reputation to maintain, a place in Society to keep, a head to hold high.

Even if his brothers wanted to make it as difficult as possible for him.

"I was?" Aylesbury blinked. "Well, I suppose I was."

"I wouldn't worry about it, you weren't saying anything interesting," said Lindow with a snort.

William glared at Lindow, but the look did not appear to make much of a difference. If anything, it just encouraged him.

"I saw the lady too, and what a beauty," Lindow said in a low voice to Aylesbury. "In fact, she put me in mind of a woman I had the opportunity to . . . well . . . and she had the most exquisite hands . . ."

William's shoulders slumped as he let the nonsense of his two brothers wash over him.

It wasn't their fault. Not completely. The world rewarded young men who displayed idiocy and rakish behavior. No man ever lost his voucher at Almack's for a hint of scandal, nor was he refused entry to their club, the Dulverton, because a woman had been found slightly ruffled in the drawing room.

More's the pity.

Rules, that was what Society offered, what William had embraced. Rules for respectability, for how to speak to others, how to enter a room, eat with an oyster fork—rules for everything.

All one had to do was follow them. Was it truly so difficult?

"—and then I said, 'My good sir, if you truly wished to win this round—'"

"You would also have cheated!" Lindow finished. He and Aylesbury guffawed, attracting more stares from others walking in Hyde Park.

And that was perhaps the final straw.

William did not consider himself a harsh man. He wished to hold his brothers to a high standard, true, but it was the precisely identical standard he held himself to. Each and every day, he did what was right. Why couldn't they?

"I suppose that is why the news of you cheating the Duke of Axwick made the newspapers," William said quietly through gritted teeth. "Honestly, Aylesbury, you could have chosen anyone to con out of their money, but you had to choose—"

"How was I supposed to know the old man was meant to stay away from the card table?" Aylesbury said, raising his eyebrows in the perfect image of innocence. "And besides, I only took a few pounds from him."

William sighed. "Enough to appear in the scandal sheets, so more than enough!"

He was being pushed right to the edge of his limit, and the worst of it was his brothers knew it.

Lindow grinned. "Oh, come on, Cothrom. We're not that bad, are we?"

"Don't you start," said William with a growl, trying his best to keep his voice low. "You may be interested to know that I have no fewer than four gentlemen each demanding that you marry their daughter. How do you intend to keep them all happy?"

His younger brother's eyes gleamed. "My word. A harem, do you think?"

William shoved his brother's arm as Aylesbury snorted. "I'm being serious, Lindow!"

"So am I," countered the man. "Who wouldn't want a gaggle of ladies waiting for you every evening?"

"You know, that's not a bad idea," said Aylesbury conversationally, though William could see he was only speaking in such a way to vex him. "In fact, when I marry—"

"You'll never marry," scoffed William.

"You never know, I might be forced to one day," said Aylesbury with a wink. "And when I do—"

"No one will wish to marry you if we don't get your wild antics under control," said William, breathing slowly to regain his control. "It would help your reputation to no end if you did marry—I beg you, marry, settle down, and stop causing so much trouble!"

Planning a wedding, as much trouble and expense as it was, would be the least of their problems. And matrimony would have to come to them all, eventually.

Presuming they still held their place in Society, that was. And the way his brothers were going, it would not be long before the name of Chance would be completely obliterated from Almack's, the Dulverton Club, Lady Romeril's invitation list . . .

Well. That last would not be a complete disaster.

"You should marry," he repeated, seeing that he had been entirely ignored.

Lindow snorted. "You get married!"

"There's nothing I would like more, but you rascals need far too much oversight," William snapped. "Besides, finding the perfect woman, one who has never strayed from the expectations of Society—"

"Hark at you and your nonsense," grinned Aylesbury. "Just find a woman you like and marry her! How hard can it be?"

William sighed as his brothers' conversation grew louder, and a couple in a carriage passing them looked back curiously. They weren't the only ones. It appeared that every single person in Hyde Park was intrigued to see what the Chance brothers were arguing about.

Dear Lord, there was even a woman by that bench pretending to look for something in her reticule, all in the hope of overhearing them! Surely no one took that long to find a mirror, or a comb, or whatever it was women kept in such things.

"Look," William said curtly, desperate to bring this to a good resolution, "all I want to do is go . . . oh, I don't know, three days without seeing our name in the papers."

Lindow's eyes sparkled. "Not even for positive things?"

"If you can manage to be mentioned by *The Times* for a positive reason, I would be all for it," William said, a reluctant smile creasing his lips. "You think you can manage it?"

Lindow shrugged. "Does almost knocking out a man at the Almonry Den Boxing Ring count?"

William's jaw dropped.

"You didn't! You clever old thing, tell me all about it," said Aylesbury with a grin. "Who did you knock out? I heard Big Max has returned from his time on the Continent, did you see . . ."

William groaned.

Damn it all to hell, but he hadn't even known his younger brother had been so foolish as to enter the ring of in illegal boxing fight in the most notorious Almonry Den. What on earth was the man thinking?

Was he going to spend the rest of his life trying to keep these brothers of his in line?

"What I don't understand," he muttered, half to them, half to himself, "is how I have only three brothers, but an infinite number of problems."

It was only when silence struck that William looked up. There was an awkward look on Aylesbury's face, and thunder on Lindow's.

"You have two brothers," the latter said coldly. "There are three of us."

William's stomach lurched. *This old argument again.* "You know full well—"

"I know nothing of the sort," Lindow said darkly. "He's not our brother."

"He's a Chance," William said heavily. It was the same debate over and over again. "He bears our name, he's our father's son."

"You keep talking about how important it is to keep this family respectable, yet you would accept *him* into the family?" Lindow said, his cheeks now red.

"An argument for another day," Aylesbury said awkwardly, trying to laugh. "The point is, we promise to try to keep scandal at bay for—shall we say a week?" He gave Lindow a congenial nudge.

It was well done, even William had to admit that. At least, he would admit it in the privacy of his own mind. It was galling to be outdone by Aylesbury, of all people. He, William, was supposed to be the one keeping them in line. He was the eldest. He was supposed to be getting them to agree to keep the Chance name highly regarded.

"Oh, maybe a week," said Lindow, bad temper almost immediately forgotten. "Is that good enough, Cothrom?"

William glared. "Good enough. Go on, be off with you."

Without waiting for a reply, he turned and started toward home.

Well, that could have been worse, he tried to console himself. It could also have been a great deal better, of course. You never knew with Aylesbury and Lindow. They were both determined, opinionated men who had no compunction in rebelling against all that Society demanded of them.

And Aylesbury was a marquess, for God's sake!

William's blood burned in his veins as he walked, and he forced himself to slow down. His pace, and his temper, started to subside.

After everything he had done for them—the hours he had spent worrying about them, the debts he had paid off, the fathers he had convinced not to call them out over daughters William was absolutely sure had indeed been ruined . . .

Well. It was a miracle there wasn't a whole new generation of little Chances about the place.

Hyde Park was beginning to fill up. William could see ahead of him that the path ahead was almost blocked, there were so many carriages demanding to come through.

Better to take the Lancaster Gate.

Leaving the path and veering to the left, William promised himself a nice, relaxing afternoon reading in the library. Or going over the accounts. How much precisely had Aylesbury borrowed against his title? Again. Was it possible to go to the creditor, and—

William shook his head irritably as he entered the small woodland that lay between him and the Hyde Park gate. No, he mustn't think any more about his brothers' problems. He'd had enough of that today.

No, the rest of the day was about him. No one else. He could spend it mercifully alone, in the silence of—

A sudden jolt as something crashed into him left William winded, but his instincts took over. His hands reached out around the unexpected woman who was about to fall to the ground. His hands touched her arms. Skin on skin. Her hands splayed against his coat.

And all air left his lungs.

She was . . .

Beautiful. There was no other word. William was not sure sufficient words had been created for a woman such as this. Hair as white as a diamond, eyes gray, searching, panicked as she thought she was about to fall. Skin soft as silk. Her warmth crushed against him was enough to make him take a desperate breath, and William's eyes roved over her as he tried to gather his bearings.

It was impossible. A woman like this did not suddenly fall into one's lap. Where had she come from? Where was she going in such a hurry? Why was she here, unchaperoned?

"Dear God," said William, unable to say anything else.

Because desire was rushing through his veins just as forcefully as anger had only minutes before.

No one could blame him—a woman as elegant as this pressed up against a man . . . no one could resist.

Resist lowering his lips, slowly, claiming hers and tasting precisely how—

"Dear me!" said the woman in a loud voice. "Now you'll have to marry me!"

William blinked. "Wh-What?"

She couldn't be serious. *Out of the question!*

And then his mind, somehow lost in the confusion of desire and surprise, managed to make itself heard.

He, a gentleman, was standing with a woman in his arms. A woman he did not know. A woman who was panting wildly. And so, somehow, was he. And they were standing alone. No chaperone. In a woodland. Where anything could happen . . .

William shoved the woman away from himself so violently that she almost fell over.

It wasn't very gentlemanly, to be sure, but he was not about to lose his reputation.

It wasn't difficult—one's honor could be easily stained by one simple mistake. Why else did he guard against any hint of impropriety at every instant? Why else would he constantly have to argue with his brothers, trying to get them to be more careful, to take their appearances in Society seriously?

Because all it would take was one mistake, one slip, and all of a sudden, you've lost your reputation.

William swallowed. Though he was not going to marry a woman merely to avoid some scandal.

The very idea!

The woman, however, did not appear to be of the same mind. "You will have to marry me!" she said again.

"I most certainly will not," William said gruffly, placing his hands behind his back.

That was it. Demonstrate he had no intentions toward her beyond that of preventing her falling to the ground.

And kissing her.

The little voice that reminded him of that particular instinct was not welcome, but try as he might, William did not appear to be able to push it aside.

Damn it.

"You took me in your arms," the woman said, pointing most determinedly. "We are all alone here, you might have intended—"

"I intended nothing, woman," said William irritably.

Perhaps if he had not just had a debate with his brothers, he would not be feeling so prickly. As it was, he'd spent all morning concocting the perfect arguments, only to have them torn apart by Aylesbury and Lindow in less than ten minutes, and he was now most irritated.

Not that it was the fault of this woman, of course. Whoever she was.

"Everyone knows," the woman was saying, "if a gentleman and a lady find themselves in a compromised position—"

William glanced about them, pulse hammering. It slowed as he saw what he had hoped for.

No one was there.

No one had witnessed the sudden embrace he and this woman had shared. No one save she could have seen the way he'd looked at her, and he had to hope she had no idea he'd wanted to—

"I think you were almost about to kiss me," said the woman slowly. "And then you would most certainly have had to marry me."

She held her head high, as though her point were clear and irrefutable.

The trouble was, in almost any other situation, William would have agreed with her. If he had discovered one of his brothers in a similar clinch, he would have been marching that Chance brother down to buy a special license and make an honest woman of the poor dear who would be joining the family.

Not that he was about to admit to that particular piece of secret hypocrisy.

"I was not about to kiss you," William lied stiffly.

It was one lie. He could be forgiven that.

"And if you had," the woman said quietly, taking a step toward him, "would you have married me?"

William opened his mouth to reply, then realized he had absolutely no idea.

Would he have?

She was beautiful. She attracted him, there was no doubt about that. The stirrings in his loins when she had been nestled in his arms could not be denied. He was a stickler for the rules of courtship, however, and the rules were quite clear.

A hint of desire managed to break free from his icy heart and melted him. The mere thought of kissing this woman, of having her pressed up against him once more—

Almost too late, William took a step back. The woman had crept closer, perhaps even hoping to kiss him, to lure him in.

"How dare you!" William said, trying to keep his voice stern and push aside all delightful images of the woman kissing him. "You—you are attempting to entrap me!"

"Nonsense," said the woman dismissively, taking another step toward him.

William backed away, hitting the trunk of a tree and wondering what on earth was happening.

Things like this simply did not occur! Elegant ladies in blue gowns and straw bonnets did not accost gentlemen in Hyde Park for kisses! Or at least, if they did, he hadn't ever been included before.

This was ridiculous!

"I am not going to marry you," William said, hardly able to believe those words were coming out of his mouth. "It is absolutely outlandish to suppose—"

"You wanted to kiss me, so why not do it?" the woman said, taking another step closer.

William swallowed. His escape routes were swiftly diminishing with every step she took. Pushing past her wasn't an option—she would merely claim he had once again touched her. And it would be true.

This was madness. He was about to be made to propose to—

No. No, he was the Duke of Cothrom. He was a Chance. He was not so foolish.

Stepping to the side and seeing the surprise in her wide eyes, William congratulated himself on an escape well made. Just a few more steps, and he would be out of the woodland. Out of danger.

"Sir, you must—"

"I must nothing," said William, almost falling over his own feet in his eagerness to get away.

If this had been any other situation, he would have laughed. Him, running away from a beautiful woman! Any man running away from this woman would need his head examined. She was intriguing, alluring, and most anxious to be kissed. An intoxicating combination.

And perhaps if William had been a different kind of man, he might have obliged her. Aylesbury or Lindow certainly would not have missed the opportunity to taste those lips.

William swallowed. No wonder they persisted in their disreputable behavior. If it were half as fun as this, he could well understand it. But just because he saw the attraction, that did not mean he was going to capitulate.

He was the Duke of Cothrom. He was a Chance.

He was, most of the time, the only thing holding the family back from ruin. And he was not going to start going around kissing young ladies just because they dared him to!

The woman appeared to be reading his thoughts. "You . . . you aren't going to marry me, are you?"

William hesitated, just for a moment.

They had moved out of the green leafy canopy of the woodland, and in the bright light of day, it was even clearer to him just what a beauty this woman was. There was an elegance, a refinement to her he had not expected a moment ago as she'd stepped toward him with the eagerness of a harlot. In any other scenario, he might have sought her out. Wished to know her better. Requested an introduction, met her father, and . . .

And things could have been very different.

William drew himself up. But things were not different. They were how they were, and he had no choice but to remind this woman, kindly but sternly, of her responsibilities to herself and to Society.

Really!

Perhaps she had heatstroke. Perhaps the sudden warmth of this spring day was playing havoc with her senses, William thought wildly.

But then, it had not been that warm a day when he had left to meet his brothers an hour ago. So why was he so overheated now?

"I am not going to marry you," he said stiffly. "And honestly, you are a fool for thinking that that sort of trick would work."

The woman examined him closely, a hint of a smile dancing across her lips. "And you aren't tempted?"

William swallowed.

Temptation was one thing. Giving in was another. And he was not about to permit himself that weakness, no matter how much he wanted to. He hadn't got this far in life, sacrificed so much, held himself to such a high standard for so long, merely to give it all up for the chance of a kiss with a . . . a woman he did not know!

"I am not tempted in the least," he said, lying for the second time that day, a personal worst. "And I'll have you know I am far too respectable—far too respectable, I repeat—to be taken in by such a ruse!" Even though he almost had been. "Good day to you!"

And without another word, William turned on his heel and marched away.

To his relief, the Lancaster Gate was close. It meant that stepping onto Bayswater Road prevented him from giving into the second temptation of the day which he had not expected.

The temptation to look back.

Chapter Three

May 7, 1812

A LICE STOOD BY the wall for at least ten minutes before she was able to catch her breath.

Well. She had done it. And her lady's maid had told her it was impossible.

"I'm telling you, m'lady," Jane had said, using the title Alice absolutely knew she did not deserve, no matter how many times she had been told not to. "It's impossible."

"But I am determined," Alice had replied just an hour ago, holding up a pearl earbob to one ear and a diamond one to another. "And when I am determined, I always get what I want."

She had spoken without her voice quavering, which she thought was impressive. Particularly after the disaster in Hyde Park only a few days before.

"I am not going to marry you. And honestly, you are a fool for thinking that that sort of trick would work."

Alice had swallowed, forcing away the remembrance of such an embarrassing situation. She had been a complete fool to think Hyde Park was the solution. Plenty of ladies and gentlemen surely found themselves there without an accompanying chaperone, and they did not find themselves forced to marry.

No, she would have to be a great deal smarter than that.

A ball. That was the perfect place. Lots of nice dark corners, balconies, side rooms. Lots of places to find a man, kiss him senseless, then ensure they were discovered.

The only problem was, she was hardly about to receive any invitations.

"I don't see why you can't wait until you're invited, all proper," said Jane, tidying up the last curl of Alice's hair. "Then—"

"You know perfectly well that Miss Fox-Edwards is not going to be invited to any balls," Alice said with a wry look. "You know me better than that, Jane. You . . . you know."

Her lady's maid's gaze softened. "I know, m'lady."

Alice managed to prevent herself from correcting her servant again, and instead looked at her own reflection in the looking glass. Her maid had been with her since . . . since before it all happened. And she had not disappeared or found another situation, though both reactions would have been quite within her right. But Jane was far more loyal than that, and so Alice had no hesitation in sharing her plans with her.

Even if her maid did not believe it possible for her to sneak into a ball uninvited.

"You'll be found out, caught, sent out in disgrace," said Jane, her face a picture of worry. "You really think it will help your reputation if you are found in such a way?"

It most certainly would not. But it was not as though Alice had much of a choice.

A ball would be the best place to find a husband—to entrap one, as the irritatingly disobliging gentleman had put it. Alice would have corrected him if she had in all conscience been able.

In truth, she had very little time until the owners of the London townhouse she had borrowed would return. An old favor to her father, they had said. She had but three weeks. And as she was not going to be invited to any balls, particularly at this point in the Season, her only option was to wander into a private ball and hope for the best.

And *this* kind of ball would offer her an advantage.

"You're sure about this?" Jane asked quietly, carefully lowering the silk turban onto Alice's head.

With just a few deft movements, her blonde hair was completely obscured. Alice gave a sigh of relief, the tension she had not known she was carrying in her shoulders starting to dissipate.

That had been her greatest concern. A masked ball would do wonders for diminishing the likelihood that anyone would recognize her, but the Fox-Edwards white-blonde hair was perhaps too distinctive. Thank goodness turbans were fashionable. The light green silk of the turban completely covered her hair.

Made her anonymous.

"I am sure," Alice said, far more firmly than she felt. "I have to do this, Jane. And I will be a good wife. I offer nothing but devotion and loyalty. Any man would be fortunate to have me walking down the aisle to them on their wedding day."

She caught the bitten lip of her maid.

"And . . . and after? When the truth comes out?"

Alice swallowed. "I shall be late if I do not leave now."

Better to leave than to think about . . . after.

As it turned out, Jane had been right, after a fashion. The footmen of the Earl of Chester were checking invitations at the front of the large London townhouse which had been decorated in red ribbons and candles all along the windowsills. Alice had watched as each carriage halted, guests were carefully handed out, and invitations presented.

Invitations which had gold edging and could not be aped by a scrap of paper.

Alice sighed as she hid in the gardens of the townhouse next door. She should have thought of this, should have brought . . . something.

"Welcome, welcome," said one of the two footmen who were checking invitations.

A young lady curtsied low as she was entreated to walk in, clearly thrilled to be attending an earl's ball.

And that was, perhaps, why she did not notice her gilded invitation slipping through her gloved fingers.

Alice held her breath as the invitation wafted in the night's gentle breeze. The piece of paper came to rest in the middle of a yew bush, right before her.

Holding it tightly and waiting until another carriage slowed before the impressive house, Alice slipped out of the garden. She stepped around the carriage so it was unclear whether she had arrived with the two ladies who were even now showing their invitations to the footman on the left, and she approached the footman on the right.

The footman who had not already seen the invitation that was now clasped between her fingers.

"My lady," he said, bowing as he examined the invitation. "Please, welcome."

Alice almost didn't move, so expectant was she of a disaster. And yet there was no disaster.

How could there be, when she was... what did that say? Lady Letitia Cavendish?

Whoever the woman was, it did not matter. Alice raced into the building before someone could call her back and spent the next ten minutes standing at the side of the ballroom, trying to calm herself.

She had done it. She was inside the Earl of Chester's ball.

It was, according to the gossip she had read in the newspaper yesterday, the last ball of any significance of the Season. It was not going to be that well attended, as sufficient elegant names had already departed for their country estates. But there were people here. Gentlemen. And not all of them, as far as she could tell, were wed.

Tension melted from Alice's brow as her eyes flickered around the room from behind her green silk mask.

Well, now all she had to do was find a willing—

Her heart skipped a beat.

Him, she had not expected.

It was the man from Hyde Park. The man who had made it perfectly clear he had not only no interest, but a resolute determination not to marry her.

Alice swallowed. He was handsome, she had not been incorrect in her estimation. Even wearing a black silk mask with an elegant black ribbon tie, he was unmistakable. He was carrying himself with a sense of importance which suggested he was not only a gentleman, but something more. A baronet, perhaps.

Her stomach lurched. Well, it would be a perfectly suitable match for herself, the daughter of a baronet. It was a shame really she had been unable to captivate the man.

He had liked the look of her, certainly. Alice had known enough of men to know when a man wished to kiss her. For a moment, she had been almost certain the gentleman had been about to give into his baser desires and kiss her. Then she would have had him—

A look, a glance, and the whole ballroom shook.

Alice grasped at the wall as though that could prevent her from falling. As it was, the floor did not precisely move. Just her stability on it.

The look the gentleman—the man from Hyde Park—had just given her...

Well, it would floor even the calmest woman. It had been hot and interested and full of desire and eagerness.

And just as soon as his eyes had met hers, he had looked away.

What was this man? Someone who could be so cold, so aloof, so reserved—yet so aching with heat that she did not know how anyone else in the ballroom was still standing?

She raised a hand to her head to confirm her hair was sufficiently pinned, and was almost surprised to feel not hair, but soft silk. Of course. With her turban on, and her mask... why, there was a chance . . .

A chance he would not recognize her.

Quite what made her do it, she was not certain. Her legs definitely did not feel as though they were strong enough to carry her, yet Alice walked forward with as much sophistication as she could manage.

Right toward the man.

And he noticed. He was watching her. Alice found she was holding her breath, so desperate was her eagerness to capture his attention. She shifted her hips, ever so slightly, as she walked.

The man's eyes widened.

She was close, just a few feet away . . . and then she was past him.

Alice helped herself to a glass of punch as pretext for why she had wandered so close to him, but even she was surprised when she heard a man behind her clearing his throat.

Dear me, am I that good? It was something she hadn't even considered. Her panic at Mr. Shenton's demands had left her little room for rational thought or any assessment of her own qualities. Before Alice had had time to draw a proper breath, she had arrived at London, determined to marry and leave behind the blackmail of the man who should have been her support, not her struggle.

Then again, perhaps not that good. She managed to hide her disappointment as she turned around to see not the gentleman she had been aiming for, but a footman. Had she been discovered?

"I seem to have misplaced my invitation," Alice blurted out, chest tight with panic. "Oh dear, I—"

"May I introduce His Grace, the Duke of Cothrom?" said the footman with a low bow, stepping to the side to reveal—

Alice's lips curled into an unbidden smile. "You again."

It was a foolish thing to say. The gentleman from Hyde Park, the gentleman she now knew was a duke, raised a quizzical eyebrow just visible under his mask. "We have met?"

"We—no, we have not," said Alice, the footman melting away

with the first part of the introduction now performed. "But I have heard of you, of course."

The compliment did not appear to be received well. "You have?"

Alice stared, transfixed, as what was visible of the Duke of Cothrom's face darkened. Did a man like him expect to be unknown in Society? Who had not heard of the Duke of Cothrom? The whole Chance family, as it happened, was well known. Alice had read conflicting reports about the exact number of brothers, but most of them seemed to be getting themselves into a pickle every week.

Her hopes rose. Here, then, was a man who was accustomed to family members getting themselves into scrapes and getting out of them again. He would not mind that—

"I suppose you must be thinking of my incorrigible brothers," the Duke of Cothrom said. "I would much rather you get to know me on . . . my own merit."

Alice swallowed.

Gone was the stiff, prim and proper gentleman she had accosted in the woodland of Hyde Park. It was the same man, most definitely, but here he was different. Warmer. Less concerned with propriety.

Why, he had not even asked her own name!

"My lady," said the Duke of Cothrom, presuming a title she did not have. "Would you do me the honor of joining me for this next dance?"

Alice's lips actually parted at this. What was it he had said to her, only days ago?

"I'll have you know I am far too respectable, far too respectable, I repeat, to be taken in by such a ruse!"

And now here he was, casting aside the rules of Society he had already made abundantly clear he clung to so dearly! What was going on?

"You shock me, Your Grace," said Alice quietly, buying time and hoping beyond hope he didn't see her confusion through the mask. "I . . . we have not been introduced. Not properly."

"I couldn't find the Master of Ceremonies," said the Duke of Cothrom with a shrug. "I thought a footman would do."

Alice glanced about them. There was no one nearby to suggest anyone was listening to their conversation, to hear the flirtatious nonchalance with which he spoke. What was this—did he have a twin?

"But . . . you don't even know my name," Alice pointed out, taking a step closer to murmur this rather outrageous fact to the gentleman.

Which was a mistake. Every inch she grew closer, she found herself pulled more fully into the gentleman's orbit. A tantalizingly intoxicating orbit. Did the man know how attractive he was? How she wished to lean closer, and closer, and closer—

"No, I suppose I don't know your name," said the Duke of Cothrom. "And I suppose in most scenarios, that would be most uncouth. But I admit . . . I admit to you, my lady, that the wearing of the masks and the anonymity . . . it introduces a level of . . . excitement."

Alice's heart pattered painfully. "Risk."

"I could not have put it better myself," murmured the duke. "I am a man who spends his life playing by Society's rules, and in the main I am happy to do so. The rules keep us safe. A game without any rules is anarchy."

"And yet here," Alice said, hardly trusting her voice to speak but knowing she must. "Here, with a single rule removed, you can do the things you always wished you could."

The Duke of Cothrom's light blue eyes flashed, and for a moment Alice thought she had gone too far.

This was a dangerous sort of game she was playing. She certainly did not know the rules, not now. How could one outplay a gentleman who seemed to adhere so closely to the rules all the time . . . yet gave them up now?

And why was her stomach twisting so?

"It is rather freeing," the Duke of Cothrom agreed quietly. "After tonight, I will return to the rules I have always followed and respected. Which means tonight . . ."

His voice trailed away, and his gaze dropped suggestively down Alice's gown.

Wild thoughts were whirling through her mind, but she managed to put them aside. All but one.

This was her chance.

"You intrigue me," she managed to whisper.

That much was true. The severe and unbending man she had met in Hyde Park had been attractive enough, but this version of him? The part of him that, by his own admission, he rarely allowed to surface?

This was a man she could maneuver.

"In that case, am I to presume you are accepting my invitation to dance?" said the Duke of Cothrom, offering a hand.

In that moment, Alice knew she could retreat. She could decide to do the smart thing and politely decline. She could return to her rented lodgings, instruct Jane to pack up her things in the morning, and they could be back in Brighton by the end of the week. And she could begin concocting another scheme to protect them.

But this was her best chance, and Alice knew it. She had not come all this way, sacrificed time with those she loved, just to shy away when she was about to achieve what she craved.

Safety. Stability. A home.

Alice took his hand and was relieved to be wearing gloves. If this was how hot the Duke of Cothrom made her through two layers of gloves, goodness only knew what he would do to her if he touched her skin again.

"I accept," she said as lightly as she could manage.

They were not alone in moving to the middle of the ballroom. The musicians had been taking a little break from their playing, but the Earl of Chester was leading what appeared to be a sister to the head of the line, and Alice recognized many of the others who formed the lines.

The Duke of Sedley, the Duke of Ashcott, Lady Margaret Dulverton, the Earl of Clarcton looking most depressed, Lord Galcrest, the Viscount Bythesea, Viscount Braedon . . .

In short, most of the refined Society London had to offer, certainly everyone who was still in town.

And herself.

Alice tried not to smile as she curtsied to the Duke of Cothrom as the music struck up. Well, she could not maneuver the man into a compromising position during the dance. She probably could not even increase his desire for her. After all, they would only be—

The moment she stepped forward and clasped hands with the Duke of Cothrom, Alice knew three things.

Firstly, she was greatly mistaken. Dancing with this man was certainly going to increase her attraction, and she could see that mirrored in his eyes.

Secondly, she had perhaps underestimated the forcefulness of the man's character. This was a man who could not be so easily swayed.

And thirdly, she didn't care.

The contact of his fingers against hers, even through their gloves, was thrilling. Jolts of desire, of longing, of the heated need Alice had promised herself she would never feel again, soared through her.

The ballroom spun, but she managed to keep hold of herself enough to step backward then turn, progressing through the dance as expected. To move as though her very skin was not tingling, alive in a way it had never been before.

"You dance well," said the Duke of Cothrom as they stepped together again.

Alice tried to laugh. "My dancing instructor as a child would be most glad to hear it."

"What, no compliment for me?"

This man's personality was so utterly different, she was finding it rather difficult to keep up.

"I was not aware you required one, Your Grace," Alice attempted to quip as their hands clasped once more. *All she had to do was ignore the burning sensation in her palms.* "But if you do require one—"

"Oh no, I cannot possibly accept one given under duress," said the Duke of Cothrom, eyes twinkling through the mask. "I would rather it were given freely."

"A request does not mean it is not given freely," Alice pointed out, losing herself in the conversation just as much as in the dance.

Goodness, it had been so long since she had flirted! Years. A lifetime ago.

"The question is, how would you like to be complimented?" Alice continued as they stepped to the side and permitted the couple to their left to move forward. "Your footwork, perhaps, or your sense of timing?"

The Duke of Cothrom met her eyes, and Alice found that she was momentarily speechless. How could such a look end all possibility of conversation?

"Perhaps," said the gentleman said, tilting his head to one side. "Perhaps I want something deeper. It could be that I crave your good opinion in a way that goes beyond a simple compliment."

Alice's breath caught in her throat.

This was too much. She had never intended for hearts to get involved in this deception. She needed a husband, not a lover. Not a man who spoke in honeyed tones that dripped across her body as though his very fingers were trailing down her collarbone to—

"You undo me," Alice whispered, unconscious of the words slipping through her lips until it was too late.

The Duke of Cothrom's eyes flashed for a moment, their sky blue transforming into a sudden dark, like the depths of the ocean. "Dear God, you make me want to—"

The dance suddenly required them to be apart, and Alice railed against the terrible timing. If she didn't know any better, the Duke of

Cothrom had been about to say something—something wonderful.

Not that she should be thinking of such things, she scolded herself as she waited impatiently for the rhythm of the dance to bring them back together. No, she should be focused on one thing and one thing only.

Encouraging the man to propose. Or forcing him to.

When they finally stepped together again, Alice was most disconcerted to find her voice was breathless. Why? Had she not moved but little?

"I suppose with the masks on, we may speak more boldly," Alice said, her hands slipping into the duke's as she pressed into his side, the two of them promenading down the set. "A-And yet I find, I cannot be so open as—"

"Oh, you are a lady of impeccable breeding and family, that much can be seen even through the mask," said the Duke of Cothrom, his breath on her neck. "I should not have presumed—"

"But I want you to," Alice murmured.

Her gaze met his and she knew she had gone too far. And at the same time not far enough. Not far enough for the deception she was attempting to weave around him... not far enough for her own feelings.

Because this was a man she could grow to care for, that much was clear. A man with morals and yet a man whose passions ran deep. A man who desired her, and yet managed to resist when he knew it was improper.

A man, in short, with a conscience.

Not something that was easy to find.

"I wish I knew your name," the Duke of Cothrom murmured as they came to the end of the line and parted. "For then I could ask if I could call you by your first name."

Alice swayed slightly, though she should have been standing still in this part of the dance. Oh, this was a man far beyond what she could have expected to encounter. She had chosen him in Hyde Park because he was there, and she had then hoped to catch him when she saw him here, at the Earl of Chester's ball, to prove a point.

But what was she proving now, other than that she was entranced by him?

Noise. The dance itself was over, the other couples gently applauding the musicians.

The Duke of Cothrom stood before her, mere inches from her, his attention so intense she found she could not look away.

Not that she wished to.

"You, my lady, intrigue me," he said quietly, just under his breath though loud enough for Alice to hear. "And very few ladies manage to do such a thing."

"I . . . I am honored," Alice said, her voice catching in her throat.

This was all too public—if he were not careful, there would be talk—

"I like you," said the Duke of Cothrom. "You are a woman I like. And you are beautiful. And I like you."

Alice blinked.

What on earth did that mean?

Chapter Four

"You, my lady, intrigue me." William did not know what was possessing him to speak so boldly—it was so against his nature. But this woman . . . she drew it from him. "And very few ladies manage to do such a thing."

He watched carefully and was rewarded with the telltale signs he had been seeing, even through the mask, since he had first spoken to her.

Interest.

She was interested in him.

"I . . . I am honored," the woman said, her voice uneven.

Delight soared through William. He had never expected anything like this: a connection made in such a public place, and with a woman he did not, in any real way, know.

It was the sort of encounter one heard about but never saw. And now it was happening to him.

There was something powerful happening in his stomach, though precisely what, William could not tell. Standing here, mere inches away from a woman whose name he did not even know . . .

What was happening to him?

This was not like him at all. He was, as his brothers had so often reminded him, far more interested in being stuffy and right than loose and having fun. Yet here he was, contravening almost every rule he had ever put in place for himself, every expectation of himself as a gentleman. And she was looking at him like . . .

Like she did not care about convention at all. Like she could sense how he felt for her, the growing need in his loins, the desire to crush her to him and taste her, to know what this woman felt like when whimpering against him.

And the memory of what Lindow had said mere days ago echoed in his mind.

"Just find a woman you like and marry her! How hard can it be?"

"I like you," said William simply, unable to help himself. "You are a woman I like. And you are beautiful. And I like you."

It sounded so ridiculous when he said it like that—but there was the simple truth.

He liked her.

He had never met a woman he liked like this. And William was not a complete fool—he knew his own mind. He knew when he thought "liked," he meant, "found so attractive and easy to talk to that he could quite happily spend hours and hours with this woman, her company sufficient and her presence intoxicating."

Though "liked" was rather a paltry summation, now he came to think about it.

But he was not some fool who believed in love at first sight, or anything so ridiculous.

And yet . . .

The woman's cheeks were burning—at least, from what he could see around the green silk mask. "Oh. Oh, Your Grace—"

"Please, you do not need to say anything," William said hastily. The last thing he wanted was to frighten her with the sudden depth of his feelings. Feelings he might be able to name but did not quite understand. "It's just . . . this is . . ."

The woman stared, her gray eyes wide and trusting.

Dear God, she was wonderful. Compared to the last woman he had encountered, this one was an angel.

William almost laughed aloud when he thought to compare this polite, respectful woman—who had been refined enough to be nervous at dancing with a man she had not been introduced to—to the wild thing he had encountered in Hyde Park.

"*Everyone knows if a gentleman and a lady find themselves in a compromised position—*"

Why, compared to that hellion, this woman was a picture of perfection! Delightful, a wonderful dancer, a conversationalist who managed to border on flirtation yet stay the right side of it.

She was far superior.

And something rather strange entered his mind. A thought that was not precisely his, but at the same time could have come from nowhere else.

A woman he liked.

"My lady," William said, stepping closer to the quivering woman and marveling at her withdrawal from any hint of impropriety. "It would do me great honor if you would tell me your—"

"There you are, you rascal!"

His shoulder was jolted as a hand suddenly grabbed him and pulled him away from the woman he had been about to say something ridiculous to. The wrenching movement shot a bolt of pain across William's shoulder blades, and he turned on the miscreant who had manhandled him, about to curtly berate him.

Then William groaned.

"You know, I thought you'd be happier to see me," said Lindow with a grin. "Aren't you always saying I should spend more time in polite company so their elegance can rub off on me?"

William sighed. "I meant so that you could become more polished, not that you could go about disgracing yourself!"

He glanced around them but could see no one watching the two Chance brothers.

Yet.

"What do you want?" William said heavily, pulling a hand through his hair.

Lindow frowned. "I haven't asked for anything yet."

"You are here, and you have pulled me aside from a delightful conversation," said William wearily. "You only do that when you want—"

"Delightful conversation?" Lindow glanced over William's shoulder, and his smile became wicked. "My, my."

"Do not speak to her," said William stiffly, glancing over his shoulder, unable to help himself.

The young woman whose name he still did not know flushed a dark pink, the color dancing down her neck and across her collarbone. She looked away, and William turned back to his brother. She ought to flush, being gawped at by an idiotic Chance.

Well. Two idiotic Chances.

"Good God, Cothrom, well done," Lindow was saying far too loudly for William's liking. "And I always thought you weren't that good with the ladies. Have you—"

"Speak another word about her and I may cut out your tongue," growled William.

His brother ignored him completely. "I actually did come over here to ask you for something, as it happens, but that is a complete coincidence. I resent the implication that I only ever ask—"

"What do you need?" said William with a sigh, pulling out his pocketbook. Carrying the damn thing had become a matter of course these days, as his brothers always in need of funds. "And how much?"

This time, Lindow did not bother to attempt to pretend. "About fifty pounds."

"*Fifty*—"

"It's not me!" said his brother, lifting his hands in mock surrender. "He was already at Chester's card table when I arrived—I couldn't have stopped him!"

William groaned. Which was quickly becoming a habit—a most unpleasant one—whenever Aylesbury was involved. He hadn't even known Aylesbury was here.

"His gambling really is getting out of control," said Lindow happily. "I'd want to take him in hand, if I were you."

William shot his brother a dire look, and the younger man had the good grace to look a little bashful.

How many years had Aylesbury been trying William's patience? How many hundreds of pounds had been taken out of the Cothrom estate to pay off his brother's debts? It wasn't as though the Aylesbury estate didn't have money he could use!

Although now William came to think about it, maybe it didn't. That would certainly explain why a few credit notes had come to his door, rather than to the second Chance brother.

"Fifty pounds," said William darkly, pulling several notes from his pocketbook. "This is all I have on me, but send me his vowels and I'll have them paid. And I suppose you have done the right thing and moved Aylesbury as far from that card room as—"

"Well, I would be more than happy to," said Lindow, a flicker of awkwardness shifting his grin. "Except . . . well . . ."

If it were possible, William's hopes sank even further. "What now?"

"Well, he managed to owe the debt to . . . to Gilroyd."

William sighed, and replaced his pocketbook, now fifty pounds lighter. "Of course he has."

The Duke of Gilroyd. One of the most notorious card players in the entire *ton*. Everyone knew he always won—what on earth had Aylesbury been thinking, playing him? And Gilroyd always collected on his debts. Always. It wouldn't surprise William if Aylesbury was being kept in the card room Chester had somewhere about here, unable to leave unless he coughed up the money or wrote a voucher for double the amount.

God save them . . .

"Look," William said firmly. "I am tired of this."

Lindow's grin became mischievous once more. "Say no more, old thing. I am more than happy to take that lovely woman off your hands and—"

"You know that's not what I meant, man, and don't look at her. You don't deserve her," snapped William.

His brother's eyes glittered. "And you do?"

William chose to ignore that particular pointed question. He wasn't precisely sure what he deserved. A rest from constantly and consistently bailing out his brothers, as far as he could tell.

"Aylesbury has got to stop running up gambling debts," he said instead. "And you have got to stop seducing women—"

"Cothrom! The very idea!"

"—and refusing to make honest women of them," William continued stonily.

Dear God, but it was shameful to be having this sort of conversation in the middle of a ballroom at a private party. It was shameful to be having this sort of conversation at all. Thank goodness the lady in question had meandered to a table in search of a drink—otherwise he'd be mortified. When were his brothers going to get it into their thick heads that they needed to start pulling their weight to keep this family's reputation?

Lindow snatched the crumpled notes from his fingers. "Thank you, old—"

"I'm not that much older than you," William pointed out darkly.

The musicians had started up again. *Blast*. He had hoped to ask her, the woman, for another dance. Now he would have to wait until this one was over—and that was if someone else hadn't already asked her.

Blast, blast, blast—

"You can't blame him, you know."

William started. Most unusually, Lindow was looking at him with an expression of . . .

Was that solemnity?

"Blame him?" William repeated. "Of course I can blame him. Aylesbury is old enough to know better, old enough to pay his own—"

"He's bored," said Lindow flatly. "We both are."

William blinked.

Bored? Dear God, how he longed to be bored! How could his brothers be bored when they were off living reckless lives with other irresolute individuals? How did two men who racked up such debt every month they stayed in London, bedding the women they bedded and drinking the vast amounts of wine they drank, end up bored?

"Bored," he said quietly.

Lindow shrugged. "Bored."

"Well, poor Aylesbury," William said, temper running thin. "If he wants to keep himself occupied, all he has to do is take over the job of keeping you in line! It's not a responsibility I ever wanted, and he's welcome to it!"

His brother flinched.

William sighed, regret for his outburst already pouring through him. Thank goodness the music would have covered much of what he had said. The last thing he needed was to undo all the good work he had done for the family reputation, speaking politely and elegantly to so many people at Chester's ball.

"I am sorry," William said quietly. "I do not mean to preach—"

Lindow laughed, but it was a hollow sound. "Really? Because you do it so often."

William chose to ignore that comment. His temper was the one character flaw he loathed about himself, though arguably it was tied up with the other passion he forced deep within. If he were ever to let himself go, really allow himself to do precisely what he wanted . . .

Well. Would he be that much different from his brothers?

"If you just went and got married," said Lindow unexpectedly, "it would force Aylesbury to fend for himself. Me too, actually, now I come to think about it."

William blinked. No, he must have imagined it. There was no possibility his brother, the reckless George Chance, Earl of Lindow, a man who never had enough coin on him and who was, as far as William was aware, being sued for breach of contract by at least two gentlemen on behalf of their daughters, was recommending something so pedestrian as . . . marriage?

"I beg your pardon?" William said slowly. "I'm sorry, I think I misheard—"

"If you were married, you'd have your wife to think about. Children, too, I suppose," said Lindow, shivering as though he could think of nothing worse. "Old Aylesbury would have to get by. He'd have to worry about his own decisions, his own consequences. Do you see?"

William did see, and it was something he had never considered before.

Oh, he would get married. One day. But he was only two and thirty, and there was still plenty of time to choose a woman who could become the Duchess of Cothrom and provide him with an heir or two. Perhaps not three. He had enough experience with multiple brothers to know what a disaster that could be.

But marrying sooner rather than later—it hadn't really been on his agenda. It had seemed superfluous. Unnecessary. The idea that matrimony would not only give him the benefit of a wife but the reduction of responsibility when it came to the other Chance brothers . . .

It was certainly worth thinking about.

"Cothrom?"

William blinked.

Lindow was carefully and slowly waving his hand before William's eyes. "Lost you for a moment there."

"I was just thinking," snapped William.

His brother winked. "Don't pull a muscle."

Shoving Lindow none too gently, but just gently enough that a casual observer may believe it was a brotherly sign of affection, William nodded at the clasped notes in the younger man's hands. "Go on, take those to Aylesbury, and tell him that's all he's getting from me this week."

"Right. About my own debts—"

"Oh, be off with you," said William with a weak laugh.

Lindow grinned, inclined his head, and headed into the crowd.

Brothers.

If their father had not made such a specific request of William, he would certainly not have worked so hard and so long to keep the blackguards in line.

The trouble was, he liked them. And William wasn't entirely sure, but he had the impression that this was rare. Aylesbury, Lindow . . . even Pernrith. In a way. A complicated way.

They were good men. They were also incorrigible, dissolute, and reprehensible in every way.

Except Pernrith.

William sighed. Being released of his promise . . . it was something he had presumed would only come when the idiots themselves were married. Even then, he would not be surprised if he were called upon to be a second in an illegal duel once in a while.

He had never before considered the possibility that his own marriage could—

"I hope everything is well," came a genteel voice.

William's pulse skipped a beat as he turned to see the woman in the green silk turban and mask. She was not dancing with another. She was not conversing with another. She had not wandered off. She . . . she had been waiting for him.

Precisely why this fact gave William so much joy he was not sure. Was it perhaps the politeness of such a decision? The respectability of waiting for a conversation to finish before she returned to his side? Whatever it was, William could not think of a way that the woman could have made herself more endearing.

"Tell me," he said in a quiet, urgent voice. "Tell me your name."

The woman looked up with gray, questioning eyes. "Why?"

Because I need to know, William wanted to say. *Because there's something about you, something I have never found in anyone else. Because not knowing your name means your beauty is somehow incomplete.*

And because I want to know you better. Know all of you. Know you better than anyone in your life has ever known you.

He swallowed back the words. Probably not the best approach.

"I think it only right, now we have danced and conversed," he said, a little of the stiffness he had attempted to leave by the door creeping back into his voice. "After all, you know my name."

A slight smile curled her lips. "Yes, I do, Your Grace."

William fought the desire to request that she call him by his first name. This was preposterous. And his stomach was being ridiculous. And so was his—

"I suppose there is no harm in you knowing it," said the woman most inexplicably.

Curiosity sparked in William. "What do you—"

"My name is Alice," said the woman with a shy look. "Alice... Alice Fox-Edwards."

Alice. Alice Fox-Edwards.

Warmth spread through him at the newfound knowledge.

"Miss Fox-Edwards," he said quietly.

It was a surprise, in truth, that she was not a Lady Alice. She certainly held herself in a manner which suggested noble breeding. There was a confidence in her and a cultured shyness that suggested she had been raised by the very best. And had she not mentioned a dancing master?

Her cheeks were pink as Miss Fox-Edwards looked up defiantly.

Which did not make any sense. There was no reason, as far as William was aware, for her to be so defiant.

Miss Fox-Edwards continued to flush. "I am sorry, it is just... it is so bold, for you to know my name, without a formal introduction."

And William melted.

This, truly, was a woman after his own heart. She understood the bounds of propriety, and though they had flirted together while dancing, she clearly agreed with him that no mask could entirely suppress the requirements of polite Society.

She was... perfect. Likeable. Beautiful. Refined, clearly from a good family. She danced well, her conversation was both respectable and playful. If the way his body had already responded to her was any suggestion, William would find no problems in that quarter, either.

And the most ridiculous, wonderful, and wild idea crossed his mind.

It was only a flicker. If he had not been gazing into Miss Fox-Edwards's eyes at the time, perhaps he would not have noticed it.

But as it was, he had been, and he did. And now William could think of nothing else.

Unfortunately for him, his lips did not afford him any additional time to consider. They simply spoke out the thought which had fluttered through his mind.

"Miss Fox-Edwards, will you marry me?"

As perhaps he should have expected, Miss Fox-Edwards flushed a dark pink beneath her silk mask, stepped back, and spluttered, "I-I b-beg your pardon?"

"I know, it is perhaps a rather strange question, but I am in earnest," said William quickly, following her footstep.

His pulse was thundering, mind whirling, hardly able to believe he had done it. But he had. And he spoke the truth—he was in earnest. A good, elegant, beautiful wife to stand by his side, entertain him in the evenings, and fill his nights with pleasure. To give him children, and most importantly, force his brothers to take responsibility for their own mistakes.

What could possibly go wrong?

"You... you..." Miss Fox-Edwards swallowed, and William forced himself not to stare at the way her throat bobbed, enticing his lips to touch the crest of her clavicle. "You don't know anything about me."

She was quite right, and in many other scenarios, William would have to admit his proposal represented a rather impulsive decision.

"True, but I think many happy couplings are begun with two people who hardly know each other," he pointed out, gesturing around the ballroom. "Arranged marriages, introductions, a few dances, a dinner party, and the invitations are sent out. Why should our partnership be any different?"

He watched Miss Fox-Edwards hesitate.

But she had not said no. If she had taken against him, considered him most unsuitable or mad even for asking, she would have said so. She would have stepped away.

She wanted to say yes.

"Besides," William said, stepping closer than was perhaps appropriate, but reveling in the intimacy the physical proximity brought, "I think I have seen enough from our dance together to know that it would be a... a pleasant connection."

Perhaps he had gone too far. He had always attempted to force down his desires, knowing no woman would be sufficient to satisfy him. His urges, his need for physical release... no woman, let alone a well-bred wife, would wish to allow him into her bed every night.

But Miss Fox-Edwards—now she had matched his desire, William was almost certain. When they had danced together, it was not only his breathing which had become short—and not due to the rigors of the dance.

His gaze flickered over her. When he looked back at her face, a jolt speared through him.

She was looking at him. And clearly liking what she saw.

"You are in earnest?" Miss Fox-Edwards whispered.

William nodded. "I am."

Well, he had no patience to find a bride in the normal way, attending countless balls and being introduced to misses by their mamas and papas. He had no wish for the excruciating awkwardness of a matchmaker, and with his mother sadly gone, there were no female relatives to make delicate introductions.

No, Miss Fox-Edwards was as good as any. Why not? They had just as much a fighting chance to make a marriage enjoyable as anyone.

William slipped off his signet ring, the heavy gold band which flattened on the top to hold the Cothrom coat of arms. Wishing he were not wearing gloves, he took Miss Fox-Edwards's hand in his own, and slipped it onto the fourth finger of her left hand over her glove.

It was a perfect fit.

"There," he said quietly, looking into her dark gray eyes. "We are engaged to be married."

Miss Fox-Edwards stared at the signet ring on her finger, then looked up. "Well. In that case . . ."

She slipped her fingers from his hands and lifted them to her turban, where the ribbon for her mask was.

If her beauty was so radiant even through such a getup, he could only imagine the perfection that lay beneath—

The mask came away into her hands, and William gasped.

Oh, God.

It was the woman—the woman from Hyde Park. Her hair was covered up by the turban, of course, so he had not recognized it, but it was definitely her.

There was a smug sort of shy look on Miss Fox-Edwards's face. "I suppose we should start planning the wedding."

Chapter Five

May 8, 1812

I T WAS THE sunlight that woke her.

With each passing day, the sun was rising earlier and earlier. Strands of sunbeams crept around the corners of the curtains, spreading delightful gold into Alice's bedchamber.

When she glanced over, bleary eyed, at the carriage clock on the little bedside table, she saw it was only just past seven o'clock. It was not a time she typically relished being awake, but for some reason, Alice was filled with a sense of happiness, peace, and calm. It was so alien after such years of strain and struggle that she was startled by it.

Sitting up did not change the sensation. If anything, Alice only felt more comforted, more relief seeping through her.

Why on earth was she so happy?

Alice shook her head, as though dislodging an unpleasant thought. It was a sorry state of affairs indeed if that was her concern: that she was too happy.

But with the debts upon her father's name, the imminent departure from this property, the extortion from Mr. Shenton, and the expectation that she and those who depended upon her would soon be destitute, there were not numerous reasons to be cheerful.

Alice looked at her hands, folded above the blanket on her bed.

They were her hands. She knew them well. The little scar on the back of her right hand from the cat she had played with when she was small, the fingernails cut delicately, and the skin kept smooth and soft thanks to the concoctions Jane created for her.

All the same, except...

On the fourth finger of her left hand was something new. A ring. A signet ring, large and heavy, barely fitting on her delicate finger, with a crest upon it.

"Miss Fox-Edwards, will you marry me?"

Relief crept across Alice's face.

"I did it," she whispered into the early morning air.

Somehow, and she was still not sure how she had managed it, she had enticed a gentleman to propose matrimony to her.

And not just any old gentleman, either.

"May I introduce His Grace, the Duke of Cothrom?"

Alice drew her knees up and her ankles in as she stared at the ring on her finger. The Duke of Cothrom. Goodness. Now that was a match to which she would never have aspired... yet she had managed it.

A duke!

She sat for a little while in silence, staring at the ring, thinking of everything it represented. Food and warmth, shelter and protection. Perhaps a nice house in the country where they could hide away from Society.

She never had to worry about anything anymore. Except...

Alice swallowed. It would be too much to hope that the Duke of Cothrom would not hear any of the rumors going around about her. She was implicated only, nothing was proven, she was quick to remind herself. But from the little she already knew of the Duke of Cothrom, Alice supposed he was not generally in favor of wives with scandals whispering in their past.

Well, she would just have to overcome that when the conversation happened.

"Good morning, m'lady," murmured Jane as she quietly crept into her mistress's bedchamber.

Alice looked up, unable and unwilling to hide her delight. "Good morning, Jane."

"And a bright and blessed morning it appears to be, too," Jane said conversationally, in a normal voice now she had ascertained that her mistress was quite awake.

Alice grinned and glanced back at the heavy gold ring on her finger. "Yes, I suppose it is."

"Now, you must tell me everything about that ball of yours last night," Jane said as she started to busy herself with readying the toilette table. "I'm guessing you got in, you clever thing, for you were not back until late and much too tired to speak of anything. Did you—"

"Jane," Alice said gently, waving her left hand.

"—obviously you can't tell me everything. It's not right for a woman in my position to know all the goings on of you people, but—"

"Jane," Alice said again, waving her hand more vigorously this time, stifling a laugh.

Her maid did not even look around. "And with only a few weeks to go before we have to return to Brighton, have you considered your next—"

"Jane!" Alice said, a laugh escaping her. "Look at me, will you?"

Jane did so, hands flying to her mouth as her eyes widened. "Is that—that isn't—is it?"

Alice grinned fondly at the ring which represented not just her salvation, but Jane's, and others', too. "It is."

Jane's eyes were still wide. "You didn't."

"I most certainly did," Alice said, slipping out of bed. "I said I would, didn't I?"

Their delighted laughter probably rang out through the house—Alice didn't know, she didn't care. A weight which had been pressing on her for months was gone, the tension in her shoulders finally starting to dissipate. All the fears, the panic of what would happen to them . . . it was over.

She had done it.

"I'll take tea in the morning room," she said to Jane after her hair was thoroughly pinned up. "Let Cook know, will you?"

Alice descended the staircase alone, which was probably all to the good, for the hallway was not empty. Standing there amongst the umbrella stand, longcase clock, hat stand, and two paintings of Brighton was—

"Your Grace," Alice murmured as she reached the bottom step.

The Duke of Cothrom nodded curtly. "Miss Fox-Edwards."

Alice stared, heart barely beating as she took in the most unexpected appearance of the man who, just a few hours ago, had asked to marry her.

He . . . he hadn't changed his mind already, had he?

Instinctively, Alice brought her hands together and clutched the ring. If he asked for it back, she would have no recourse. There was no brother, no father to make the Duke of Cothrom comply with the offer he had made.

Even if it had been made in haste. Impulsively. At a ball.

Oh, Lord, was she about to lose the very thing she had only just secured?

The Duke of Cothrom bowed, and just in time, Alice recollected herself. She curtsied low, and wished to goodness she weren't so flustered.

Dukes were not supposed to just turn up at one's home, let themselves in, then wait in the hallway at—Alice glanced at the longcase clock—eight o'clock in the morning, were they?

The silence elongated as she stood there, wretchedly hoping the Duke of Cothrom wasn't about to do the unthinkable and end their engagement.

Before it even truly began, Alice thought dully. *Before I had any chance to impress him, to show him how pleasant I could be as a wife.*

And yet he said nothing. The Duke of Cothrom merely stood there, glancing at her, then flicking his gaze about the place. In silence.

Was it possible the Duke of Cothrom was . . . shy?

"What are you doing here?" Alice blurted out, unable to bear the tension any longer.

She regretted the words the instant they left her lips, but there was no taking them back. And she had a right to ask, didn't she? Fine, perhaps not in such an uncouth manner, but still.

The Duke of Cothrom inclined his head. "To find out a little more about the woman I am about to marry."

His light blue eyes met hers, sparkling in the early morning air, and a rush of desire suffused through Alice's chest.

Goodness. The way he looked at her . . . it was territorial. Possessive.

He was a powerful man, and not just due to his title. It was not something she had much experience in, but—though Alice would feign admit it to a living soul—she wanted to.

"Ah," she said aloud, flustered and not sure what the proper etiquette was. Surely this was early, even for an engaged couple to meet? "Well . . . well then. Would you like to join me for tea in the garden?"

The Duke of Cothrom's eyes widened. "In the garden?"

Alice censured herself privately, but there was nothing for it now but to barrel forward. "It is a habit of mine when I am in the country, and I admit that I rather prefer it, if the weather proves clement. Will you join me?"

She gestured farther down the hall, where the back door opened to a terrace.

For just a few heartbeats, the Duke of Cothrom hesitated.

What could he possibly have against gardens, Alice wondered. Or was it merely that the practice was unusual, and he had a dislike of doing anything unorthodox?

If so, she would have to trot him down the aisle as soon as possible . . .

"Yes. Garden, tea. How pleasant," the Duke of Cothrom said politely. "Lead the way."

It was a relief to turn her back on him and walk calmly—as calmly as she could manage on the surface, at least—to the back door.

While she had the benefit of hiding her face from her betrothed, Alice tried desperately to calm herself.

She had hoped for time this morning to think over the events of last night, compose herself, and prepare a story for the Duke of Cothrom as to her background. A few lies, nothing more.

But having him so immediately presenting himself . . .

Alice opened the back door and inhaled the fresh air, felt the sunshine on her face, and tried to remember she had done the most difficult thing. The Duke of Cothrom, following her outside and breathing in deeply in turn, had offered her marriage. In public. Even with no male relatives to enforce such a thing, there would surely be too many witnesses for him to cry off.

Stepping over to the collection of chairs and small tables that were on the small terrace, Alice gestured to them. "Please, take a seat."

The Duke of Cothrom did not look at the seats themselves, but her hand.

Alice looked too, then winced. She had gestured with her left hand. The hand bearing his signet ring.

Somehow its solid weight was a comfort to her that nothing else could be. He had given her his ring. He would not merely have come to take it back, would he?

"Thank you, Miss Fox-Edwards," the Duke of Cothrom said quietly, taking a seat by a little table.

Alice slowly lowered herself into the opposite seat and flashed a brief smile.

He did not return it.

Her heart sank. Well, she had been prepared to marry any gentleman who would treat her with a modicum of respect. Warmth would have been a bonus. Love had most certainly not been expected.

Still. It would have been pleasant to find herself engaged to a gentleman who smiled more.

"Miss Fox-Edwards, I am sure you can understand why I must—"

"Do you wish to rescind your offer?" Alice said in as brave a voice as she could manage.

That must be what he was about to say. Her initial fear at seeing him in her hall was coming true. Well, she couldn't wait for him to say it politely. She had to know, one way or the other, and if asking the question gave the Duke of Cothrom permission to get straight to the point—

But the dark-haired man looked bewildered. "Rescind? Why should I wish to do that?"

Alice stared, hardly able to believe it. "You . . . you don't?"

The Duke of Cothrom shook his head. "No, there was no thought of—"

"Because if you wanted to—"

"Do you wish to be free?"

Alice swallowed and looked away from the gentleman seated opposite her and out toward the garden.

It was a pleasant enough garden. Little care or attention had been given it since her mother died, which Alice regretted. She should have kept it in better repair, she supposed, but gardening was not something that came naturally to her. Besides, in Brighton, she had a man for that.

She'd *had* a man for that.

A large oak tree at the end of the garden gave a great deal of shade to some plants, and a gravel path meandered toward the house. Peonies which had stopped flowering a few weeks ago were still resplendent in their greenery, and the shrubs were sweet with the scent of their small flowers. Tulips had dotted the path in the early spring, and now bright annuals with blues and reds and yellows brought happiness to her.

Selling the house had been painful, but she had little recourse to do anything else. This way the debts were paid, and the Marshes had been kind enough to let her stay on while they were visiting their daughter in Lincoln.

It was not her garden any longer.

When Alice turned back to the Duke of Cothrom, she ensured that she was smiling. "I have no wish to be free of our agreement, of course. But . . . well, your sudden arrival here, outside visiting hours—"

"Ah." The Duke of Cothrom—*was he flushing, ever so slightly?* "I suppose that is most uncouth of me, and beyond the borders of refined behavior, but . . . well, I wanted to see you."

Something flickered. *He wanted to see her?*

"To ask you some questions," the Duke of Cothrom continued. "I . . . I think it only right that I know a mite more about you before our engagement is announced."

Alice nodded mutely, hardly able to believe it. *Announced*. Their engagement announced.

This really was going to happen.

"Tea, m'lady," said Jane.

Alice jumped. She hadn't noticed the door to the house open, or her maid walking through it with a tea tray in her arms.

If the Duke of Cothrom's jolt was anything to go by, he had been just as startled.

"Thank you, Jane," said Alice hurriedly. "Just pop it here, thank you. That will be all."

As her maid stepped back toward the house, behind the Duke of Cothrom, she gestured wildly with wide eyes. Alice managed to stifle her giggle and looked resolutely at the teapot.

"Shall I pour?" She and the Duke of Cothrom sat in silence as she carefully poured the tea. "Your Grace, do you take—"

"Cothrom."

Alice stared. "I . . . I beg your pardon?"

"Cothrom," the Duke of Cothrom repeated with a tight smile. Very tight. "I think, given that we are engaged to be married, it is permissible for you to refer to me thus."

Refer to him thus. Ah.

It was most strange. Alice had been confused last night by the difference between the prim and proper gentleman she had accosted in Hyde Park, and the rather forward gentleman she had met at the Earl of Chester's ball. Now she was bewildered.

Which was the true Duke of Cothrom? The reserved, stiff man, or the man who had whispered such . . . such things to her?

"Perhaps I want something deeper. Crave your good opinion in a way that goes beyond a simple compliment."

"Well, Cothrom," Alice said, pinking at the way he inclined his head in approval as she spoke. "Milk, sugar, lemon?"

Their tea made, Alice took a slow sip of the piping hot liquid and tried to relax. It was just a conversation with her future husband. Just tea on a terrace.

Why, this was in a small way an insight into their future together.

The thought was a shock to her system. The rest of her life . . . with this man. Well, she could certainly think of worse.

"You threw yourself into my arms."

Alice blinked. "I—I beg your pardon?"

"In Hyde Park," the Duke of Cothrom said calmly. "You threw yourself into my arms. Why?"

Well, she should have expected this—but now the question was before her, it was not entirely clear how to navigate it.

"I *fell* into your arms," she countered, trying to keep her breathing level. "I did what any unchaperoned woman should and attempted to . . . to protect my honor."

He examined her closely, his sky-blue eyes serious.

Would he see through her deception? It was not precisely a lie, after all. Was it?

No, he was an intelligent man. He certainly wouldn't swallow such a ridiculous statement. He—

"I see. Yes, of course," said the Duke of Cothrom with a slow nod. "Yes. Of course."

Alice's eyes widened slightly. *Goodness.* That was unexpected.

"Tell me, Miss Fox-Edwards," said Cothrom in a businesslike manner, placing his cup back on its saucer. "Your parents. They are well? In London?"

"They are sadly no longer with us, Your—Cothrom," Alice amended, her cheeks pinking at the suggestion of intimacy.

If the duke saw it, he certainly didn't show it. "And you have siblings?"

"No siblings at all, I am afraid," said Alice with a wry look. "I am an only child, something I have regretted since my parents died."

For some strange reason, Cothrom looked almost relieved. Or was it a trick of this early morning light?

No, it was definitely relief. Alice watched as the man's shoulders eased downward and the tension in his jaw somehow melted away. Her eyes lingered at that point where his jaw curled up under his ear, then meandered to his chin, to his throat, the suggestion of prickly hair escaping from his elegant cravat. He was a broad man, as well as tall. Strong. Powerful. She had sensed some of that power when . . .

Alice swallowed and sipped again at her tea. That was it, the tea— that was why she felt so warm.

"Forgive me for being so forward," she said quietly. "But I believe if we are to be married, then we should feel free to speak openly."

Cothrom nodded but said nothing.

Alice hesitated, then continued. "I am curious as to your relief that I am alone in the world."

Fine, she perhaps could have phrased that a little better. But still. It was odd.

Clearly Cothrom thought so too, for his cheeks reddened. "I take no pleasure in it directly, of course, Miss Fox-Edwards, but—"

"Alice."

It did her good to see the man confused by a single word.

"I . . . I beg your pardon?"

"Well, if I am to call you Cothrom, do you not think it right and proper that the intimacy is mirrored?" Alice asked teasingly. *Well, it might do the man some good, too.* "You should call me Alice."

She watched as the man's throat bobbed, and a strange sense of power crept over her. Goodness, it was pleasant to see a man like him so turned around. It was only a name, wasn't it?

"Very well," Cothrom said quietly, fixing her gaze with his own. "Alice."

Something hot and sticky and delightful soared through Alice—a sensation she had never encountered before. Dear God, but hearing her name on his lips, spoken like that, like a prayer, like he was begging for something—

"You are right to sense that I am relieved, in a small way, that you have no family," Cothrom continued, as though he had not just struck a most unusual chord now humming through her body. "I cannot permit even the slightest hint of scandal near my family, as I am sure you can understand. I must be sure, completely certain, that there are no skeletons in your past."

Try as she might, Alice could not prevent her breath from hitching.

Well, this was it. If she were to survive this conversation intact, and most importantly survive with their engagement intact, then this was the moment to speak up.

And she could. She knew she could.

All it would take was . . . lying was such a strong word.

"Ah," she said brightly, as though she were delighted to hear him say such a thing. "In that case, I must tell you about . . . about my second cousin."

As she had expected, Alice saw Cothrom's brow immediately furrow. "You must?"

"She was also called Alice, and she had a flirtation with a gentleman a few years back, a flirtation which did not end well, I am sorry to say," Alice said as blithely as she could over the agonizing thumping of her pulse. "She went abroad after the—well it was not a scandal so I shall not call it that. Let us term it . . . disappointed hopes."

Cothrom's brow was still furrowed. "That is . . . yes, I believe disappointing is the right phrase. But there was no scandal—no actual suggestion of wrongdoing?"

Alice swallowed. *Just a few more lies.* "Naturally. But as you can imagine, bearing her name, there may be a few in the *ton* who confuse the two of us. They may believe that it was I, you understand, when in fact I have never flirted with a gentleman who has not subsequently proposed marriage."

She permitted herself a small smile and lifted up her teacup to prominently display Cothrom's own signet ring on her finger.

As expected, the man flushed. "Yes. Yes, I see."

Alice peered over her teacup, fortifying herself with the hot liquid.

Goodness, he was handsome. It was probably a very unladylike thing to think, but he was. Greek statues could have been modeled off him, that sharp jawline, that penetrating stare.

"And I assure you, I have no parents or siblings to cause a scene," Alice added as she lowered her teacup, forcing the point home. "And—"

"But what about you?" Cothrom interrupted, leaning forward slightly. "Your life until now, I mean."

Alice hesitated. *Some truth would not hurt.* "My father was a baronet, I came out into Society about four, five years ago, and I returned that Season back to Brighton to care for my father. Other than that, there is not much I can tell you."

Well. It was not a lie.

Cothrom was gazing at her closely, as though attempting to discover her dissembling. His intensity caused a flutter in her stomach.

Perhaps she needed to eat something. That was surely the explanation for—

"You are very beautiful," Cothrom said suddenly. A red tinge touched his cheeks.

Alice stared. She was not an expert on dukes—far from it—but they were not usually this reserved, were they?

No, perhaps reserved was not the right word. Upright. Proper. Always holding himself back.

What was it he had said at the ball last night?

"I admit to you, my lady, that the wearing of the masks and the anonymity . . . it introduces a level of . . . excitement."

"I mean, you are a beautiful woman, and have been out in Society for more than enough time to . . ." Cothrom babbled before his voice faded. "Why are you not married, Miss . . . Alice?"

This time Alice was prepared for it. The question, that was. Hearing again her name from Cothrom's lips once more shot something delicious through her body. How did he do it?

"I was . . . waiting for you."

"No, really," said Cothrom, finally smiling. "I mean, that is very flattering, but—"

"Look, if you want it, you can have it back," said Alice, deciding to force this conversation to its conclusion.

She was still uncertain as to whether the Duke of Cothrom was looking for an excuse to break it all off. But she needed to know, once and for all, that he was committed to her. Committed to this.

Alice slipped off the signet ring, placed it on her right palm, and with a slightly shaking hand, offered it out. "Take it," she said quietly. "If you want."

Try as she might, she could not prevent the slight quaver in her mouth.

This was a gamble—one she could lose. She did not know this Duke of Cothrom well enough to sense if he would understand what she was truly asking. Whether he would truly marry her.

Her gaze swept over the tall man. She could see in his eyes, the way his pupils flickered, that he was weighing it up, the advantages and disadvantages. A business decision, not one of the heart.

This certainly had nothing to do with love.

Before Alice could say anything, before she could attempt to convince him of her worth, how pleasant it would be to be married to her, before she could say anything—

The Duke of Cothrom reached out.

Her hopes sank. *Well, it was going to be another scandal, one he would weather but she would not.* There were enough people at the Earl of Chester's ball to hear his proposal. When there was no wedding—

Cothrom's hand reached hers, his fingers brushing against her own as a tingle shivered across the skin of her hand. And then he was closing her hand. Enclosing it around his signet ring.

Alice stared, meeting his eyes with frank astonishment.

"Miss . . . Alice," Cothrom said quietly, "I will be honest. I did not expect my engagement to occur this way, but I do need to marry at some point, and there is sufficient Chance wealth not to require an heiress."

Still uncomprehending, Alice whispered, "Then what do you want?"

"I want a good woman," Cothrom said simply. "Someone I like. Someone I can . . . can care for."

And a shimmer of something that might have been attraction or desire moved between them. The air shifted, grew warmer, and Alice found she did not want the gentleman to remove his hand from hers.

Well. It was a start.

Alice smiled. "I can be that woman."

Chapter Six

May 15, 1812

"Y OU ARE A complete idiot."

William scowled. He was usually the one saying that, and it was most disconcerting to have it thrown at him across his own smoking room.

"I am not," he began.

"Yes, you are," said Lindow firmly. "What on earth were you thinking?"

"He wasn't thinking at all, of course he wasn't!" Aylesbury said before William could get a word in edgeways. "For the first time in his life, the man wasn't thinking. We should be celebrating!"

The two men fell about in laughter, and William tried to smile. Tried.

It was his own fault. He had invited all three—despite Lindow's opinion—of his brothers to Cothrom House to tell them about the engagement. The trouble was, the gossip of London moved far more swiftly than he had expected. They already knew.

Which meant they had already been preparing their roasting comments.

"Oh, have another drink, Cothrom. It's not the end of the world," said Aylesbury easily.

"I don't know, I would describe marriage as just that," teased Lindow.

"All the more reason for a drink!"

William sighed, ignoring their laughter but not their pointed requests for another drink. It was a little early for such things—just after luncheon—but he supposed he should have expected it. *Any excuse.*

As he stepped across the oak paneled room toward the drinks cabinet, William glanced once again at the door. He had hoped... well, the invitation had been most welcoming. As welcoming as he could make it. And yet still Pernrith had not come.

"He won't come," said Lindow quietly from behind him.

William did not turn around as he opened the drinks cabinet and started pulling glasses toward him. "He might. You don't know that—"

"He won't," Lindow said flatly. "He's not a part of this family."

"And whose fault is that?" William shot over his shoulder. "If you could just make him feel welcome—"

"I won't ever do that, and you know that, so please drop it," the younger of the Chance brothers said through what sounded like gritted teeth. "He's not our full brother. Our father betrayed our mother, sired a—"

"That word is not to be bandied about in my house," William said, as calmly as he could manage as he turned back to his brothers with three glasses and a bottle of brandy. "Thank you."

Lindow glowered but had the self-restraint not to continue.

William sighed as he stepped over and handed glasses to him and Aylesbury, pouring a healthy portion of brandy into each. "Come now, I did not invite you all over to argue."

"No," said Aylesbury abruptly, evidently just as eager as he was to move the conversation on. "We're here to commiserate!"

"Celebrate," said William stiffly.

"We're here discussing your imminent imprisonment," said Lindow darkly. "I'd call that commiseration!"

Damn it all, but they were infuriating. "To Miss Fox-Edwards," said William tightly, lifting his glass.

Both of his brothers did so, as well. For a moment, he allowed himself a sense of relief that they were finally behaving like civilized human beings.

"Yes, to Miss Fox-Edwards," said Aylesbury with mock seriousness before throwing back the entire glass of brandy.

"To Miss Fox-Edwards," Lindow said with a grin. "And all who sail in her—"

"Lindow!" William censured.

There was nothing he could do. Lindow and Aylesbury were chuckling like schoolboys, and William's headache was only growing with the sip of brandy he'd taken.

"Don't take on so like a mother hen," Aylesbury said with a placating lift of his hand.

Lindow dropped into an armchair. "Yes, after all, you're the one who has decided to do the irresponsible thing and offer marriage to the first woman you spoke to after our little conversation."

Ah. Yes, well. They had a point.

William dropped onto the sofa and beheld his brothers, wondering if he could explain it to them. Perhaps if he understood it better himself, he'd have a better chance of doing so.

But that was the trouble. Something strange had come over him when he'd been dancing with Alice—with Miss Fox-Edwards, he must remember to call her that in public. Something had overcome him, some desire he had not known before.

Oh, he'd known desire. Hot lust, easily sparked, easily solved.

But this? This had been different. His tea in the garden with her the following day had proven his instincts, though slightly confused, had been right. Miss Alice Fox-Edwards was a perfectly respectable woman with no relatives likely to cause a scene, and one distant cousin who was thoughtless and thankfully out of the picture.

She was therefore perfect.

"—never thought you would be so . . . so reckless," Aylesbury was saying.

William blinked. Both his brothers were staring. He shrugged. "It did not feel reckless at the time."

Although it had felt similar, he imagined. There had been a rush of something new, a delight in leaving behind the expectations of Society, just barreling forward with the first idea that had come into his head. Was that what recklessness felt like? If so, no wonder his brothers were so reckless.

"I never would have thought it of you," said Lindow, wagging a finger.

William gritted his teeth to prevent himself from listing the innumerable occasions when Lindow had been far more reckless. "I know."

"If anything, I'd say you were thoughtless," Aylesbury said expansively, placing his brandy glass on a console table. "I mean, you met the woman that very night! Spent what, an hour with her, in total?"

William hesitated. It was tempting to mention he had met Alice beforehand. It would make the sudden engagement sound far more reasonable. Rational. Explainable.

The circumstances of that meeting were so unusual, however, that it may not actually help. Besides, he had not recognized her at the ball, not with the mask and the turban.

No. Perhaps not worth mentioning.

"You were thoughtless," came Aylesbury's words.

William nodded curtly. "I know."

"You could be making a huge mistake," Lindow pointed out.

"I know."

"You might not even like her after a few months," Aylesbury said, shivering.

"I know."

"And you could bring ruin on the whole family if it turns out she's a wrong'un," said Lindow, with barely concealed glee.

A nerve throbbed in William's temple. "I know."

Lindow and Aylesbury exchanged a look. Then they fell about laughing again.

William tried to contain his temper, he truly did. It was just his brothers' way, he knew. After so many years, he should really be accustomed to their ribbing.

But somehow, when it came to Alice, it crossed a line. A line William had not even known he had. But the act of mocking her, teasing him about her, lit a fire in him that decades of dedicated self-control could no longer hold back.

"It is not a laughing matter!" William exploded, rising suddenly from his seat.

If he had hoped his outburst would quieten his brothers, he was sorely disappointed.

Aylesbury grinned. "Well, at least it's not me making a huge mistake this time. It's rather pleasant for it to happen to someone else."

"Yes, is this how you feel every time you see us being little disasters?" piped up Lindow. "It is most enjoyable."

William did everything he could to slow his breathing, but he did permit himself a slight eye roll.

Brothers!

All three of them were nightmares, in their own way. Aylesbury was constantly needing money, money William could ill-afford now he was to be wed. Lindow was the black sheep, if it were possible to pick one, constantly getting himself in trouble with the ladies. And Pernrith . . .

Well. Having a half-brother from your father's notorious affair was difficult to manage at the best of times, but Pernrith didn't help himself. He was a viscount! He needed to be here, part of the family, working out what was best for the family.

William gritted his teeth. Though he wasn't entirely sure he wanted another opinion on his hastily arranged marriage.

"Look," he said quietly. "Admittedly, I did not imagine I would step into the Earl of Chester's ball a free man, and leave it—"

"With a ball and chain newly forged," interrupted Lindow.

William glared. His brother sipped his brandy with an apologetic expression. "Fine. I was caught . . . unawares."

"You were *caught*," said Aylesbury, far more quietly than William had expected. "There is no crime in that. Simply break it off."

Break it off.

William sighed. It was a course of action he had considered, naturally. Waking in the early hours of the day after the ball, he had run through a number of different routes out of his hastily offered engagement.

Leave town. No, that would bring ruin on the lady.

Break it off quietly, secretly. No, there were people at that ball who had seen her.

Marry her, then divorce her. Definitely not.

And that only left . . .

"I will marry her," said William quietly.

Lindow's smile faded. "Dear God, I thought you were joking all this while. You are truly going to marry her?"

"I knew he wasn't jesting," said Aylesbury shrewdly. "This is Cothrom we're talking about. He doesn't joke."

"I most certainly do joke, just not with you two," William said curtly, tightening his fingers around his brandy glass as though that would tether him to the ground. "But I believe in following the rules, in sticking to what Society expects."

"So . . . so you'll marry her, just because you ought?" The way Lindow said it, it was as though William had been given a sentence of transportation. His brother's face surely could not have been more horrified if he had been.

"I made her an offer, in public," said William quietly. "I will honor it."

And not only because it was the right thing to do, though he would not share that particular detail with his brothers.

Because there was something about Miss Alice Fox-Edwards. She had given a perfectly reasonable explanation for her strange behavior in the woodland of Hyde Park. A respectable woman *would* feel startled to be suddenly in the arms of a man she didn't know, William reasoned. Her cry of matrimony was what Society expected.

And there was something else. Something he felt whenever he was in her presence. He had gone to see her that morning in the hope—nay, the expectation—that he had dreamt it.

But the moment she had descended those stairs, bright eyed and ready for the day . . . when they had drunk tea together . . . the feeling of her hand in his, that sudden yearning for her, a connection he could not have predicted . . .

William blinked. Both Aylesbury and Lindow were staring now, genuine concern on their faces.

"Dear God," faltered Aylesbury. "You . . . you're not in love, are you?"

"No," William said instinctively.

"Love? Of course he's not in love. He barely knows the woman," Lindow scoffed. "You're in lust, aren't you, Cothrom?"

"No," said William hurriedly. "No, it's not—"

"Then I don't see why you've got to marry her," said Aylesbury, leaning back in his chair and fixing his elder brother with a curious expression. "There's just no rhyme or reason to it."

No rhyme or reason to it.

Though William was loathe to admit it, his brother was right. In a way, there was no logic to what he was doing.

But perhaps . . . perhaps this was something that went beyond logic. Perhaps—

A chiming clock distracted him from the nascent thought, and William groaned to see the time. "I must depart."

"Depart? We've only just arrived," protested Aylesbury.

"Yes, I've only just started going through my list of hilarious quips about this ridiculous marriage," said Lindow, pulling—*dear God, was that a list he was taking from his pocket?*

William snorted, despite himself. His brothers were dependable. Dependable to be idiots, but dependable, nonetheless. "I invited you to be here at eleven and you arrived past one o'clock. You can hardly complain if I have another appoint—"

"I think you will find we will complain, and shall," declared Aylesbury with a wink. "Though if you leave us alone in the excellent company of that drinks cabinet you have over there, I think I can be mollified."

"I already am," Lindow said with a wink of his own in William's direction. "I've guessed where he's going."

William did not bother to favor that with a response. "I shall see you tomorrow for dinner?"

"Only if we can have it here," said Lindow, rising and approaching the drinks cabinet. "For some reason, I have discovered that if you don't pay your cook, they go off and leave you."

"How bizarre!"

William groaned, but he didn't have time to sort this out. He would have to fix it tomorrow. "Try to leave me something in the drinks cabinet for when I return."

"We shall try," said Aylesbury, placing a hand on his heart with a mischievous expression.

Lindow snorted. "I make no promises."

And it was with that comforting reminder that his brothers were complete reprobates that William pulled on his gloves and hat and left Cothrom House.

It did not take him long to reach Marian Gardens, where Miss— where Alice was lodging. His butler, Nicholls, had been able to discover the location remarkably quickly when William had returned from the Earl of Chester's ball, and though he had taken the carriage that morning, this afternoon, William preferred to walk.

The fresh air and gentle pace would give him the opportunity to reflect.

His brothers' teasing echoed in his ears, but though William knew most of what they said was true—he had been reckless, he had been thoughtless, and his decision certainly could bring disrepute to the family—he still felt no regret about what he had done.

Which was most odd.

Even more so because there was something odd about Alice Fox-Edwards, as well. Oh, William could readily believe her story about Hyde Park—that wasn't bothering him. But there was something else, something more. Something she wasn't telling him, he was certain.

And the only way to get it out of her would be to . . . well, *force her* sounded so uncivilized.

Before William knew it, he was standing outside her front door.

"You are late," said Alice as she opened the door.

This was rather surprising to William. Not the statement that he was late. He'd known he was going to be late the minute he'd left his own home, just as he also knew he wouldn't publicly blame his brothers for it.

No, it was the fact that Alice had opened her own door.

It appeared she could guess his confusion. "Oh, I . . . my footman has a toothache, and my . . . my housekeeper is assisting my cook."

William inclined his head. "How unfortunate for you."

He had intended the words as polite patter, nothing more, but Alice inexplicably raised an eyebrow. "Why? I'm not the one with a toothache. Ready for our walk?"

William swallowed, and then nodded instead of attempting to trust his tongue.

That was the thing about Alice. She was at the same time both forward and shy. She had appeared most appropriately reserved at the ball, and yet there was something forceful about her. Something

William knew he should censure, but could not help but find ... interesting.

The moment Alice stepped out of her lodgings, she slipped her hand into the crook of William's arm. "Where to?"

William opened his mouth, but no sound came out.

She'd done that with such a level of intimacy, he hardly knew what to do with himself. Did all young ladies know how to do such a thing? As though it were natural? As though they had been that way for weeks?

There was a knot in his throat that did not seem able to dissipate, no matter how many times he swallowed. It was most unaccountable.

"Cothrom?" Alice said gently as they reached the pavement.

William drew himself up.

He was a duke. He was a Chance, a family of brothers who did not shy away from anything. Except, it appeared, young ladies.

Oh, hell.

"How about Hyde Park?" he said. "It is close by, and it would be . . . pleasant to walk there."

With you on my arm. So we can make new memories there, memories that don't include you barreling into me, demanding that I marry you.

Not that he spoke these thoughts aloud.

By the look on Alice's face, cheeks pink and eyes averted, he did not have to.

"Yes. Yes, of course."

As they walked arm in arm down the street toward the nearest gate to the park, William attempted not to think about the weight on his arm. The sense of delight it gave him. The warmth spreading up his arm and across his torso. The pride he felt as others glanced at them, and saw a beautiful woman on his arm.

Perhaps this marriage nonsense wasn't such a bad idea after all.

Hyde Park was packed. Though the heat was pushing some to return to their cooler country estates, the beautiful weather was drawing out anyone who was anyone into the open air. Horse riders swept by, carriages trundled, and a great number of pedestrians mingled, forming and unforming groups as gossip and well wishes traveled faster than lightning.

For a time, they walked in silence. Then Alice said something which sparked a reaction within William he could not have predicted.

"Ah," she said, pointing over to a copse of trees, the sunlight glinted off his signet ring on her finger. "Where we first met."

And William did not know what made him do it. If asked, he would have spluttered some sort of incoherent babble or said nothing. It was like . . . hot fury, but he wasn't angry. Spurred on by something far too similar, and far too different.

"Cothrom!"

No one heard Alice gasp his name, she spoke too quietly for that—and William was not surprised. All the air must have been pulled from her lungs as he lunged, pulling her suddenly into the woodland.

Where no one could see them.

"Cothrom, what on earth—"

"This is where we first met, you're right," said William, breathing harshly as he pushed Alice up against a tree, glorying in the desire pooling through him. "You asked me—nay, ordered me—to marry you."

Alice stared through blonde lashes, soft pink lips parted. Invitingly. "Yes, but—"

"And there was nothing more in that?" William asked insistently, desperate to know before he gave into the temptation which had begun in this very place just days before. "You did not . . . I don't know, lie in wait for me, or—"

"William!" Alice gasped, using his first name without even asking. "The very idea—"

"What did you want from me?" William said, taking a step forward and pinning her to the tree trunk with his very presence. "What did you want?"

He was panting, his lungs tight, and something was building, an ache, a need, and he knew he shouldn't give into it, knew what was right, what was due her as a woman . . .

And Alice was looking with such . . . it was not fear. Nor was it surprise—that had faded. It took William a moment to recognize it.

Dear God. It was desire.

"William," Alice murmured. "William, I—"

He did not give her a chance to say another word. William finally touched her body with his own, moaned at the sensation of her breasts pressed up against his chest, and covered his lips with her own.

It was a crushing kiss, one far more passionate than he should have bestowed as their first kiss—but it did not seem to matter.

She could have shied away, pushed him back, declaimed him as a gentleman who presumed too much, all of which would have been perfectly respectable responses. But Alice did not do any of those things.

Her lips parted. Her head tilted, welcoming him in. Her hands were splayed against his chest, just as they had been the first time they had met here, in this woodland, in Hyde Park.

But this time they were pulling him closer, and he wanted to be closer. William's eyes closed as he lost himself in the kiss, tingles of sparking pleasure roaring through his body as his tongue deftly plunged into her welcoming mouth.

Sweet fire. Hot honey. A sort of giddy headiness he had only previously associated with mead.

When William stepped back, breaking the kiss much against his wishes, Alice's hair had become unpinned where he had pressed her into the tree.

They were both breathing heavily.

"Wh-What . . ." Alice swallowed, her eyes unfocused. "What were you saying?"

William gave a laugh, pulling a hand through his hair and wondering how he could have allowed himself to lose control like that. *He could not lose control again.* "I have no idea."

Chapter Seven

May 20, 1812

THE THIN, DELICATE ribbon moved smoothly through Alice's fingertips. The glinting light from through the modiste's shop windows made the navy fabric shine, almost shimmering as she turned it between her fingers. First one way, then the other.

At first, it just looked like an ordinary piece of ribbon. Dull, a dark navy, nothing much to look at. Then a slight twist, and the silver that had somehow been woven through the threads glittered, transforming it into the most beautiful thing she had ever seen.

Alice swallowed as she forced herself to put the ribbon down.

The last thing she needed was to gain attention as a thief when she was merely dazzled by a little luxury.

"And I told her, I said, we'll never get an appointment just turning up," a woman with thinly pursed lips said to another, perhaps her daughter, who looked dour. "One cannot simply turn up at Madame Jacques and expect her to be available! Why, she is one of the best—"

Alice took a gentle step along the wall of seemingly unending ribbon samples. It took her mercifully away from the irritable chastising of the couple of ladies, but unfortunately brought her into earshot of an entirely different pair.

These two were about her age. They looked joyful, almost carefree. One held a straw bonnet, and the other was attempting to persuade her friend that nothing but a new ribbon would do.

"Look at that color, it simply does not work!" she said earnestly. "Now if you'd just had me with you when you went to buy the wretched thing, you would never have—"

"I like it," the first woman said stubbornly. "And I'm not asking you to wear it—"

"I would ask that you do not wear it anywhere near my presence, unless you intend to remove and burn it!" giggled her friend.

Alice allowed a small smile to drift across her face as her fingers gently moved over the great number of buttons on display.

Strange. It had been . . . what, four years since she had been able to jest and quip in public like that?

A lifetime ago.

The modiste's shop was bustling, divided into two halves. The front half, the shop, was filled with fabric, ribbons, buttons, thread—all the tools of her trade. Waiting customers could spend their time reviewing the different materials that would one day become the most sumptuous of gowns. It was packed with at least ten people, as far as Alice could see. She was doing her utmost not to meet anyone's eye.

The counter divided the place in half, and behind it was the fitting area. Only one lady was invited back there at a time by Madame Jacques, which would explain the first woman's disgruntled point that arriving without an appointment was foolish.

Alice swallowed. *Unless, of course, you have a card signed by the Duke of Cothrom . . .*

"Madame Jacques will be with you shortly," the shop assistant had said the moment Alice had provided the card, blushing, when she had entered. "She will not be long."

It had been long, but Alice was hardly in a position to complain. Just being permitted entrance into the stylish and fashionably popular Madame Jacques's was more than she could have hoped.

And after that kiss . . .

"Wh-What . . . *what were you saying?*"

"*I have no idea.*"

Alice knew her cheeks were pinking. There was nothing she could do to stop them—it had been a curse ever since she was a child. The moment heat started to blossom on her face, her cheeks did their absolute best to announce it to the world. Raising a hand to her face, Alice almost cringed further at the boiling temperature of her cheeks.

Everyone would see! Worse, someone may take it into their heads to ask her precisely why she was flushing so deeply. And it was not as though she could tell them.

"Oh, because I have tricked a duke—a duke!—into proposing to me, and now I've kissed him, and he is far more than anything I could have hoped for."

Not a conversation she could ever have. With anyone.

Turning close to the cabinets that lined the walls, Alice pretending to show an intense interest in the sample of muslin that was before her.

All she had to do was remain as invisible and uninteresting as possible while she waited for Madame Jacques. And that meant she could lose herself in thoughts. Thoughts of . . .

William.

Alice swallowed as desire rushed through her body, accentuating every sensation against her skin. The smoothness of her clothes, the tightness of her stays—

She really shouldn't be thinking about him at all.

If only the Duke of Cothrom were not such a delicious kisser. It would be much easier to concentrate whenever she was around him, Alice told herself sternly. And it would make using him in this way far less distasteful.

As it was . . .

It was working well, Alice thought as her stomach tied itself into a knot. The plan had been to find a gentleman, and it was working. The moment she had access to funds, she could pay off Shenton and that would be the end of it. She could live happily ever after. They both could. All three of them.

As long as William never found out about—

He never would, Alice cut off the thought, trying to settle her raging panic. She had been most clear that she wished to wed swiftly. By the time Shenton discovered her plan, it would be too late.

And William would never know what she had done.

It was easy to get lost in such thoughts. Perhaps she would have continued thinking that way if not for something spoken just a few feet away which caught her attention: her own name.

"—Miss Fox-Edwards, they say, though I don't see why such a woman as that should get to marry a duke," a woman was saying snippily by the buttons. "I have never heard of her! Why should a woman barely known in London claim the hand of—"

"You have never heard of her either?" interrupted an older woman with a gleam in her eyes that Alice looked away from. "The name is familiar to me, though I cannot precisely remember . . . there was a scandal—no, a hint of a scandal—"

Alice tried to take a slow and calming breath, but it was all for naught. Her lungs simply would not cooperate, her body shifting painfully from carefree delight in the memories of William to desperate panic within seconds.

There had been no scandal. No true scandal, anyway. No scandal anyone knew of.

But try telling that to half the gossips in the *ton* . . .

"Yes, I heard something about her," said a third woman who had joined the first two. "I am sure it was outrageous, for why else would I remember?"

Alice closed her eyes, just for a moment, fighting to force down the nausea rising as the conversation continued.

Was this to be her life? Constantly waiting for the sword to fall, knowing that one day William would have the truth presented to him?

Not that anyone other than herself knew the truth.

Well, herself and one other person. A person she despised and could not risk—

"—not sure it will last," the first woman was saying dismissively. "The Duke of Cothrom has refined tastes. If there is a whiff of scandal, the man will be backing out of that engagement faster than—"

"Bold words from you, Mrs. Pullman," boomed a new voice, one Alice had not heard in the modiste's before. "Did not your own daughter survive a failed engagement?"

The whole place went silent.

Slowly, hoping the new arrival to the conversation would sufficiently distract those in the modiste's, Alice glanced over her shoulder.

The woman was tall, elegant, and well past her prime in the eyes of the *ton*. Yet her silvery hair and the unfashionable nature of her gown did not detract anything from the power that she so evidently wielded.

Alice's gasp caught in her throat. *This had to be—*

"Lady Romeril," said a woman with flushed cheeks, curtsying low to the doyenne of Society. "I-I did not see you—"

"No, I suppose you were too busy besmirching a woman's reputation," said Lady Romeril in a lofty tone.

Alice swallowed.

Lady Romeril. She had met her but once, years ago, and the woman still demanded the respect and attention of any room she was within, clearly.

She held many of the cards of the *ton*. Giving and taking away Almack's vouchers was just the start. Alice had once heard that anyone in Society could be made—or broken—by simply a look from the well-respected woman.

She had not believed it then. She believed it now.

"I do not speak to offend the lady," the poor woman who was being subjected to Lady Romeril's glare said in a hurried voice. "I would certainly not wish her to think I was—"

"Then you are both foolish in the extreme, and the height of rudeness," boomed Lady Romeril, not caring to let the woman finish her sentence.

Apparently that was too far. Alice's lungs tightened as she watched the two women.

She was not alone. Every single person in the modiste's had turned away from their conversations and was staring at Lady Romeril and her combatant. Even the shop assistant at the counter had let the ribbon they were supposed to be measuring fall between their fingers.

Oh, this was a nightmare. Alice had never intended to be so . . . so prominent in Society. Not after leaving all those years ago in what could have been disgrace.

And now she was present to witness an argument between Lady Romeril, of all people, and another woman. About her!

It was mortifying. Alice's body responded to the tension as she knew it would: by stiffening and making it impossible for her to escape.

She should never have come to the modiste's . . .

"I am not foolish, nor rude," the woman was saying, though her flushed cheeks suggested she secretly thought otherwise. "I—"

"You are foolish, because you have not noticed Miss Fox-Edwards is just a few feet from you," said Lady Romeril with a crooked smile. "And you are rude because I believe you would have spoken ill of her regardless. Miss Fox-Edwards."

With a sickening feeling spreading through her, Alice caught the gaze of Lady Romeril as the woman turned to curtsy to her.

Could this get worse?

The woman who had spoken so ill of her was spluttering. "M-Miss Fox-Edwards, I-I n-never—I would not have—Lady Romeril h-has quite misrepresented—"

It was all Alice could do not to turn around, away from the stares, the whispers, the scene Lady Romeril had so elegantly constructed, and march out of the door. Away from the modiste, away from everyone staring, away from the chance that William—that the Duke of Cothrom—might one day discover—

"I will beg for your forgiveness on Mrs. Pullman's behalf, even if she will not ask it, Miss Fox-Edwards," said Lady Romeril magnificently, sweeping her hands about the shop. "And on behalf of all those who have been whispering behind your back, as well. I do assure you, they are quite numerous."

Alice's fingers were numb. She glanced down and saw why. She had brought her hands together before her, unconsciously, and was gripping her own hands so tightly that the ends of her fingertips were white.

When was this nightmare to end? How on earth was she ever to escape it?

"Th-That... that is quite all right," she said aloud, hoping to goodness her voice would hold. "I—"

"After all, His Grace, the Duke of Cothrom, chose you, of all the ladies in the *ton*, to be his bride," said Lady Romeril, clearly not caring a whit to hear what Alice actually thought. "He must think you are impeccable—a cut above the rest. The only woman he could consider as his bride."

Alice blinked in the dazzling glare of Lady Romeril's look, and knew she had to speak. She had to say something. The silence in the modiste's was deafening. A pin, if it had been dropped in that moment, would have been most palpable.

As it was, no obliging pin was discarded.

Alice swallowed, mouth dry, shoulders slumping under the weight of such attention.

Speak, Alice!

"I-I..." She swallowed again, hating her darkening cheeks and trembling fingers. "I—"

"There you are, Miss Fox-Edwards," said a low, deep voice as a hand gently wrenched hers apart and placed one on a strong arm. "I thought you would have finished by now."

Alice turned. She looked up into the face of William Chance, the

Duke of Cothrom.

There were gasps around the modiste's. Only then did Alice realize hers had joined them.

"Are you ready to leave?" William asked in that low, deep, comforting voice.

Alice considered attempting to speak, then simply nodded.

How much of that had he heard? When had William entered the modiste's? Well, it was over between them now, wasn't it? But the last thing she wanted was to give Mrs. Pullman, and all the others here, a show of the disintegration of her engagement.

William strode forward with that elegance and confidence only nobility appeared to have, and Alice clung onto his arm, pulled along in his wake.

And her mind spun. *And what . . . oh, God, what was the world going to say when he broke off their—*

"I apologize," William said stiffly.

Alice blinked as they stood on the pavement, the door to the modiste's clanging behind them. "I—I beg your pardon?"

"It is intolerable that you should have to suffer such ignoble behavior, but I am afraid that is the way of the world," said William, his face a picture of distaste. "It is something you will need to grow accustomed to as the Duchess of Cothrom."

It was a good thing Alice was holding tightly onto the man's arm, for without his support she'd have been liable to droop.

What on earth was he saying? William—the Duke of Cothrom could not seriously still wish to marry her after that nightmare?

"Come, let us walk, there are some pretty gardens along here," said William, seemingly not needing her to respond.

Their footsteps became even and measured, and after a full minute of walking in silence, Alice's pulse had slowed sufficiently for her to form words. "What the . . . how did . . . you?"

Oh, bother. Not coherent words, apparently.

William glanced at her as they entered the little garden in the center of Berkley Square, and there was something rather odd in his expression.

Was that . . . a smile?

"You are in shock after suffering such unpleasantness," he said gently. "It speaks well of you, as a lady, to be so astonished by hearing such rudeness."

Alice hesitated, then nodded.

Well, what was she supposed to say? That it was not the rudeness itself she had feared, but the fact that he would one day hear about the gossip?

"Your countenance, your flush, everything tells me you are a well-bred, delicate woman of principle," William said quietly, his voice soft, as though what he was saying was not for the ears of another. "You confirm all my suspicions. My hopes."

Alice could not halt the sudden intake of breath. "Cothrom, I—"

"You are reproachless," he said, his voice thick with emotion. "Anyone who is about to be a duchess will be subject to envy. I am just sorry you had to hear it."

It took almost another full minute for Alice to understand what on earth was going on.

Then it hit her.

William believed she had been . . . *slandered*. He felt sorry for her! Worse, he was so impressed with her response to the supposed lies that he considered her absolutely spotless.

Her heart fluttered. It was precisely what Alice had hoped for, what she had worked so hard to achieve. The trust of a man like William. Yet now that she had his trust, now that he was so publicly declaring himself loyal to her . . .

A dark, bitter distaste for what she had done started to creep into her.

It was wrong.

Alice pushed the thought away as she and William slowly walked along the path, her arm on his, the early roses starting to lend their perfume to the air.

It was true that it wasn't particularly moral, what she was doing—but she was hardly hurting anyone! She would be a good wife, an excellent wife to the Duke of Cothrom. She would be loyal, quiet, demure, and spend most of her time in the country, if she could manage it.

And it would end the threatening letters, the fear of blackmail, the terror that at any moment her whole life could be torn apart.

Alice swallowed. All she had to do was ensure that William Chance, Duke of Cothrom, never found out the truth about her. How hard could it be?

"You are very quiet."

She tried not to laugh, but it was difficult. "I . . . well, I am rather surprised by the turn of events. I . . ."

Alice's voice faded as she caught a glimpse of her future husband's expression. It wasn't adoration. Not quite. But it was certainly a similar flavor, and it was something she simply did not deserve.

If he knew the truth . . .

But he never would. Alice had promised herself, even after the wedding, with the blackmail sorted and the entire affair behind her, she would never tell him.

The memory of the kiss floated back into her mind.

If a marriage with William was going to contain a few more of those kisses, surely both of them would benefit. It would not matter that years before they had ever met, she had—

"I am heartened by your distaste of such gossip," said William sternly. "False though it may be, there was no excuse for anyone saying such things. Your cousin's legacy, I suppose."

"Yes, yes, my cousin," Alice said peremptorily. "Second cousin. Removed, somehow."

She saw a dark shadow pass across his face.

"A pity," he said as they turned a corner. "She has done you much wrong by even offering a hint at a stain on your character."

Alice's stomach twisted in a knot. Before she could stop herself, she said, "You are very focused on propriety, aren't you?"

William halted, just before they reached the gate on the other side of Berkley Square, and fixed her with a look of genuine astonishment.

"No more than the next person, I presume," he said coldly.

Alice bit her lip. It had been the wrong thing to say—and yet it was true.

"Besides, I have a responsibility," William continued, his expression softening. "One that you cannot possibly . . . but no, perhaps, one day, you will."

Alice continued to stare. *What on earth did he mean?*

"Alice, if I may still call you that . . . Alice, you are to be my wife," he said quietly. "You will share in the joys, the privilege, of being a Chance, and I am afraid that means you will also necessarily partake in the ills."

The ills? What on earth could the man be talking about?

"The ills," Alice repeated.

William nodded, his expression dark. "Propriety may not be fashionable, but it keeps us safe. Safe from harm, from accusation, from losing the delicate reputations our father carefully built. I must protect my family, Alice."

And that was when her hopes started to sink again. "You must."

"I must, and I have, and I shall," William said fiercely. "One misstep, Alice, that is all it would take! One mistake, one hint of true scandal, and the Chance name would be over. There's no real fighting chance in reclaiming your position when it comes to the *ton*. You must always be on your guard, always seeking to be impeccable. And that is why having you as a wife is such a relief."

Alice blinked. She could not have heard that correctly. "I am sorry, did you say, relief?"

And most unaccountably, the man flushed. "Well, I call it relief.

Comfort, then. To do life alongside someone who has the same values as I, someone who understands the importance of always being perfect. It will be . . . pleasant."

His light blue eyes met Alice's, and she could see the flash of desire in them. The longing to close the gap between them, to share in another kiss.

And yet propriety, if nothing else, held him back.

Oh, dear Lord. What was she doing?

The guilt Alice had managed to hold back since their engagement—aided, of course, by that scintillating kiss—resurfaced, this time twice as intense.

She was doing something wrong. She was contaminating this good, rather stiff, gentleman. And if she were not careful, she would drag him down with her.

"Just remember, Alice. I have the document, and you won't get it without paying a great price."

And the echo of Shenton's words forced her resolve, stiffened her spine, and made her smile up at the man who trusted her, despite having no evidence she was as good as he said.

"I look forward to it," Alice said quietly, squeezing her hand on William's arm. "To being your wife. To upholding the Chance name alongside you."

Chapter Eight

May 22, 1812

"Absolutely not," William said firmly. This was one of the benefits of talking with Nicholls. Unlike any of his brothers, the man actually listened to him. When he said something was correct, his butler listened. When he said he disapproved, his butler—

"I am sorry Your Grace, but I am afraid you are incorrect," said Nicholls in his most delicate voice.

William glanced up from the newspaper he had been perusing, folding it carefully in his lap before saying anything.

He had intended for it to be a prominent gesture, to remind the servant precisely who was the master and who had risen early that morning to polish all the silver in the house.

Perhaps it would have worked better if he had managed not to get entirely entangled, the paper not quite folding smoothly, so that William was covered in a cascade of unpleasant folding noises and small irritable mutterings he soon realized were coming from his own mouth.

He dropped the newspaper, ill-folded, onto the drawing room floor. "And what do you mean, I am incorrect?"

His butler met his eye, but only just. "It is a situation, Your Grace, when the words you say and the decision you make are incompatible."

"Nicholls," began William in a warning tone.

This was the trouble with having an intelligent man for your butler. *Lord save him from intelligent men!*

"I merely mean, Your Grace," said Nicholls quietly, "that in the order of precedence, it is simply not possible."

"Not possible?"

"Not without giving offense, you understand," his butler added. "And I would, of course, not wish to be accused of not following the appropriate rules."

William opened his mouth, hesitated, considered the variety of arguments he could give, and closed it again.

Damn it, but the man was right. Dash it all, but he was.

"Most irritating," he muttered.

His butler inclined his head. "Indeed . . ."

The delicate trailing off was sufficient. William rose to his feet and started to pace around the drawing room.

"All I wanted was a simple dinner," he said quietly. "Introduce Miss Fox-Edwards to the family. You know the sort of thing."

"I do indeed, Your Grace," said his butler, who remained standing by the doorway, hands folded behind his back. "And in any ordinary situation, his *lordship* would . . . not have been invited."

William halted, shot a glance at the man, then resumed his pacing.

Once again, the infuriating man was right. But he had to invite Pernrith, he just had to! The arguments if he did not . . . though having said that, neither Aylesbury not Lindow was going to like it . . .

William pulled a hand through his hair, wishing to goodness things weren't so complicated. "What would you advise?"

"A time travel machine, Your Grace."

"What the devil do you—"

"You need to go back in time and uninvite his lordship," said Nicholls smoothly, though there was a twinkle in his eye. "That should just about clear everything up."

William halted in his pacing, about to launch into a diatribe about the proper respect given to the son of a duke—then chuckled dryly as he saw his butler's expression.

"Point well made," he said ruefully. "And perhaps I will take your advice in the only way I can—in the future. For tonight, however, we need to make a decision. Seating."

"Most of it is simple enough," said his butler with a shrug. "You will be at the head, and Miss Fox-Edwards will be on your right."

"And Aylesbury on my left," William nodded, leaning against the mantlepiece where a small fire burned to keep the chill off the room. "He's the second-born Chance, that's easy."

"Ordinarily, my Lord Lindow would sit on Miss Fox-Edwards's right, as he is the next oldest brother of yours, and Lord Pernrith on Lord Aylesbury's left," said Nicholls, a twist of awkwardness in his tones. "However . . ."

William exhaled. "However."

However, neither of them was willing to say, *Pernrith was illegitimate*. He was never legitimized by their father, but William had taken the decision almost five years ago to give the man a courtesy title. One that none of the other Chance brothers had been using.

It gave the Viscount Pernrith some legitimacy in the eyes of the *ton* but could not give him the legitimacy of a true Chance.

And Aylesbury would make a fuss if Pernrith were seated more prominently than Lindow, as precedence must be maintained . . . but also if he found himself sat beside a man he so openly disliked. Really there was no way to win there.

The trouble was, neither of them liked him, though Lindow had a tendency to be more vocal about it. Both of his brothers resented the rather prominent evidence Pernrith gave—simply by existing—of their father's disloyalty to their mother. It was . . . complicated.

"I give up," said William heavily. "Set the table, and I'll accompany Miss Fox-Edwards to the dining room. Aylesbury, Lindow, and Pernrith can sort out the rest for themselves."

He was not surprised at the raised eyebrow of his butler, but there was nothing the man could do to dissuade him.

The bell rang.

"That will be Aylesbury," William said with a sigh. "Try to prevent him from stealing a bottle of my best claret from the cellar, and if he asks for any money—"

"Direct him to you, as ever," said Nicholls smoothly, bowing. "Of course."

William had a few blessed seconds of calm, but it wasn't enough. This introduction had to be perfect.

Alice had not understood the necessity, but he had explained it was imperative she meet his brothers before the wedding. It was only right, seeing as she had no family.

"All three of them," he had said only the day before.

And Alice had frowned and said, "Three of them, Cothrom?"

Perhaps he could have done a better job of explaining Pernrith to her. *Perhaps he could have done a better job at bringing Pernrith into the family in the first place*, William thought wretchedly.

Or perhaps he should never have—

"There's the blackguard!" Aylesbury crowed as he strode into the room, Lindow at his heels. "You'll never guess where we've—"

"You've been at the Dulverton Club," said William wearily.

Lindow grinned as he threw himself onto a sofa. "Told you he'd guess!"

"Well I don't see how the blazes you managed it," Aylesbury said irritably, sitting beside his younger brother and glaring at William. "You're not having us followed, are you?"

There would be no need, William thought dryly. *The men coming to me with your debts are far more efficient than any tailing I could attempt.*

"Not quite," he said aloud. "Now listen, this evening is very important—"

"Yes, yes, you want us to approve of this woman you suddenly felt a rush to propose to," Aylesbury said, waving a hand. "Is she truly that pretty?"

"Yes," William said instinctively.

His chest tightened. *Blast*. He hadn't actually intended to say that.

"My word," said Lindow, lifting an eyebrow as the front doorbell rang again. "You're keen. Well, I can't wait to see her again. You need your brothers' approval, do you?"

"Yes," said William. He should explain, let them know before he arrived. "And—"

"Here she comes now," said Aylesbury, sitting up. "Why good evening, Miss—what the devil are you doing here?"

He had sprung up to his feet, and Lindow—again—was not far behind him.

William stepped forward hastily, placing himself between the two Chances on one side, and . . .

Well. He supposed he was half a Chance.

Frederick Chance, Viscount Pernrith, sadly did not look surprised at the unpleasant welcome he had received. "Cothrom. Aylesbury. Lindow."

"I do not think you were invited—" began Lindow instantly.

"I invited him," William said quietly, raising his hands to the two men who had spoken. "I wished him to be here—I wanted all of you to meet—"

"Miss Fox-Edwards is not yet here?" Pernrith asked, glancing about the room.

"No," snarled Lindow. "So you can leave now without any fuss, you—"

"Miss Alice Fox-Edwards," intoned Nicholls, suddenly appearing in the doorway.

Quick as a flash, all four of the Chance brothers turned, argument forgotten.

William gave a long, heavy sigh as Aylesbury and Lindow stepped forward to introduce themselves to the woman who would be their sister in just a few short days.

Well, it could have gone worse. It most certainly could have gone better, naturally, but that went without saying whenever Aylesbury and Lindow were in the room.

It was just still so difficult. William, as the eldest, had long ago lost the impression that their father had been perfect. Having said that, even he had found it disconcerting to discover that the previous Duke of Cothrom had been unfaithful to their mother. A fourth son to his name, born just weeks after Lindow. It was not something Aylesbury had been old enough to understand when the news had broken.

But they were now old enough to know better, William thought wearily as he watched Pernrith hang back, patently believing he was unwelcome.

And yet what had he truly done to alter the situation? William, the oldest son, had given Frederick a title the moment their father had died, but perhaps it was not enough. Perhaps his avoidance of impropriety had blinded him to—

"Your Grace," murmured Alice, curtsying low before him.

William swallowed. That was the trouble with Alice's beauty. It crept up on him, making it impossible to guard against the flare of his nostrils, the sudden intake of breath, the hardening of his—

"Ahem," he said aloud, as though that could dislodge the sudden rush of heat pooling in his loins. "I mean, Alice. I mean, Miss Fox-Edwards."

Did Aylesbury have to snicker so loudly?

"So delighted to be here," said Alice with a wry look that William hoped to goodness he was the only one to see. "I am honored indeed to be included in a family dinner, as this clearly is."

Her eyes flickered to Aylesbury and to Lindow, then over to Pernrith who had not yet stepped forward and introduced himself.

Panic flared in William. "Ah, yes, this is—"

"Viscount Pernrith, I presume?" Alice said lightly, curtsying to the illegitimate Chance brother. "I hope I will gain your favor, alongside that of my lords."

Her attention moved across all three brothers, and William felt the panic start to subside.

It was well done. Evidently his brief and awkward explanation yesterday had borne fruit.

"He is our brother, of course, and a Chance. Not a full brother—the title, it was meant to . . . and Lindow, he doesn't like . . . but you'll see all that tomorrow. Just be charm itself, as you always are."

And she was. William sat back on the sofa, partly dazed, as Alice gently drew Aylesbury out of his shell, teased Lindow something terrible, and listened with true interest to what Pernrith had to say, the temperature in the drawing room slowly returning to normal.

She was, in short, nothing less than perfection.

William swallowed, hardly daring to speak in case it broke the spell. *How did she do it?* How did she step into an awkward situation, an awkward family situation, no less, and suddenly make everything easy and light? It was unfathomable.

It was, perhaps, what had drawn him to her in the first place. He could barely keep his eyes from her. When Alice laughed, he felt the tug in his stomach. When she leaned closer to one of his brothers to better hear them, he felt the twist of envy.

No wonder he had proposed so suddenly.

Yes, it was all going splendidly—

"—heard the strangest thing about you, actually," Lindow was saying, nodding his thanks to Nicholls who had just passed him—against William's orders—a third glass of whiskey. "A rumor I didn't wish to believe from the haberdashers!"

William's mouth went dry.

No. It had been shocking enough to hear that Alice had such a besmirched cousin, and he had no wish to hear the story again—and he was certain she didn't either. That must be why her cheeks were so red, her expression unfathomable.

Because he had been most clear, had he not, that Alice herself would have to be impeachable. And had she not said there was nothing in *her* past?

"I cannot permit even the slightest hint of scandal near my family, as I am sure you can understand. I must be sure, completely certain, that there are no skeletons in your past."

"Ah, I think dinner is almost ready," said William hastily, rising to his feet. "Why don't we—"

"I didn't hear the gong go," said Aylesbury lazily, leaning forward. "What did you hear, Lindow? Not buying ribbons from a disreputable seller, are you, Miss Fox-Edwards?"

William's gaze snapped over to Alice.

And his heart sank. *Why did she look so . . . so guilty?*

"Yes, I heard that there was a little scandal—well, perhaps we should not call it a scandal. A whisper of a scandal," said Lindow with a lilting grin. "Miss Fox-Edwards, can you defend yourself? This would have been . . . oh, about four years ago?"

Surely the whole room could hear the thundering of his pulse. William's mouth opened, but nothing but a croak left it. A croak that went unheard because Alice—

"Oh no, do not tell me that you also have been taken in, my lord," said Alice calmly.

If his expression was anything to go by, Lindow's curiosity was only growing, and William saw Pernrith stifle a grin out of the corner of his eye.

"Yes, I am afraid there was something rather shocking that occurred four years ago," Alice said evenly.

William had been taking a fortifying sip of brandy. The sip became a drown, if there were such a thing. At the sound of her words, his wrist had jerked most horribly, and the delightful amber liquid had been poured not just down his throat but up his nose.

Hell, he always hated scandal being spoken of. Did he have to listen to it again?

"Are you quite all right there, Cothrom?" Alice said lightly.

Placing the almost empty glass on a console table, William tried to breathe. His nose and mouth burned. "Perfectly all right, I thank you."

"So there is a secret in your past, how fascinating," said Aylesbury, glancing at his elder brother with something akin to triumph. "Dear me. I suppose our righteous brother—"

"Self-righteous," cut in Lindow with a grin.

William tried to smile, but his fingers were tingling painfully, and his pulse was roaring in his ears. Though his brothers could laugh—of course they could. Was there anything they couldn't laugh at?

"Unfortunately, your information is incorrect on one vital matter," said Alice smoothly. "I have a cousin, also called Alice. Second cousin, actually. It is she who . . . well, a disappointed love. Nothing more troublesome than that."

Her bright eyes met his, and there was such certainty in there, such delicate embarrassment, such resolute openness, that William's insides melted.

He had chosen well. Yes, she was ashamed of whatever situation this cousin of hers had managed to find herself in—but she would not accept the blame of another.

Dear God, he had chosen well.

"I apologize for my brothers putting you in such an awkward position," William said stiffly as the dinner gong finally rang in the hall. "You are not responsible for your cousin's actions. Only your own."

For just a heartbeat, a shadow appeared across Alice's face. Most inexplicable.

Then it was gone, and she was smiling and taking his arm, and William could feel nothing but sparks of desire for this woman who was to be his wife.

Only when William and Alice entered the dining room and he helped her to her designated seat did he remember.

Oh, damnation. The seating.

As Aylesbury took the seat on William's left, they both looked at the two men still standing.

William swallowed. "I—"

"I'll sit here, if no one minds," said Pernrith smoothly, taking the seat beside a stony-faced Aylesbury. "I believe Lindow has the right of precedence."

The tension in the room was palpable, though William would have admitted himself slightly relieved. *Well, the problem had solved itself.* Pernrith had openly spoken of his lesser status, and none of them had shouted at each other.

Yet.

William caught Alice's eye and they shared a look. A private look. A heated—

He quickly looked away. What did he think he was doing—indulging in silent flirtation in public?

The dinner itself was relatively calm. There was a small amount of consternation when a footman almost dropped a tray, and William found his cravat was far too tight when Alice accidentally brushed one of her fingers against his, but there it was.

He had managed it.

A dinner. With all four Chance brothers. In one room.

Without fists being thrown.

He should be congratulated. He certainly felt as though a round of applause was in order when both Lindow and Aylesbury managed to cordially bow their heads to Pernrith upon their leaving.

It was with great relief, however, that William shut the door behind all three of his brothers.

The armistice wouldn't last forever. Best that all three be gone well before ten o'clock than for Alice to witness—

"You made it sound as though your three brothers are constantly at each other's throats," said a voice behind him conversationally.

William winced, then turned to smile awkwardly at Alice. "I did, I suppose. And usually I am correct."

It was most difficult to continue speaking, however, with her standing in the candlelight like that. He had never seen a woman with such finely spun hair, so blonde it was almost white. Her gray eyes were sparkling, as was her knowing smile.

"Will you take a glass of sherry with me?" William asked cordially.

His nerves tightened as he awaited her answer. True, it was slightly scandalous, the two of them remaining and conversing unaccompanied. But they were engaged to be married. The humiliation would not be great if it were discovered.

"Of course I will, William," Alice said. "But only if you tell me the details behind those brothers of yours, and why I could have sliced some of that tension with nothing but a spoon."

She turned without waiting for a reply and entered the drawing room.

William swallowed. It would absolutely not be a good idea to lay out the thorny and impulsive history of the Chance brothers. Keeping that to himself was imperative.

Though try telling that to his tongue, the moment he sat in an armchair opposite Alice Fox-Edwards.

"It all began with Pernrith, I suppose," he said quietly. "He is the product of an . . . indiscretion."

"Your father, I presume," Alice said lightly. "Unusual, for him to be such a close part of the family."

William hesitated. "It has not been without its difficulties. As for close . . . in a way, I am not sure I *would* describe him as part of the family. If Lindow had his way—"

He bit down on his words just in time.

Lord Almighty, he almost spoke out of turn there. It was not his job to criticize his brothers—it was to protect them from their own stupidity! If only there was someone here to protect him from his own.

Alice said nothing but raised an eyebrow.

Damn, but she was perceptive.

"It has not been easy, being the head of the family since my—since our father died," William said, sipping the sherry and thanking God for its restorative powers. His mind sharpened, then just as quickly melted as he met Alice's gaze. "Trying to give each of us a fighting chance to be respected within the family and respectable to those outside the family . . . it has been difficult."

"They are very different kinds of men, each unique to himself," Alice said softly.

William nodded. She was playing with the stem of her sherry glass in a most alluring and disconcerting way. Her fingers moved up slowly, then down. Up and down. Up and—

Oh blast.

Quickly crossing his legs and hoping beyond hope she had not noticed the uncouth bulge in his breeches, William tried to smile. "They certainly are, and most difficult. At times I feel as though I am fighting against their very natures."

"And what is your nature?"

William cleared his throat, but it did not clear his mind. His natural instincts wanted him to leap up, step over, push her against the sofa, and kiss—

"I don't know what you mean," he said aloud.

Another lie. Really, he mustn't get into the habit of this.

"Well, you are such a prim and proper gentleman, William," said Alice with a slow, teasing look. Her fingers did not cease their movements. They were causing an aching tension in William where there certainly should not be any. "And yet there must be something about you. Something different. Something within yourself that you are fighting. Some other nature, if you will."

His eyes widened, sensuous fingers forgotten. For the most part.

Now how on earth did she sense that?

It was incredible. The whole *ton* saw William as nothing more than a stick in the mud, he was sure. He knew the rules of Society, and he followed them. There was nothing else to him.

Except there was. And Alice had spotted it.

"I . . . I protect my family, and that is sufficient." His voice hadn't always sounded so gruff, so strained.

What on earth is this woman doing to me?

Alice examined him for a moment, then placed the sherry glass on the console table beside her. "Well, this has been a delightful evening, Your Grace."

Your Grace. William could not help but notice the return to formality, even as he almost stumbled over his own feet to see her to the front door, butler waved away.

"My carriage awaits to take you home," he said quietly.

Alice paused in the open doorway, and there was a smile almost . . . almost like molten mischief on her lips.

Before William could say a word, she had stepped forward and placed a kiss on the corner of his mouth.

"I know there's more to you, William Chance," she whispered. "And I will find you out."

Chapter Nine

May 28, 1812

ONLY WHEN THE large blob of ink had entirely obscured the letter Alice had been writing did she realize she had been holding her pen for too long.

Far too long.

"Botheration," she muttered, folding the paper carefully so the ink did not spill out onto the small writing desk and dropping it into the wastepaper basket beside her, though she wasn't sure why she bothered.

When Alice had made her plans to come to London and find an unsuspecting husband, she'd been forced to sell most of her extraneous possessions. Fine writing desks were a luxury she could ill afford.

This small travel writing desk was more than sufficient for her needs. Even if the hinge was broken, and the ribbon was fraying, and there was a gash mark across the lid that looked as though in a past life, someone had taken a swipe at it with a knife. The plain fact was that a little ink stain upon the thing wouldn't make a huge amount of difference to its quality.

The real tragedy was the paper.

Alice tutted at the small pile of paper to her left. "Careless."

She could hardly justify wasting any more paper, and that meant no more daydreaming about a particular duke.

"And yet there must be something about you. Something different. Some-

thing within yourself that you are fighting. Some other nature, if you will."

Alice brushed a lock of hair from her eyes as she sat back in the hard wooden chair in the small drawing room of the house that would soon no longer be hers.

William Chance, Duke of Cothrom.

With every interaction with him, she discovered something new, something precious. It did seem rather ridiculous that this whole charade had been concocted with the intention of finding a sap she could easily woo and convince to propose to her. Instead, she had ended up with a strong-willed gentleman whom she had somehow still managed to woo.

Even after he discovered her identity at the Earl of Chester's ball . . .

A slow smile crept across Alice's face as she considered the dinner, just a few nights before.

An introduction to the entire Chance family had felt like a rather tall order, yet William's brothers were far easier to sway than he had been.

And his care for them, his dedication. The genuine spirit he had for protecting his family name, the ferocity with which he would do anything, even sacrifice his own happiness for them . . .

Alice's stomach lurched.

It was a characteristic she knew well.

Steeling herself for the task ahead, Alice leaned back over the small travel writing desk and picked up the pen which had so recently been dripping ink all over the place.

Try as she might, she could no longer put off writing this letter.

Frowning as she started to write in a clear, bold hand, Alice spent about ten minutes carefully considering each word. It had to be perfect. It was the only letter she could afford to send this week.

When she finally placed down her pen, Alice gave a long sigh. She'd hardly noticed the air she'd been holding in, keeping her lungs taut, but now the wretched letter was written, she could breathe easy.

She would breathe far easier when her daughter could be brought home.

Dear Mrs. Seaby,

Thank you for your last letter. I am delighted to hear you have found some plums, and that little Maude is eating them. Please be careful to ensure she is never permitted to eat them alone, however. I would hate for a stone to become lodged in her throat. You will be careful, won't you, Mrs. Seaby?

I have been enjoying the weather of late. I hope it has been warm with you. I will endeavor to have a shawl for Maudy sent to you, but if it does not arrive and the temperatures change, you may use the one I left.

Plans for my marriage continue apace, and I am delighted to say that the date is set for June 12th. Of course, I will not be able to have the honor of your presence, or Maudy's, but know I will do my utmost the moment I am a wife.

Please find a pound note enclosed. It is the last of my money. If you require more, would you be so good as to keep a tally? When I am married, I will naturally pay off all debts.

Thank you, Mrs. Seaby, for your kindness.

I remain faithfully yours,
Alice Fox-Edwards

Alice examined the letter. It was not overly cautious, she hoped. Being a mother from afar led to worries and concerns she could never have predicted when her little one was carefully curled up in her arms.

Closing her eyes, Alice took herself back to the last time she had held Maude. Her child. Her darling one.

She could almost feel the weight of the girl in her arms, almost smell the delicate scent of her hair. Almost hear the laughter, the giggles that provoked tears in both of them.

Her conscience wrenched as though about to be pulled from her.

Alice blinked back tears as she opened her eyes. She would do it—she would offer up her heart from her chest if that was what it took.

But she couldn't.

Or was she? Was she, in fact, doing just that?

"You are," Alice whispered, eyes flickering unseeing across the letter. "But it's William Chance's heart you could be ripping out."

She swallowed. She had never meant for something like genuine affection to grow between her and the man she marked as her husband. That had never been part of the plan.

Perhaps that was why the guilt stung so much.

But she couldn't back down now—she couldn't call off the wedding. The Duke of Cothrom was about to become, though he did not know it, the benefactor to her child. All her pin money, once she had access to it, would go to Maude.

And then everything would be—

"There you are," said a quiet, warm voice. "I am so accustomed to you answering the bell, I worried you were indisposed."

Alice rose so hastily her chair tipped to the floor. The noise was nothing to the thundering of her pulse, the panic pouring through her.

William—William, here?

Her instincts drove her to act.

"William," Alice said, trying to speak lightly as she turned back to the writing desk, quickly folding the letter to Mrs. Seaby. "I did not hear the bell, my apologies—"

"What have you there?" asked William curiously, stepping into the drawing room. "Not a letter to another gentleman, I trust?"

Her best, most carefree smile was plastered across Alice's face. "Of course not!"

The letter remained in her hand, folded once and so obscuring the words, but not safe.

Where could she put it? Where could she hide—

"May I see it?"

Alice blinked. "I beg your pardon?"

William's cordial expression had faded, and there was a look of gentle mistrust on his face. As though he knew she was hiding something.

Of course he knows you're hiding something, Alice chastised herself silently. *You've acted in the most guilty manner possible!*

"The letter. I wish to see it," said William.

His voice was low and utterly serious. He had stepped closer, now just a few feet away.

Alice steadied her breath and resorted to the only manner which she knew: flirtatious.

"Why, William, I do believe you are jealous!" she said playfully, tapping him with her free hand as the other—containing the letter—moved behind her back. "Well, I am sorry, but until you marry me, my correspondence is—"

"I am not jesting, Alice. Show me the letter," said William, his voice controlled.

No. Not entirely controlled. She could hear the quaver in his voice, sense the distress in his tone.

This was madness! A man could not just demand to see the private correspondence of a lady!

Perhaps a duke could, a treacherous voice whispered in her ear. *Perhaps a duke should, if he were marrying a woman with a secret . . .*

"Give it to me, Alice."

"N-No," Alice said, taking a step back.

She would not let him. It would all be over between them, everything she had tried to build—the genuine connection they had found. The marriage would be over, and Shenton—

"Alice!"

William lunged forward. Thanks to his longer arms and dexterous movement, he snatched the letter for Mrs. Seaby from Alice's fingers before she could stop him.

Red hot anger coursed through her veins. "What about privacy? What about respect for—"

"If the letter was innocent, you would not wish to hide it," William said quietly, face impassive. "You know my guiding principles, Alice. You know I could never permit—"

"You immediately think of scandal, of course," she said bitterly, blinking back the tears which had so recently sprung from happiness. "You cannot imagine innocence!"

"You immediately tried to hide the letter," William pointed out, most unfairly. "Why not let me see it, if there is truly no scandal within?"

How dare the man speak in such a reasonable tone while behaving so rudely!

"Marrying you doesn't mean every secret—"

"So it is a secret?" William said quietly, lifting the letter and gesturing to it.

Alice swallowed. *Oh, how could this have gone so wrong?* "I . . . I . . . When you asked me to marry you—"

"From memory, it was you who first demanded matrimony," said William slowly. "Why was that, Alice?"

It was all tumbling down around her, but Alice would not permit this engagement to end merely because she had been caught with a letter. Oh no, she was far cleverer than that.

Wasn't she?

"Why not?" she asked boldly, meeting his gaze despite the dread seeping through her lungs. "Gentlemen can demand ladies marry them. Why not ladies?"

"Because that is not the proper order of things, and you well know it," William said, his voice growing curt. "Damn it all, Alice, but you know my position! Keeping the Chances' good name, it is all I do—"

"You might try to trust me," said Alice tartly, lashing out through her pain. *Oh God, what would he do?* "You might trust my discretion, my discernment—"

"And it will be all the easier once I have read this letter," William said, unfolding it and looking away.

Alice swallowed, her throat dry, as she watched his eyes flicker, taking in every line.

It was over. There was nothing she could do to avert this disaster, one of her own making.

Why had she not taken more notice of the time? She had known William was due at three o'clock. Why had she wasted so much time in daydreams?

Her heart was in her mouth as she watched the tension in William's jaw slacken. He blinked rather rapidly then folded the letter, offering it out to Alice.

Try as she might, Alice could not be calm. She snatched the letter back, placing it behind her back again.

As though that would make any difference, she thought dully, meeting William's gaze as defiantly as she could. It was all out now, the truth. It was over.

"When," William said quietly, "were you going to tell me about your ward?"

Alice's jaw dropped.

She closed it hurriedly, her mind whirling. *Ward?*

But of course, William was an honorable man. He would not look at her and presume the very worst: that she had a child, secretly hidden in the countryside. He would think of the most logical and most respectable solution.

A ward.

Alice swallowed. It was not her lie—and if she were careful, it would never have to be.

"Alice," William said gently. "When were you going to tell me about . . . about this Maude?"

Hearing her daughter's name in William's mouth stirred Alice to action. But first, she slowly lowered herself onto the sofa. Her knees could only take so much strain.

"After the wedding," Alice said quietly. "I . . . I was going to use my pin money. Nothing would have come from your accounts—I was determined about that."

"How old is she? This child?" William asked.

She had expected anger, rage. Perhaps a little pique that she had kept a secret from him.

Yet there was none of that in William's eyes. In fact, as he stepped forward and slowly lowered himself to sit beside her on the sofa, there was naught in his expression but affection.

It was most unaccountable. A miracle! But . . . strange.

"Just . . . just over three years."

"And you are sending her money," William said flatly.

A spark of anger rose once again in Alice. Was William going to be one of those men who wished to dictate how she spent every penny? Was even her pin money not truly to be her own? Some ladies spent a small fortune at the modiste, the haberdasher, the bonnet maker, the jewelers. Was she to be forbidden from buying a shawl for a cold child?

"Yes," Alice said defiantly, lifting her chin to look directly into his eyes. Blue eyes. Sky-blue, dazzling eyes. "I care for her."

He held her eyes unflinchingly, and though it was difficult to hold on, Alice did her best.

This was it. The moment. When she would have to face the reckoning of what had happened all those years ago.

But as the silence dragged on, unbearably so, Alice found it more and more difficult to hold her tongue. Why was he doing this—looking at her in silence, saying nothing, revealing no judgment? Was it only so when he finally spoke, his censure would be all the more devastating?

The letter was now crumpled behind her, trapped between her

and the sofa. Alice would have to write it out again later, there was no possibility of sending it in the post like this. Another piece of paper wasted.

Though depending on how this conversation ended, she may have to consider rewriting it. Perhaps she would be telling Mrs. Seaby she was on her way home. After all, her reputation would not survive the ending of an engagement with a duke.

"You have little," William said quietly. "It makes no sense."

Alice blinked. "I beg your pardon?"

"This house is pleasant and well situated, and though you are smartly dressed, you are not rich, Alice, are you?" William said. His voice was low, the warmth of a summer's day, the gentleness of a breeze. "I see no luxurious furnishings here. And yet you send a pound—not an insignificant amount of money—to your ward."

Alice hesitated. She still had not lied—not truly. She had hardly corrected the man, that was to be sure. But that was hardly her fault, was it?

"I think it is only right," she said, determined not to look away and admit defeat, "to care for those in your dependency. Even if it means . . . personal sacrifices."

Like not eating three meals a day. And not lighting the fire unless you come to visit, Alice could have said. *Like not having a footman, or a housekeeper, and making do with myself and Jane. Like knowing that my bills are racking up and unless you marry me, William Chance, I may find myself in debtors' prison.*

Or worse. With Shenton over my head, crowing that my reputation and that of my daughter are ruined forever.

"Personal sacrifices," repeated William.

He had the most bizarre expression. Alice could hardly understand it. There he sat, gazing, somehow closer to her.

Far closer than she had thought. A shiver ran down Alice's spine as she realized William's knees were so close to hers, they were almost touching.

His hands were in his lap, clasped together. Almost unconsciously, knowing she could never be so forward and presumptuous to take them in hers, Alice nonetheless released the letter, leaving it behind her, and folded her hands in her own lap.

Mere inches away from his.

Lord, she was fooling herself. This wasn't working. He couldn't possibly believe in and accept her "ward." The Duke of Cothrom, as she must now think of him, would thank her for her time, politely inform her that their engagement was at an end, and that would be that. She would have to—

"Alice," William said stiffly.

And he didn't just speak. He had moved, his hands had taken hers, and the warmth of him—Alice almost gasped.

The intimacy of such a thing... if she had not been certain she was awake, she would have believed she was dreaming. William Chance did not do such things. Their kiss had been an anomaly, to be sure. He had been most clear it would not happen again.

Not until they were married, anyway.

"I must apologize," said William.

Alice's eyes widened. "I beg your—apologize?"

He nodded curtly, real contrition in his expression. When he spoke, it was in a rush, as though he had been holding back the tide but could do so no longer. "You can imagine what I thought—the letter, I assumed it was—but you are an honorable, good woman, Alice. And I never thought—to find someone who understands responsibility as I do, who doesn't just understand it, but lives it, even when it is difficult..."

His voice trailed away, and Alice realized to her astonishment she was being praised.

Praised. By the Duke of Cothrom. For her "responsibility."

"Ah," she said weakly. "Well, I wouldn't put it—"

"I never thought I would find someone who understood," William said, eyes aglow with something Alice might have called affection. "I didn't realize we were so alike. Alike in our obligations—"

"And in other ways," Alice said, a flash of inspiration coming to her. All she had to do was distract him, pull William away from this line of thinking about her "ward." She knew just the thing. "I think we share morals and . . . and desires, don't we?"

William looked at their intertwined hands.

Slowly, Alice told herself as she gently stroked her thumb over the back of William's hand. *Just enough to show him what you mean, but not enough to evoke censure.*

That was always going to be the balance with William, wasn't it? The man didn't *have* a moral compass, he *was* a moral compass. It would never do to—

William groaned, and it was so heartfelt, pulled from such a deep place, that Alice gasped. "Don't tempt me, Alice. The things I have considered—the longing I have for you—"

And he leaned forward, and Alice's pulse skipped a beat as he pressed an eager kiss against her neck just below her ear.

William's breathing was short, his hands tight on hers, and in the midst of the pleasure he was sparking as he trailed kisses down toward her collarbone, Alice quite lost all sense of what she was doing.

Honestly, how could she maintain it? The man certainly seemed to know what he was doing. Tendrils of temptation were twisting through her.

"But I mustn't," William said, panting as he drew back and fixed her with a devoted yet regretful look. "I . . . I mustn't."

And just like that, Alice realized she had entirely underestimated William Chance, Duke of Cothrom.

It was not that he did not wish to do the delicious things. It was that he desperately wished to and would not permit himself to.

The man was full of passion, yet his strength of character did not permit him to let himself go.

Now that was interesting.

"Do it again."

She had not intended to say those words. It was not part of her plan for to ensure William truly would marry her by way of this type of seduction. But she wanted him. She wanted his lips upon her skin, his warmth, his presence, the feel of him pressed up against her, losing control. What did it matter if a consequence of their shared pleasure was to bind him even more strongly to her?

"I mustn't," William said quietly, though he kept a hold of her hands. "I . . . well, I desire you very much, Alice, and I . . . if I give into such longing—"

"I don't mind," said Alice quickly, thinking rapidly. Yes, that would be an excellent way to ensure their marriage. And besides, if that little taster was anything to go by, she would very much enjoy being bedded by the Duke of Cothrom.

William's smile was roguish, just for a moment. "But I do. Alice, I want our first time to be special. Don't you?"

Alice tried to return the smile. *First time. Ah.* "Of course. In . . . in that case, shall we go for our walk?"

Taking a deep breath, and apparently gathering the strength to let go of her, William released her hands and rose. The mask came back down, and he was William Chance, impeccable model of propriety once more.

"I think that is an excellent idea, Miss Fox-Edwards," he said, offering an arm. "In public. Where we cannot—where I cannot—be tempted."

Chapter Ten

May 29, 1812

"Y`ou ... you look ...`" *Beautiful. Stunning. Angelic. Delectable.* William swallowed. "Good."

"Good?" Alice repeated, her shoulders dropping as she stood on the pavement outside her lodgings.

Coughing did not clarify the matter, William discovered to his irritation. Nor did it help him recover from the sight of the beautiful woman before him.

Though beautiful wasn't quite the word. There did not appear to *be* a word that summarized the elegance of Miss Alice Fox-Edwards dressed up for the party he had invited her to.

Well, the party that Lady Romeril had invited her to. God help them.

Alice was wearing a gown of simple elegance and refined style. Scalloped edges around the hem and sleeves, and a simple string of pearls around her neck. There was some sort of embroidery across the bodice that was most exquisite. And it was fine. Perfect. Just the sort of elegant gown a lady should wear to such an occasion.

The problem was that William wasn't certain whether he preferred the silken concoction on Alice—or off her.

She smiled, dipping slightly to brush a leaf off her skirts which had caught there in the late spring breeze. The movement was refined. It also gave William an eyeful of a curving breast, threatening to spill out of her stays at any moment.

Steady, man, William tried to tell himself. *You'll have her in just a few days. Not even two weeks.*

And until then, it's cold baths for you.

"Are we ready, then?" Alice asked, looking up from her leaf removal.

William swallowed. *Damn it, man, pull yourself together!* "Yes. Yes, I think so."

It had been agreed between them that there should probably be at least one but no more than three public outings for the two of them together. After all, they were to be married. It would be most strange if William did not include Miss Fox-Edwards, his betrothed, in the invitations he received.

But he had not quite prepared himself for this. Not readied himself for the intoxication that was having Alice in his carriage, alone.

Just the two of them.

Where no one could see them.

William stiffened, forcing himself to sit on his hands like a child as the carriage rocked merrily away. Alice swayed with the movement.

William inhaled the heady fragrance he associated with the attractive woman. Honey, and a spice he could not recognize. A hint of lavender, rounding out the intense *Aliceness* of the whole thing. He'd never breathed in anything like it. When he lay in bed, furiously not making love to her as he would wish, that heady mixture was all he could smell.

One day, Alice would be leaving that scent on his pillows. His sheets. His very skin—

"Are you quite well, William?"

William blinked. Alice was examining him with a curious air. "I beg your pardon?"

The teasing smile that curled on her lips made his manhood stiffen. He crossed his legs. "Are you looking forward to this evening?"

"Very much," said Alice, glancing out of the window as she spoke. "I have never been to this part of London—at least, not in a long time.

Lady Romeril's dinners are said to be . . . exquisite."

William swallowed, his gaze drifting past the elegant neck, the teasingly close bust, to the refined wrist and intricately enmeshed fingers. Though enclosed in gloves, it was easy to see every finger. Fingers that he wished were once more in his possession as he pressed a kiss—

This was ridiculous, William told himself. He'd gone and made a complete fool of himself just days before, when Alice's ward had been revealed. He'd almost told her, in fact, just how in her sway he truly was.

"I . . . well. I desire you very much, Alice, and I . . . if I give into such longing—"

No, the time had come to regain the upper hand.

Over himself, William thought weakly as his body responded yet again to the slightest of movements from the woman opposite him.

This was supposed to be an elegant, refined, and most of all respectable dinner. And it would be. All he had to do was keep his hands to himself.

Much to William's chagrin, it did not take the carriage long to arrive at Lady Romeril's door. He had wished for another ten minutes or so. Ten glorious minutes of polite conversation with the world's most beautiful woman, in a box where no one could see what they were doing.

A man could dream.

Instead, he was jumping onto the pavement and extending his hand. "Careful . . ."

His voice trailed away as he realized just how ridiculous he was being. *Careful?* It wasn't Alice who needed to be careful.

It was himself.

As Alice stepped onto the pavement the swish of her gown's skirts revealed, just for a moment, a dashing hint of ankle.

William stared, bewitched. Just the smallest glimpse, but it was enough to rouse him. Who else had seen that part of Alice? No one.

Just him.

It was the beginning of an intimacy he could not wait for. Dear God, when he had his fingers trailing along that ankle, and higher, and higher—

"Your Grace?"

William started, shaking his head as though ridding his ears of water. "Wh-What?"

Alice was stifling a smile—a most knowing one. "We are ready to go in, are we not?"

Shaking himself internally as well as externally, William drew himself up to his full height and offered her his arm. "We are."

Because he was being ridiculous, he told himself as they stepped up to Lady Romeril's home and were welcomed by a bowing footman in her outrageously green livery. Getting worked up about an ankle? What was he, a green-gilled youth of eighteen?

He was losing his head, and that would never do. No, he needed to retreat back into the high walls he had created for himself years ago, in the full knowledge that allowing his desires to have full rein would have little benefit for him or his family.

His desires had to be restrained. The heat within him, quenched.

While having a woman as delectable as Alice Fox-Edwards on his arm.

William inhaled slowly as he inclined his head to a few notables as they entered Lady Romeril's drawing room. The Duke of Axwick, the Earl of Chester, Viscount Braedon—oh, and the Duke of Penshaw. Where had he been all this time?

That was it. All he had to do was forget he wished to get under the skirts of the woman beside him, and—

"Ah, there you are," boomed a voice that made William wince. "I rather thought you would be here earlier, Your Grace."

William felt Alice's hand tighten on his arm and was strangely comforted by it. Lady Romeril was a force of nature, everyone in

Society agreed on that—and it was a wonderful force of nature, of course.

No one would dare speak a word against Lady Romeril.

But still, she was a rather extreme force of nature. Like a gale. Or an avalanche.

As their hostess barreled toward them, pushing aside lesser guests with her gaze fixed on them, William prepared himself for the well-meaning onslaught.

"Goodness," muttered Alice in a voice so low only William could hear her. "Will be any survivors, do you think?"

Swallowing a snort and wondering how he himself would survive this conversation on two fronts now, not just the one, William bowed low as Lady Romeril reached them. "My lady."

"Yes, yes, you're very delighted to be here, I am sure," said Lady Romeril, waving a hand and not giving him a second glance. "So, we meet at last, Miss Fox-Edwards. Officially."

William glanced at his betrothed and saw only the smallest hint of embarrassment tinging her décolletage.

Pride rose. Yes, that was precisely the response he would wish for in his future bride. Embarrassment could not be helped. But one's display of it could.

"I am very grateful for the invitation this evening, Lady Romeril," Alice said demurely, curtsying low—far lower than was necessary, in truth. "What a delightful room."

Their hostess, however, was not about to be distracted by compliments to her home. "This old place? It's nothing, I assure you. I was delighted to read of the engagement, though of course His Grace had also been kind enough to send word. As he ought."

William nodded stiffly. It was a peculiarity of Lady Romeril's that the nobility had discovered—either at their own peril, or through the gentle hint of another. Despite being very little to most of them, Lady Romeril demanded—nay, expected—to be informed of all births, marriages, and deaths. It was trying, but there it was. William had got so in the habit now he quite forgot it was unusual.

Alice seemed to hide her surprise very well. "Read of it, Lady Romeril?"

There was just a hint of confusion in her voice that William did not understand.

A footman appeared at his side and momentarily distracted him. "A glass of champagne, Your Grace?"

William shook his head. The last thing he needed in the presence of Lady Romeril was to lose his sense. "No, I thank you."

It was only a momentary exchange. The encounter with the footman probably lasted no more than ten seconds. Five, more likely.

But appeared to be sufficient time to entirely destroy Alice's equilibrium. When William turned back to his future bride and Lady Romeril, it was to see one with a face of utter confusion, and another full of pain.

What the devil had happened?

"I-I was not aware . . . I did not know," said Alice, all her confidence seemingly drained.

William squeezed her hand on his arm in the hope of comforting her, though he was quite at a loss as to why it was necessary. What on earth had Lady Romeril said to—

"I presumed you had known," said Lady Romeril, shooting daggers.

What the blazes—

"And just in *The Times*, you say?" Alice said hesitantly, looking between them in bewilderment. "Our engagement, you announced it in *The Times*, William. Your Grace, I mean."

In any other situation William would have frowned at the intimacy spoken in public, but the woman seemed genuinely distressed. "I—yes, I think *The Times* was only—"

"Oh, Miss Fox-Edwards, how delightful to make your acquaintance—and with the duke! I read about the engagement in *The Times*, of course," said a woman William didn't recognize, approaching their group. "How wonderful! And the date is set, I presume?"

William did not reply but glanced at Alice—and was astonished to see her face paling and her demeanor most changed.

What on earth had happened?

She was marrying a duke. William was not arrogant enough to presume he was the most charming man in the *ton*. He certainly wasn't the richest, and though his looks were fair, there were gentlemen apparently who were more handsome than he. But still. He was hardly a beggar, hardly a bore, hardly displeasing to behold. And he was a duke!

He had presumed Alice would be pleased by the announcement, but it appeared more likely that she was about to faint away.

"I must introduce you to the Duke of Wincham—he's about here somewhere," Lady Romeril was saying over the patter of the woman William did not know.

"—quite the best thing to be married in silver, of course, but then you will know that. A duke! Such a conquest, I must congratulate—"

"And the Marquess of—there he is, the naughty man," persevered Lady Romeril, raising her voice louder to be heard over the din. "Miss Fox-Edwards, you must—"

William moved the moment he realized it was happening. As Alice's eyelashes fluttered the strength in her arm suddenly decreased and he was just quick enough to get his arm around her waist when—

"Oh! Oh, Miss Fox-Edwards has fainted—Miss Fox-Edwards has fainted!" Lady Romeril announced to the room at large.

Careful to keep his steadying arm around Alice, William shot a glare at his hostess. "Fresh air, my lady."

"What a thing to happen, and in my drawing room, too," Lady Romeril was muttering. "What was that, Your Grace?"

William gritted his teeth. "Fresh air."

"Oh, the balcony there is unlocked," said Lady Romeril, waving a hand nonchalantly at a set of doors. "I shall guarantee privacy for the poor woman. Shall I send for smelling salts, or a brandy, or a poultice, or—"

"Fresh air will, I am sure, suffice," snapped William as he walked, half carrying the silent woman in his arms.

Something strange had happened to him the moment Alice had succumbed to whatever panic was overwhelming her. He had been filled with a sense of... protectiveness. Possessiveness. A desperate need to keep Alice safe against all the frantic whispers that filled the drawing room as they reached the balcony door.

A silent footman opened it and William gasped as the cold evening air hit his face.

The door clicked shut behind him.

"Alice," William murmured urgently, looking into the face of the woman, he realized, he was starting to truly care about. "Alice, are you—"

"Well, now we are alone, we can talk properly," Alice said sharply, opening her eyes, straightening her now strong body, and wrenching herself from his arms.

William stood, shocked.

Gone was the fainting woman. Gone was the pale betrothed, hardly able to stand.

Before him stood a woman still wearing the same gown as Alice Fox-Edwards, who still had the face of Alice Fox-Edwards.

She also had the hands of Alice Fox-Edwards on her hips and was giving him a dark glare.

"A-Alice?" stammered William. He cleared his throat. "I don't understand what—"

"Why did you not tell me you had made the announcement of our engagement in *The Times*?" Alice said, still glaring as though he had committed some terrible crime.

What it could be, he was not quite sure. Was it not usual to do such a thing? William thought as quickly as he could, though he was still at a loss to understand precisely what he had done wrong.

"Is ... is there a better, more prestigious newspaper in which I should have announced our engagement?" he asked tentatively. "And did you—did you pretend to faint?"

The latter question was ignored. "How could you announce such a thing without asking me?"

William stared.

He was still awake, was he not? He definitely felt as though he was standing in the cooling London night air. A plant of some sort had trailed its way along the balustrade—surely he would not have dreamt that. So why on earth was this nonsensical conversation happening?

"You pretended to faint," William said. "Why would you—"

"Oh, you would rather we had this conversation in public?" Alice raised an eyebrow.

He swallowed. "I would rather not have it at all, when I am so lost within it." Petulance was not really his forte, but he could not help the complaining tone.

Who could blame him? He was utterly at a loss to understand precisely what he had done wrong—and Alice did not appear to be inclined to tell him.

But then just as swiftly as Alice had reacted in anger, she seemed to crumple. Her hands left her hips, and her arms folded before her protectively.

Protectively against him?

"I ... I was startled," she said softly, her large eyes meeting his. "I ... if I had known, I would have asked ..."

William stared, transfixed.

He had done what he thought was the right thing. Every engagement was announced in *The Times*. It was what the gentry and nobility did.

Yet somehow his adherence to rules had injured her. Injured a woman he would fain hurt in any way. And he had done it through an announcement? It wasn't as though it was very long. With no family of Alice's living, the statement had merely read:

> *An engagement is announced between His Grace, William Thomas Leopold Chance, Duke of Cothrom, and Miss Alice Fox-Edwards.*

At the time, William had felt rather ashamed that it was so little. But Alice appeared to be distressed, truly distressed, it had been published at all.

What was going on?

"And Lady Romeril, wanting to introduce me to everyone under the sun," Alice said with a dark look. "I do not care for being paraded about like—like a prize!"

And guilt washed into William's chest.

Of course she didn't. What person would?

He had seen couples like that. One would consider the other an impressive catch and would definitely lord it over their friends and connections. With every introduction came a smile of glee as their betrothed became nothing more than an object to them. A thing.

Like I was doing with Alice, William thought wretchedly. More interested in getting under her skirts than understanding her mind.

Oh, hell.

"I . . . dash it all, Alice, that isn't what I intended," William said quietly, taking a step toward her. He halted as she took a step back. *Blast. It was that bad.* "I just—I did what everyone did. I did not think—"

"I know," Alice said, through evident pain.

William could have cursed if he were not afraid of offending her.

And he already had. Through his own ignorance of her, something that could no longer be excused, he had somehow harmed her. What harm an announcement of an engagement could do, he did not know, but that did not matter. The point was, Alice was injured. By his hand.

"I would never wish to hurt you," he said gently.

Somehow that was the right thing to say. She met his eyes this time with a small shrug as she said, "I know. It's just—the announcement, and Lady Romeril—"

"She is a bit much," said William quietly.

"It's all a bit much," she said in a low voice.

William hesitated.

This was supposed to be nothing more than a practical marriage. A match that would give him the opportunity to sire heirs and, if he were lucky, a jolt to get his brothers to start behaving.

Though admittedly it was yet to be seen whether the latter were possible.

And yet within weeks, things had changed. His heart had changed.

Where there had once only been physical desire, and who could blame him when looking at Alice Fox-Edwards, there was now something much more. Much deeper.

Respect.

William took a step forward and was encouraged to see that, though Alice was now leaning against the balustrade, she did not step away.

Yes, he respected Alice. Discovering the truth of her ward, how she willingly impoverished herself if it meant caring for a child—that was the sort of person he wished to marry.

The trouble was, he may have already ended that possibility.

"If . . ." William hesitated. She was just a foot from him, but he could not cross that line, not now. He had to speak first. "If you are having second thoughts—"

"Second thoughts?" Alice said quickly, eyebrows raised.

Dear God, but he wished he had time to think about this. William was not usually a rash person. Important conversations were typically rehearsed in his dressing room, his unfortunate valet playing the role of . . . well, whomever he had to have the awkward conversation with.

Flares of tension sparked up William's spine, but he persevered.

This conversation was important.

Even if he would regret it.

"I don't want to go ahead with a marriage you are not fully committed to, Alice," William said quietly. "If . . . I don't wish to force . . . I think I would greatly enjoy being married to you, but you must not continue with this engagement merely . . . just because I asked you to marry me."

There. It was said.

He regretted it already. What did he think he was doing, giving Alice the opportunity to step away from him, perhaps forever?

His stomach rebelled against the thought just as Alice twisted something on her glove.

William's pulse skipped a beat. His signet ring.

And a desire, one he had never known before and could not control, overswept him. He would do anything, absolutely anything, to convince her to keep that ring on her finger. To make her his.

Whatever it took.

"I, for my part," he said, a little more hoarsely than he'd expected, "would very much like to keep to our arrangement."

When Alice looked up and met his gaze, there was a teasing look on her face that both reassured and thundered through him. "You don't even know what marriage to me would be like."

"I know what I would want it to be like," William said.

He stepped forward but just to the side, so he could lean against the balcony's balustrade alongside her. It was sweet torture, being this close to Alice and not touching her, but William knew he would lose all sense of decorum if he did.

Worse, they could be spotted.

"What?" Alice whispered, her eyes flickering across his face. "What would it be like?"

William swallowed. It was not in his nature to be open, but of all people in the world, Alice deserved to know. Still, it was easier to speak to his hands than her face. "I . . . well. I want to be happy—and for my wife to be happy, of course. A quiet life, in the country, if possible. Laughter, and music, and . . . and children. Lots of them, if we are so blessed."

When he looked up, Alice's eyes were shining. "I never thought . . . I would not have guessed that is what you want. Quiet, calm happiness."

William shrugged. "I may be a duke, but that doesn't mean I want to spend the rest of my life fighting for the Chance family! I want to be with someone I care about. Someone . . . like you."

For a moment, he thought he had gone too far—said too much, revealed too much.

Alice's cheeks flushed. She did look away.

His hopes sank. It had been too much to hope for. Most marriages, after all, continued for years without any hint of true affection. If he could respect his wife and be respected in return, perhaps that would be enough.

"I care about you, too," Alice said simply, slipping her hand into his. "Aren't we lucky?"

William's chest swelled. So did something else, but he was firmly ignoring it. "What are the chances?"

She grinned. "I suppose we should go inside."

His eyes widened. *Dear God! Bedding Alice was never too far from his mind, but even so—*

"To the *party*," Alice added with a knowing look. "We are at Lady Romeril's."

William blinked. "Yes—yes, we are. To the party, then."

Chapter Eleven

"So," came the soft burr of a voice in her ear. "Shall I call the carriage?"

Alice swallowed, her knees somehow shaky as she stepped down to the street after several hours at the party. It had been wonderful. A bit overwhelming, yes, but still wonderful, to stand on his arm and receive the flattering compliments of those around them, and to be a part of it all again. Part of the *ton*. And now the party was over.

He was so close—so wonderfully close. Just for a moment, she could have pretended they were just like any other couple engaged to be married.

The moment faded the moment the cold night air brushed over her skin. *This was not a normal engagement.*

At least, she knew it wasn't.

"Alice?"

Alice forced a smile as William stepped to her side, an eagerness on his face she recognized well.

Carriage. Yes, the carriage would be the perfect place for the two of them to sit. And talk. And kiss. Far from prying eyes, free from interruptions.

It would not surprise her if the Duke of Cothrom cleverly instructed his driver to take the long route home, Alice thought dryly, *and extend the possibility of their kisses . . .*

No. That was not a good idea.

She may have certain feelings for this tall man who looked at her sometimes as though she were . . . *precious* was the only way she could describe it.

But that did not mean she was about to present him with an opportunity to ruin her admittedly shaky resolve with his scalding hot lips and—

"N-No," Alice murmured, partly to herself, partly to the man examining her so closely.

William's brow furrowed as he pulled his greatcoat tighter around him. "No?"

"No," said Alice decidedly, as though that had been precisely what she had intended to say. "I mean, it is such a lovely night, after all. Why not walk?"

"Walk?"

Now it was the duke's turn to look flummoxed.

That was it, Alice thought desperately. She could not afford to lose herself in this, whatever this was. It was only right that she, at every point she could, confuse the poor man. Then perhaps she could get to the wedding day without making a complete fool of herself and risking everything.

"Well, why not?" said William with a wry look. "We've already done so many things I would not have expected. Yes, we'll walk."

Alice slipped her hand into the crook of the man's arm. Not because she adored the close contact. That wasn't it. That would be ridiculous. But because something as simple as a walk home in the moonlight appeared to William to be one of the most outrageous things a person could do.

What would he say, a horrible little voice whispered in the back of Alice's mind, *if he really knew?*

The streets were quiet. The hour was late, and revelers returning home were taking the socially acceptable mode of transport, that of a horse and carriage. Lights were disappearing in the homes Alice and William walked by, giving the sense that the world was falling asleep.

Aside from them.

Instinctively, Alice glanced up. "That's a shame."

Evidently she had concerned him, for William immediately halted in his steps and jerked his head about, one way and then the other. "Shame? What is a shame—what has occurred?"

"Do not get your breeches in a twist," Alice said absentmindedly, using the phrase her mother had used which she had also slipped into the habit of using.

"Do not get my—"

"It is only the stars, that's all," said Alice.

She had remained looking up at the sky, and after a moment, she sensed—just out of the corner of her eye—William's head tilting back as well.

The moonlight was bright—the moon was almost full. And the gentle lambswool of the clouds barely covered it. The stars, on the other hand . . .

William's arm straightened, Alice's hand slipping from it—but just before it returned to her side, his fingers caught hers. Entwined them. Heat shot through her: not just the warmth of his body, but the warmth of the moment. The connection. The intimacy.

Alice forced herself not to look down. Once she saw her fingers mingled with his, it would be impossible for her to speak.

After all her plans, her hopes . . . was something real and true happening between herself and a duke?

"I can't see many stars," William said quietly.

"I'm afraid that was my point," Alice said wistfully. "Out in the country where . . . where I lived for a few years, there were more stars."

"More?" His head twisted. She could almost feel the wry smile creasing his face. "There can't be more."

"There were certainly more visible," she said quietly. "Here we can see . . . what? The North Star, the Morning Star . . ."

As she spoke, Alice lifted her free hand and gestured toward the pinpricks of light she mentioned. Stars she had known well, known for years. Companions to her life. Wherever she went, no matter what happened, the stars would accompany her.

"But you can't see the Bear here, or Cassiopeia," she continued, pointing to roughly where she would have expected to see them. "And the sky feels strange without them, somehow. Empty. The stars are lacking."

There was a moment of silence as Alice dropped her hand to her side. The silence continued, on and on. Eventually she realized it had gone on far too long.

Forcing down the panic that instantly flared, a response she would one day hope to control, Alice glanced at the man beside her.

He wasn't looking at the stars. Or the lack of them.

No. He was looking at her.

"You know a great deal about astronomy," William said quietly.

Alice opened her mouth, hesitated, then closed it again.

What was she to say? It was hardly a critique. There was no crime in a little stargazing.

But William had not said the words with praise. It sounded . . .

"I cannot be the only one," Alice said, dropping his hand and stepping forward briskly as though leaving the conversation of stars behind.

"No, I suppose not," William said, easily reaching her side and matching her pace as they continued along the London streets. "But I never thought a woman—"

"A woman would have any interest in the stars?" She grinned and kept her voice gently teasing. "What, you think a woman cannot have interests?"

Alice was rewarded with a flush that tinged William's cheeks. On another man, perhaps, the sight would have been uninteresting. On William's visage, it only highlighted the passion and gleam in his eye, the interest in his demeanor, the closeness of his body.

She swallowed and tried to focus on where they were going.

He was really very close . . .

"You know, I never . . . well, I never had much time for women."

Alice almost tripped over her own feet. Throwing out her arms to right herself, they were grasped by William as she pitched forward, the world spinning—

And then she was balanced again. Her hand was tucked into William's arm.

"No, women have not formed a great part of my life until . . . well, until you," said William with a low chuckle Alice felt through his side. "My brothers have always taken so much of my attention. One brother in particular. Pernrith."

Pernrith. Alice could recall his face easily. A shy man, light blond hair. A man who had been mostly silent. There had been something awkward in the meeting. She had presumed a family quarrel, something plastered over but never truly healed.

"Oh?" she said lightly as they turned a corner and took a left.

William nodded. "Yes. He's my father's bastard, actually."

It was a good thing Alice had William's support, for there was a high chance of her tripping over again.

Bastard? Dukes did not go around hosting their illegitimate half-brothers, did they?

"Ah," Alice said helplessly, with absolutely no idea what to say now.

"Yes," said William quietly.

Grateful for the darkness of the evening, Alice allowed their conversation to falter. What did one say to that? How was one meant to continue?

Oh, it happened. She was not so ignorant as to suppose that every child was born, let alone conceived, on the right side of the blanket. She could not afford to be so ignorant, not any longer.

But to hear a gentleman speak about it so openly, so calmly—for that gentleman to have introduced her to said brother. For that gentleman to be a duke!

"You are offended."

"I am not offended," Alice said sharply, looking over at William and arranging her features into the epitome of calm. "No child deserves to be despised or cast out of a family due to a mere circumstance of birth. Not when they had no control over it."

There was a flash of something in William's eyes.

"I think much the same," he said warmly. "When Pernrith was brought to my father's house, Lindow was only three years old, and the two are nearly the exact same age. Only a month between them. It was agreed that he, Pernrith, I mean, would be recognized as a natural son of my father. He would have a small income, and that would be all."

Alice frowned slightly as they turned another corner onto the street where she had taken lodgings. Her heart sank. Their journey, and their conversation and time together, was almost at an end.

"But..." Alice hesitated. "But when I met him, you introduced him as—"

"I was the one who gave Pernrith the viscountcy," William said stiffly, his tone slipping once more into the formal duke she knew so well. "It was in my power to give, after our father died, and it did not seem right to leave him without a title."

And something pulsed through Alice as their steps slowed and eventually stopped outside her door.

"You did not need to do that," she said quietly.

William shrugged, a boyish mannerism which immediately made him appear several years younger. "It was the right thing to do."

Yes, that was perhaps the best way to sum up this contradictory man, Alice thought. The right thing to do. Not easy, not fun, not simple. Not emotionally taxing, nor practical in any way.

But the right thing to do.

"Here we are," William said with a half-smile, jerking his head toward her door. "I suppose I should leave you."

Should. He did not want to, then.

Hope flickered. What was it that he'd said at Lady Romeril's?

"I may be a duke, but that doesn't mean I want to spend the rest of my life fighting for the Chance family! I want to be with someone I care about. Someone . . . like you."

After all her scheming and planning, after all the fear she would be unable to find a man to save her from the predicament she found herself in . . . she had found him.

William Chance, Duke of Cothrom.

Kinder, and more noble, than half the gentlemen she had ever met.

He cared for her.

And she . . .

"Will you come in?" Alice said, gesturing as elegantly as she could manage. "A cup of tea, perhaps. Or a nightcap. I am certain I have half a bottle of brandy somewhere. Entirely legally, I assure you."

William met her eye, and grinned. "I feel assured."

She laughed, the chuckle wafting gently in the cool night air. "Well. Mostly legal. I purchased it legally. That is perhaps as much as I should promise."

Their mingled laughter flowed around them, warming Alice, taking the sharpness out of the midnight air. *Oh, that this could be her life . . .*

"I should probably go," said William ruefully. "Decorum, and all that. Propriety. The rules."

As he spoke, Alice watched his focus flicker over her. Swiftly at first, then slowly. Slowing at particular parts of her. Her lips. Her collarbone. Her breasts . . .

Oh, he wanted her. The certain knowledge fired something in Alice she knew she should dampen, knew she should ignore—but they were to be married. And the kiss William had bestowed upon her, pushed up against a tree in Hyde Park, had been most delicious.

It was only fair to them, wasn't it, to ensure they were truly compatible?

A thrill rushed through Alice as she reached out and turned the door handle. "Just a cup of tea. What harm can it do?"

She met William's gaze, and the thrill deepened, darkened, transmuted into something far more sensual than her words would immediately suggest.

Oh, she hadn't felt something like this in such a long time.

"Come on, William," Alice said in a quiet murmur, stepping into the doorway.

For a moment, she wasn't sure if he would follow her. It was certainly a most unusual request. A gentleman may offer it, of course, but a lady?

Plainly William had discovered a way around the rules which resided so prominently in his mind, for Alice breathed in his commanding presence as he moved past her into the hall.

There, that was half the battle, Alice thought as she closed the door quietly and turned to face him. Now all she had to do was work out how to entice—

She didn't have time to think. She didn't need it. The moment the door slipped into the latch, William had launched forward, his hands reaching to cup her cheeks. Alice's back slammed into the door but it was a welcome pain, a jolt of surprise, and he was kissing her.

William Chance was kissing her.

And what a kiss. This wasn't the genteel or gentle respectable kiss a duke should offer his betrothed. It wasn't calm, restrained, or ducal at all.

It was animal. Primal. William's lips parted hers in a possessive movement that made Alice gasp—a gasp which transformed into a moan as his tongue teased along her own, sparking desire through her body. His hands cupped her cheeks gently, but in a way that claimed her—demanded her.

And Alice melted into the kiss. She wanted to be claimed, she wanted to be desired. And this kiss was full of promise for the future, passion for the present.

But like all good things, the kiss which had taken her breath and reminded her just what it was to be a woman, had to end.

William leaned back, panting heavily, his hands shaking as he removed them from her. "I—I shouldn't have—"

"Yes, you should," Alice said through lips sore with the pressure of his passion.

Dear God, if that was one kiss, what would it be like when he took her to bed?

"I must go," William said quietly, his voice ragged.

"Of course," said Alice, nodding as she reached out for his lapels. "Of course."

She pulled him closer and William did not resist, and they were kissing once more, the need which had been tugging at Alice's loins aching in the explosion of their ardor.

And this time, William's hands did not remain chastely on her cheeks. No, one was placed upon her waist, holding her tightly as though she could slip from the earth's gravity and float into the stars if he did not keep hold.

And the other . . . the other . . .

Alice gasped into William's mouth as his thumb brushed across her breast, returning to the nipple which had somehow wiggled itself free from her stays. The sudden jolt of aching pleasure the briefest contact his thumb had made through the fabric of her gown was enough to pool heat between her legs.

Dear God, yes . . .

It was easy to kiss this man, easy to care for him, easy to sink into his arms and lose herself in the connection. Easy for Alice's hands to slowly move down his firm torso, feeling the straining muscles beneath, until they reached—

William stepped back as though branded the moment Alice's

hands brushed against something else that had been straining. This time, something in his breeches.

"Dear God," he muttered.

"Is anything wrong?" asked Alice, lust-hazed and reaching for him.

William affixed her with a stern look. "Yes. Yes, there is."

And she halted, hands outstretched, panic now replacing the searing passion she had so recently been enjoying.

Surely he could not have guessed—but she had hardly attempted to keep her past a secret tonight, had she? Speaking of a life spent looking at the stars in the country, her ease at illegitimacy, the way she had enticed William inside—the way they had kissed.

Alice swallowed, trying to calm the frantic beating of her pulse.

Was it all over?

William pulled his hand through his hair, and when his face was visible once more, Alice saw to her relief that he had a rueful grin upon it.

"Damn it, Alice, I am doing my best to keep to propriety," he said quietly. "At every juncture, I have been attempting to make the right decisions. The best ones for you and me, and for Society."

Alice nodded, not trusting her voice.

William's dark hair fell over his eyes as he looked at her wistfully, head tilted to one side. "Which makes it all the more frustrating, you see, that I very much wish to take you upstairs and ravish you."

Just hearing those words spoken aloud would have been startling at the best of times—but hearing them from William's mouth? A shot of molten desire burned through Alice, settling between her legs and making it difficult to stand.

Oh, God. Was there anything more arousing than a man who desperately wanted you, yet was ready to deny himself?

"I . . ." Alice swallowed, her throat dry. She did not take her eyes from William's. "I did not think there was this side of you. Animal. Base. Desperate to . . . to give into one's desires."

"Just because I keep it hidden, under control, in check," William said darkly, stepping forward, "that does not mean it is not there."

There was such a strange look in his eyes, one of longing and yearning, that Alice instinctively stepped back.

And hit the door.

And William was before her, his chest pushing her against the door, her breasts straining against him. His arms slammed into the door either side of her head and Alice gasped, unable to help herself, as she saw, just for a moment, the raw need within him.

"I have wanted you, wanted to take you as mine, since the moment you revealed yourself at the Earl of Chester's ball," William growled, his voice ragged and his hungry eyes raking over her face. "Did you know that, Alice? Do you know how much I crave you, how every second we are in polite Society I must hide my needs, hide my desires?"

It was all Alice could do to stand there and listen to such delectable words. How had she managed to choose a man who was the perfect mixture of refined gentleman and devouring beast?

"Every chance I could take to kiss you is agony," William said in a low voice, head dipping so that he spoke into Alice's ear. His breath tingled down her neck, entering the very core of her. "And I very much . . . I very much wish to take you upstairs and show you."

Alice moaned, unable to help herself, and William groaned as he sank his lips onto her neck.

Then he was gone.

Alice blinked. His sudden absence was like diving into cold water.

William had only stepped back a few paces, exhaling heavily. When he met her gaze it was with a wry grin. "So. Damn. Now you know."

It was on the tip of her tongue to tell him to take her. That she didn't care, that she wanted him to make love to her.

But before Alice could decide precisely how to say such a thing,

William took a deep breath. "We need to get married. As—damn. As soon as possible."

And Alice's heart leapt.

Guilt leapt, too. But it was easily covered with passion and lust and need.

An aching need that only William could fulfil.

You care about him, Alice reminded herself silently. *This isn't just part of a plan anymore. You have true affection for this man, and he evidently wants you. What's the harm?*

"Well," she said aloud, surprised to find her breathing just as ragged as his had been. "I am free next Thursday."

Chapter Twelve

June 5, 1812

WILLIAM STARED WITH dull eyes at his reflection in the looking glass. "No."

"You are certain?"

"Absolutely," said William, wrenching off the light orange silk waistcoat as though it were contaminated. "Next."

The orange silk waistcoat was removed from his fingers, to be replaced immediately by one of a shimmering gold.

"Next."

"But you have not even tried it—"

"I said next, Pierre," William snapped, every nerve taut. "And I meant it. Next!"

It was ridiculous. He had never been the sort of Brummell to care about clothes to such an extent. Clothes were . . . an armor. Protective for the body and for the soul. They stood between you and Society, ensuring that as long as you dressed adequately, in the correct fashions with the right fabric made by a respected tailor, you could pass through the world unnoticed.

Until today.

"This is a delicate linen blend," his valet was muttering as he slipped William's arms through the holes. "Very stylish, of course, a pleasant natural color . . ."

The man's voice faded away as William turned to the looking glass to glare at his reflection.

This was his fault.

His own, that was. Not Pierre's. The poor man had been given less than a week's notice, it was hardly his fault no wedding suit had been ordered. But that left him attempting to find the perfect outfit to become Alice's husband using only the clothes already at his disposal.

William glanced over his shoulder and saw the pile of waistcoats on the floor, discarded due to his dismissal. If he wasn't careful, he was going to run out of waistcoats.

His valet cleared his throat delicately. "Any of these would be most suitable, Your Grace. They have all been made with care from the finest—"

"Suitable isn't enough," said William quietly, turning back to his reflection and trying to compare the waistcoat he was currently wearing to the third one he had tried on, a cotton blue. "Suitable is most unsuitable."

"I see, Your Grace."

No, he didn't. How could anyone see who didn't know Alice like he did?

For the first time since his impetuous suggestion to the woman William was rather afraid he was now in love with, he started to wonder if he had been a little too rash with his suggestion.

"We need to get married. As—damn. As soon as possible."

"Well. I am free next Thursday."

It had seemed to be the perfect solution. William was struggling to keep his hands off the woman, and Alice seemed, most surprisingly, just as eager to receive his kisses as he was to offer them.

It had been difficult, always, for William to hide that particular part of his nature. That part of him that wanted to feel a woman beneath him, sink himself into her, know the connection two people could find in such a meeting. In such a mating.

It had been too long.

And then there was Alice. Just when he had been certain she

would recoil from his ardor, she had matched it.

Dear God, she'd even reached for his—

"There are but two other waistcoats you have not yet tried on, Your Grace," came the reproving tone of his valet. "Do you wish to see them on, before you make your final decision?"

If you can make a final decision, were the unspoken words William nonetheless heard loud and clear.

Damn it all. This was supposed to be one of the happiest days of his life, not the day he spent hours before a looking glass, attempting to find a balance between well dressed and fop.

There was a snorting laugh behind him. William was just about to turn and scold his valet for being so rude as to laugh at his master, when—

"I cannot believe you are actually doing this," said a conversational voice with just a hint of mirth as someone launched themselves onto his bed. "You're actually going through with it!"

William sighed and did not bother to turn. "Aylesbury."

"I mean, you hardly know her!"

His brother's comment was well-intentioned, William was sure. At least, he hoped it was. And he was not entirely wrong. How long had it been since he had first met Alice? Days? Weeks?

The time had flown by yet had been so enriched with conversation and connection and meaning . . . William had never encountered the like. It was starting to become difficult to remember a life without Alice. Which was ludicrous but still undeniably true.

"Here are the other two waistcoats, Your Grace," murmured Pierre, stepping to the side and holding out the two items.

William glanced between the two, both greenish, one with a pattern. Then he glanced at the one he was wearing. Then at the pile behind him.

He had to make it perfect—perfect for Alice. He didn't even know her favorite color.

"I mean, you decide to marry her at a ball, then less than a—"

"Yes, Aylesbury, I well know your opinion on the matter," said William stiffly, slipping out of the linen waistcoat and grabbing the green one without a pattern. "I'll thank you to—"

"You barely know this woman and she'll be the matriarch of our family," Aylesbury pointed out behind him, his voice tinged with laughter. "I never thought you'd be a fool in love!"

"Thank you, Pierre, that will be all," William bit out.

His servant bowed and immediately departed—though too late not to hear his brother's scandalously rude comments.

He would just have to hope his valet had the wherewithal to keep that information to himself. God help them, if he had to spend the first few weeks of married life quashing rumors that he had fallen in love with his wife, something dukes never did—

"Honestly, man, I don't know why you're doing this," Aylesbury said, his voice less teasing now. "Unless . . . unless you have to. Unless there's an heir to the title on the way I don't know about . . ."

William's stomach lurched as he attempted to button up his waistcoat. *Damn buttons, damn thumbs!*

"No," he said—perhaps too quickly.

If only . . .

"I am marrying Miss Alice Fox-Edwards today, and that's an end to it," William said curtly. "In this waistcoat." He looked at himself in the looking glass. "Probably."

Aylesbury sighed. "I just don't understand."

And neither did he, not really. William could not encapsulate in words precisely why it was so vital to meet Alice at the end of the aisle today, make promises to her that would bind him to her for life, take her to his bedchamber and—

Well. Perhaps that last was understandable.

But he could have a woman, a plethora of women, if that was what he wanted. He was the Duke of Cothrom. It would hardly be difficult to find a mistress. A woman for the night. But satisfying his urges . . . that wasn't enough.

What he had with Alice was not something he understood, but William had spent all his two and thirty years depending on his gut, his moral compass. It always told him when something was incorrect, and it had always been right. And there were no warning bells going off when he thought of spending the rest of his life as Alice's husband.

"I don't suppose you would understand," William said quietly, more to his reflection to his brother. "It isn't something that can be explained, I don't think. At any rate—"

"You are going to be late!" said a new voice.

"Lindow!" Aylesbury cried with evident delight.

William groaned as the bed springs creaked behind him, and his two younger brothers got comfortable. "Not two of you."

"You should just be grateful we're here, as you're running late," said Lindow sharply. "Why haven't you got him dressed?"

"What, do I look like a valet to you?" Aylesbury shot back.

"I didn't say you were a valet, but I sent you here to hurry him up and—"

"You're the younger brother, why don't you hurry him up?"

William could not help but smile. No matter what happened, no matter what he attempted, his brothers never changed. Irritating, utterly uncontrollable, and able to bicker at the drop of a hat.

And he wouldn't have them any other way.

Though if he could cease their gambling losses and convince them to keep their breeches on—

"I wasn't jesting, you truly are going to be late," said Lindow, suddenly at William's side and tugging on his jacket. "It's supposed to be the bride who is late, not you!"

William glanced at the carriage clock over the mantlepiece. "No I'm not, because it's only—oh, Christ!"

He could have sworn he had only been here twenty minutes. *How long did it take to try on waistcoats, really?*

As it turned out, far longer than the twenty minutes William thought had passed. It was more like an hour and twenty minutes. He *was* going to be late.

"Just get a jacket on, and—"

"No, I can't," William said, heat blossoming across his torso, constricting it, making it impossible to breathe. He was drowning in fabric—he had to get it off. "Lindow, let go!"

William wrenched off both jacket and waistcoat, dropping them both on the floor.

When he looked up, Aylesbury and Lindow were frowning.

"Cothrom?" Aylesbury said quietly. "You . . . you need to get dressed. You have a wedding to attend."

"I can't believe I didn't order a proper wedding suit!" William said, horror in his voice. "What was I thinking? The whole of the *ton* is going to be there, and I'm not wearing a—"

"Oh God, I was afraid of this," Lindow muttered. "Come on now, Cothrom, we can cancel the wedding, no one will—"

"I don't want to cancel the wedding," William said furiously, panic dripping into his lungs, making every movement hurt. "I just—"

"Look, you'll have to send a footman," Aylesbury was murmuring. "We can smooth the whole thing out, we've just got to—"

And desperation was clenching at William's mind—they wanted to cancel the wedding! No, he wouldn't let them, he had to marry Alice—

"Let go of me—"

"Hold him tight there, we can't have—"

"Good afternoon," came a quiet, slightly nervous voice.

All three brothers turned to see who had interrupted their struggle. Aylesbury and Lindow had each taken hold of an arm, but William was able to wrench himself free as they stared at the newcomer.

Pernrith.

He smiled weakly. "I . . . well. Good afternoon. As I said."

William could feel the tension spilling over into the room as Lindow glowered at the illegitimate Chance.

Dear God, this was the last thing he needed.

"What are you doing here?" Aylesbury asked roughly.

"Aylesbury," William began.

"No, it is a fair question," Pernrith said mildly. "I just... well, I thought you may not have time to order a wedding suit, so I thought I would bring this one."

A servant stepped in behind him, placed a box onto the bed and immediately left, closing the door behind him.

"You weren't invited here," Lindow said quietly as William stepped forward to inspect the box. "I don't know what you were—"

"Oh, my," muttered William.

The room fell silent as William slowly pulled out of the box...

"But... but... that's Father's best waistcoat and cravat," said Aylesbury quietly. "I... I knew you were given them in the will, but—"

"I thought, this way you'll be taking the traditions of the Chance family into your marriage," said Pernrith quietly, still standing by the door. "I hope it fits."

A knot tied itself into William's throat as he beheld the fabric. He knew it so well. Their father had always worn it on Sundays, at Christmas, whenever their mother decided it was a holiday and all of them should take a picnic out into the gardens.

His father's waistcoat. His cravat. Damn, they both still smelled of his favorite cigar.

He glanced up and tried to put into his expression all the words he could not say. "You will be there, won't you? At the church?"

If Pernrith was surprised at the comment, he did not show it. "I would not miss it."

Someone cleared their throat. When William turned around, it was to see a grim look on Lindow's face.

His heart sank. Was his most roguish brother truly going to make such a fuss about this—on his wedding day?

"If we're going to get you there in time," his brother said darkly, "we're going to have to dress you in the carriage . . ."

It was not an experience William ever wished to repeat. There was something rather unpleasant about having one's hands jammed through sleeves and someone—he was not sure who—forcing his feet into court dress shoes.

By the time William was deposited outside the church, he felt as though he had been through a mangle.

But he was here. And the church bells were pealing. And the bride, most importantly, had not beaten him to the altar.

"There's still time to run, you know," muttered Aylesbury as the four Chance brothers strode down the nave. "I've got a fast horse waiting at the chapel door."

William snorted as they halted at the front pew. "You haven't."

It was the silence that made him hesitate.

He turned to his brother. "You . . . you haven't, have you?"

Aylesbury winked. "Would you take me up on it if I did?"

William nudged his brother so hard, the man almost fell over.

"Now what was that for?"

"Shhh!"

Glancing up, William saw to his dismay that their laughter had echoed around the packed church. Packed full of Society. All staring and watching him.

Worse, it had gained the attention of the vicar who was even now glaring at them with a righteous look.

William inclined his head and tried to ignore the muffled laughter of Lindow, who was seated behind him. Along with Pernrith? Now that was a first.

Clasping his hands together before him in what William hoped was a clearly contrite expression, he waited.

And waited.

The organ music continued, extending on and on until he fairly hummed with it.

Where was she?

"She's not coming, you know."

This time William managed to avoid thrusting his elbow right into Aylesbury's gut, but it was a close call. Especially when he wanted to so badly.

How could he say such a thing? Alice had been just as eager to wed as he had when he'd made the impulsive suggestion that they move the wedding forward. Had she not kissed him with just as much ardor, clung to him with just as much need—hadn't she wanted him? Hadn't her hand wandered down to his—

No, no, this was not the time nor the place to be thinking of things like that!

But William had been certain, absolutely sure, that Alice wished to marry him. Perhaps he had been a little eager, a little forward. It was unlike him. She drew that from him in a way he could never have predicted.

He shuffled his feet, hating the tightness of the court shoes.

Still. He had not been so overly forward that she had retreated, had he? Would she change her mind?

A tingling ache of uncertainty flowed up William's spine.

He was not a bad man. The very worst of his soul, the worst of himself, the aching needs that his body demanded of him had always been ignored. He had always done his utmost to offer the best of himself. Keep his family in line. Keep the name of Chance respectable.

Had he still managed to make a fool of himself?

William glanced, just for a moment, over his shoulder. The church doors were closed. Alice had not arrived.

Before his gaze could return to the front of the church, it met that of Lady Romeril. She was glaring.

She was not alone. Muttering was starting to move through the church like a breeze.

He was being talked about.

Perspiration beaded on William's forehead, but he refused to permit himself to brush it aside. He would not, could not, let anyone in the place see how desperately this was affecting him.

Dear God, they were going to be talking about this for weeks! William Chance, the Duke of Cothrom . . . stood up, at his own wedding?

"You know, I never thought I would need to ask this," muttered Aylesbury as he leaned forward as if to brush a piece of fluff from William's coat. "But you didn't . . . well, say anything or do anything stupid, did you?"

William met his brother's gaze. "You know me."

"And that's why I hesitated to ask," said his brother softly, so quietly William could barely hear him. "But it's . . ."—he reached into his waistcoat, pulled out his pocket watch, and frowned—"half an hour past."

William's stomach twisted with a mixture of nausea and pain. "It isn't."

"I wouldn't lie to you, Cothrom, not about this," came the quiet reply. "Are you absolutely sure she's coming?"

It was not a question William had ever wished to consider.

His mind whirled as he attempted to run through every conversation they had ever had, every slight he had accidentally made, any offense he could possibly have given . . .

And came up empty.

To be sure, he was not always the most eloquent gentleman, but he had always erred on the side of caution, always ensured he was as polite as could be. He behaved as was expected, not only for a gentleman betrothed, but for a duke. The few times he had erred he had apologized. Been given an apology. He was a Chance, and there was no possibility he would ever permit the name to be brought into dispute.

Except . . .

William tried not to groan aloud as he closed his eyes, the weight of the realization heavy on his shoulders.

Except when he had been open, far too open, about his desire for her. Dear God, what had he said?

"Every chance I could take to kiss you is agony. And I very much . . . I very much wish to take you upstairs and show you."

No wonder the woman had turned tail and run. She had given him some platitude about getting married at once but had surely made her escape. What woman of Alice's breeding and elegance would wish to submit herself to a ravenous man like himself?

William swallowed hard, knowing in the depths of his soul he had made a catastrophic mistake. And worst of all, he had not comprehended it until now—until it was too late!

He might have had a fighting chance of convincing her if he had not been so dunderheaded as to ignore the consequences of his rash actions. But now Alice knew him—really knew him. Knew the depths of his soul, knew what he thought whenever he looked at her. And she had decided she had no wish to be a part of his life anymore, let alone his wife.

And that meant he was standing right now, before all the *ton*, waiting for a bride who was not coming.

"Aylesbury," William said hoarsely, his hand clutching that of his brother. "I—I think I've made a terrible mis—"

The rest of the word was drowned out by the sudden creak of doors—doors that were opening.

Every head in the church turned, creating a rushing sound that poured into William's ears and made it impossible to think.

And then his mind righted itself, and he turned around.

The organ music changed. Handel's March began. And there in the doorway appeared—

A woman. Just a woman. Standing there on her own.

To anyone else in the church, perhaps, that would have been all they would notice. But William was not just anyone else in that church. He saw so much more.

Alice. She was smiling nervously, creases of worry around her eyes. Eyes that sparkled, that surely dazzled everyone she looked at.

The gown she was wearing was simple, elegant. William could not have hoped for better: it was clearly of the latest fashion but was not clinging so desperately to the current mode that she could be considered trite.

The soft gentle silk, the same russet as William's waistcoat, seemed to drift across Alice's body like water. It clung to her curves and skimmed to the floor, drifting elegantly with every step that she took.

Every step closer to him.

William's gasp caught in his throat, his lungs tight, so constricted he hardly knew how he would take the next breath.

Oh, she was . . .

She was beautiful. She was elegant.

But more importantly than that, she was his—or was about to be.

And the sheer relief that she had not decided to abandon him, to give him up after discovering part of his most vulnerable side, almost brought William to his knees.

This woman. He did not deserve her, and he would spend the rest of their married life ensuring she knew that.

After approximately an age, Alice drew level with him, and William stepped forward to take his hand in hers.

"I've been waiting for you," he blurted out, unable to hold the words back.

Alice's hands were warm, but not as warm as her expression. "I know," she said softly. "But I'm here now. I'll always be here."

Chapter Thirteen

"THIS WAS A terrible mistake," Alice muttered to herself.

The sun was shining. That was supposed to be a good sign, wasn't it?

But how could she even countenance the weather when everything in her life was about to fall apart?

"Ah, Miss Fox-Edwards," said a quiet voice behind her. "I can't believe it. You're actually going through with it."

If only she had stepped into the church. If only she had not loitered, trying to breathe in slowly to calm herself. If only she had not been tempted to look up at the church with a happy smile, hardly able to believe it.

Perhaps if she had not done those things, she would not be here, standing outside the church, looking into the eyes of . . .

"Mr. Shenton," Alice said softly.

She should have known. He wouldn't permit her to escape him, he never would. There was too much power involved, too much control.

And how Mr. Shenton loved control.

A slow smirk crept across the man's face. "I didn't think you had it in you."

Alice did her best to inhale deeply and lift her chin. "I don't know what you mean."

"I think you do," Mr. Shenton said softly as carriages rattled by behind him and passersby glanced at them standing outside the church. "I told you that you'd never be free of me until you married, but I never thought you would take me so seriously. I never thought you would actually find some fool—"

"William is not a fool!" Alice said furiously, then clasped a hand over her mouth.

Her bouquet hung by her side in her other hand. A bouquet she would not need now. Not now her extortioner, her blackmailer, had turned up at her own wedding.

Mr. Shenton's dark expression flickered. "Ah, William, is it? Yes, I saw the announcement. It reached me even in Brighton. Well played, Alice."

"That's Miss Fox-Edwards to you," she said as bravely as she could manage.

His gaze flashed as he caught her in the lie. "You haven't told him, have you?"

She had expected fear to flood through her veins if she ever saw him again. She had expected to freeze, to be utterly unsure what to do. To have all the wind taken from her sails.

She had not expected Mr. Shenton to actually come to London.

To stop the wedding.

"William knows me," Alice said quietly.

"But he doesn't, does he?" Mr. Shenton pressed. "You haven't been completely honest with him, have you? You can't have. No man who knows the truth of who you are, what you are, what you've done, would even consider—"

"I have done nothing wrong."

It was more than she could bear. After everything she had tried to leave behind, after she had attempted to build a new life, escape Mr. Shenton . . .

William was in there. Poor, innocent William.

He had proposed to her under false pretenses. If she were half the person he thought she was, she would call this off. Tell him the truth. Tell him she could not marry him.

Free him from her.

A part of her ached for him, loved him. But it was not something she could tell him. Alice knew William saw their marriage as much a part of his duty as a duke as anything else. He liked her. Cared for her. Desired her.

But it wasn't the same thing as love.

Mr. Shenton was still speaking. "—should go in there and inform His Grace—"

"No," said Alice with a firmness she had not expected.

The man frowned, a dangerous look flickering in his eyes. "No? What do you mean, no?"

But she'd had enough. Years of fear, years of payments that bought silence which she knew could only last so long. Years of wondering when it would all come crashing down around her. Years of protecting Maude and fearing one day her protection would not be enough.

It ended here. It ended today. It ended now.

"I am now under the Duke of Cothrom's protection," Alice said quietly, though her voice no longer quavered. "He is about to become my husband, and I will be his wife—*his* wife, Mr. Shenton. Our . . . our arrangement, for want of a better word, is over. You cannot hurt me anymore."

You cannot hurt me anymore.

Relief soared through her as Alice spoke those words. She could hardly believe it, but it was the truth. Once she was married, there would be nothing Mr. Shenton—or William—could do to harm her. William would never divorce her, and Mr. Shenton would have his money. He would no longer be able to reach her.

And clearly Mr. Shenton saw that. His scowl was dark, ill-tempered, and accompanied by the words, "You think you're so clever, don't you?"

"I have outsmarted you," Alice said bluntly, fingers tightening painfully around the ribbon of her bouquet. "Now if you do not mind,

I have a wedding to attend, to partake in."

For a moment she really thought Mr. Shenton would do his worst. Step into the church, disrupt the wedding, make it impossible for her to be happy.

Tell William of her true past.

But with a sneer worthy of the greatest actor on the stage, Mr. Shenton inclined his head and swept away along the London street.

Alice leaned against the church wall, hardly sure how she was still standing.

It was just as she had feared, when she had discovered William had put the announcement of their engagement in the newspaper. But the worst had happened, and she was still here. Still standing.

She had not slept all night. What bride slept well the night before their wedding?

Alice had seen the evidence of her poor night's sleep in the looking glass that morning. The bags under her eyes were almost large enough to fit her wedding trousseau, and there was a pallor to her skin that was certainly not her best. No matter what Jane attempted, there was no number of potions or lotions could transform her skin.

But she was here. All she had to do was step through those doors.

"Well then, Alice Fox-Edwards," she murmured to herself, straightening and taking a deep breath, "time to get married."

The door was heavy. If her father had lived, if she'd had a brother, it would have been a gentleman at her side who would have opened the doors, but as it was, she was alone.

The creaking scrape of the door echoed through the church, mingling with the organ music which changed almost immediately.

The church was packed. Eyes whirled around to stare, muttering flowing through the nave like water, but Alice did not care about that. She was not interested in what the ladies of the *ton* thought of her gown or what the gentlemen of Society thought about her appearance.

Her gaze was fixed on one thing.

William.

And he was smiling. Joy that was most unexpected flowed through her, a joy Alice did not deserve.

After everything she had been through, all she had suffered, all she had struggled through—marriage to a duke? Not something she could have ever predicted.

As her legs slowly moved her up the aisle, faces turning to follow her like sunflowers adoring the sun, Alice did not take her eyes from William. His smile strengthened her, making it possible to take each step.

And it was a relief, finally, to reach him and have her hand be taken in his.

The moment of connection between them sparked heat which flowed to her very core. Alice looked into the eyes of the man she was about to marry, and was relieved to discover her affection for him was...

It was love.

She had not expected it. Could not have predicted it. There was no thought of love when she had arrived in London to find a husband. Love was not a secondary consideration, or a third. It was not something she could have hoped for.

Yet despite all her scheming, all her plans, she had not just hooked a husband. She had found a man who was brave and intelligent, fiercely protective, with a deep desire for connection.

And who kissed like the devil.

Who could wish for more?

After all her conniving, all her hopes, Alice was marrying for love.

"I've been waiting for you," William said suddenly, as though the words had pushed themselves from his lips.

Alice squeezed William's hand, hoping some of what she felt could be communicated through that simple gesture. "I know," she said softly. "But I'm here now. I'll always be here."

That was all she wanted, wasn't it? Someone always beside her, supporting her, ready to listen to her and be heard in turn. A partner.

William's smile was gentle, as it always was. "You know, a part of me thought you would never get here."

Alice tried not to laugh, conscious that the echo in the church would make it immediately obvious to every guest there. "You know, neither did I."

"Ahem," said a third voice.

She turned to see the stern face of a man wearing a reverend's collar.

"Now you two have finally arrived and you seem to be done with your chitchat," the vicar said peevishly, "do you mind if I cut in and marry you?"

William squeezed Alice's hand and she felt his mirth, even though he managed to control his face and look seriously at the older man. "Of course, sir. Thank you."

The vicar sniffed, though was a tad mollified by being spoken to so respectfully by a duke. Even if that duke had been so rude in the first place.

"Dearly beloved," he said loudly, scowling at the congregation as though it was a great outrage to have so many people cluttering up his church. "We are gathered here today . . ."

More words were spoken. Alice was almost certain they were, she could hear them echoing around the columns and under the archways. But it was difficult to pay attention. Standing beside a handsome duke holding her hand, gently rubbing his thumb along her own, was distracting.

The smoothness of his thumb was intoxicating—and so was the memory that it was *that* thumb which had teased such unexpected pleasure as it had grazed across her—

"My lady?"

Alice started. Both the vicar and William were staring. "I-I beg your pardon?"

The vicar's frown deepened. "Impediments. There aren't any, I presume?"

She swallowed. "None whatsoever."

It was not a complete lie. It didn't reveal the truth, certainly, but Alice was hardly going to announce that to all and sundry in the middle of a wedding. Her wedding.

"And you, William Thomas Leopold Chance, Duke of Cothrom," intoned the vicar, turning to the man beside her. "Do you know of any reason . . ."

Alice could not help but glance up at her future husband through her eyelashes. It had all been so sudden—though she supposed that was the way nobility got married. Arrangements were made, fathers and brothers shook hands, and a wedding was organized for a few weeks' time.

Easy as that.

But this? This was hardly easy. She was marrying a duke under false pretenses!

Suddenly the lack of noise hit Alice's ears like she had dropped into water. She blinked. Again, both William and the vicar were looking at her.

Alice smiled weakly. "Would . . . would you mind repeating that?"

Thankfully William appeared to be taking her lack of concentration as nerves. Which perhaps it was. Alice certainly couldn't understand why it was so difficult to pay attention when her very future was being decided.

". . . to have and to hold, from this day forward . . ."

". . . for better, for worse, for richer, for poorer . . ."

". . . in sickness and in health, to love and to cherish . . ."

". . . till death us do part, according to God's holy law."

Alice swallowed. "In the presence of God, I make this vow."

And it was over. Done. Finished.

With a few simple words and a few signatures on a piece of paper,

Alice took William's arm and knew that now, everything was different.

She wasn't just holding the arm of a gentleman. Or a duke. He was her husband.

Organ music poured through the pipes and with a start, Alice was pulled forward by William as he strode purposefully down the aisle. The congregation smiled and murmured congratulations, some bowing and curtsying, some just inclining their heads.

Lady Romeril sniffed as they passed. "So late!"

Then they were out in the sunshine, glaring after the darkness of the church. Alice blinked against the blinding light and before she could regain her sight—

"William!" she gasped.

He left her little time—or breath—to say anything else. Before anyone had left the church, before they could be discovered, William had pulled her into his arms and kissed her.

And this kiss was most unlike all the others which had preceded it.

Oh, it was still William. His touch, the scent of him, all cedarwood and masculinity and something else that was just William which Alice had not yet deciphered. It was the same passion, the same need to be close to her, the same heady concoction of desire and affection Alice so adored.

But it was still different. Reverential, and possessive, and . . . and more.

The kiss was over before it had truly begun, and when Alice blinked up with hazy eyes, it was to see William flushing.

"Sorry," he said, brushing his hair out of his eyes. "Probably not appropriate, but I admit, I couldn't help—"

Alice did not permit him to finish the question.

This was her husband—her savior, though he did not know it.

This kiss was achingly sweet, her fingers clinging onto him as though she was about to be wrenched from his arms. She loved him, and though she had not yet the bravery to say the words aloud, perhaps her lips could do the talking for her.

When Alice finally released him, William was flushing all the more.

"Damn—I mean, goodness," he said, glancing at the church behind her with an apologetic expression. "I'm glad we were able to move the wedding forward."

Alice grinned as she entwined her fingers in his. "As am I."

Wedding guests were starting to pour from the church, and her hopes sank at the realization that she would have to greet each and every one of them at the reception. Aylesbury had offered to host it, apparently, as Alice's lodgings were simply insufficient to host such a great number of people, but William had insisted. It was his bride. His reception. He would host.

The pavement was swiftly filling up with guests, but just as Alice was steeling herself to start speaking to them, William groaned.

"What is it?"

"Nothing, it's just—"

"There she is! We thought we were going to have to announce to the masses that our dear boy had been left at the altar," came a cheerful voice from behind her.

A smile crept across Alice's face as she turned to see the Marquess of Aylesbury grinning with the Earl of Lindow beside him—and the Viscount Pernrith behind them.

"I do apologize for my tardiness, I am sure," she said with a laugh. "But it is a bride's prerogative, after all, to keep her husband waiting."

"You kept him waiting far too long, I commend you," the Earl of Lindow said with a giggle. "He was sweating away—"

"I was not sweating," William assured Alice with a frown at his brother.

"He even asked me if I had a horse ready for his escape," added the Marquess of Aylesbury happily.

"I asked no such—"

"He was concerned, I think, that you had changed your mind," came the quiet voice of the viscount. "I am glad to welcome you into the family, Alice."

And Alice's heart swelled.

The family.

It was more than she could have dreamt. Having a brother-in-law she could trust, that only wanted the best for her, was more than most women could hope for.

And she had three.

"Thank you, all of you," she said demurely, seeing the other wedding guests holding back while the three Chance brothers congratulated them. "And I must especially thank you, my lord, for the recommendation on the color of my gown."

She had not expected her words to cause such consternation, but Alice watched in surprise as not only the marquess and the earl, but her own husband stared at Pernrith in shock.

"You—you told her to wear the Cothrom russet?" William said quietly.

Pernrith shifted on his feet. "Well, I knew I was going to offer you Father's waistcoat, as soon as I could find it, and I thought—"

"That was . . . that was well done," said the earl stiffly.

Alice's pulse skipped a beat as she looked between them. Oh, if their marriage, their wedding could bring a new closeness between the brothers—

"I am just sorry you have to put up with all four of us Chance boys on what is meant to be such a pleasant day," said the Marquess of Aylesbury, winking. "I didn't see your family in there, were they unable to come?"

And just as rapidly, her boldness disappeared. Her family . . .

William squeezed her hand.

"Unfortunately, Alice has been left alone in the world due to the passing of her parents," he said quietly. "But not anymore."

Alice tried to nod, show him without speaking just how much his words meant to her. Even if they were not entirely accurate.

"I've just had a thought," said William suddenly, turning to Alice. "Oh, blast, I wish I'd thought of it before!"

"You always were slow, Cothrom," said the Earl of Lindow sardonically.

He was nudged, what appeared to be painfully, in the ribs by the marquess. "How can you say that to the blighter, on the man's wedding day!"

"You say it all the time!" protested the earl, rubbing his chest.

The Marquess of Aylesbury rolled his eyes. "Yes, behind his back! We don't tell the man—"

"Alice," William said urgently.

Alice dragged her attention away from the brothers—who were most entertaining—to look at her betrothed.

No. To look at her husband.

"Alice, I've just had the most marvelous idea," William said urgently. "I'm a fool not for thinking of it before the wedding, but there it is. You don't have to be alone!"

Alice waited, but it appeared the duke had nothing else to say. "Alone? William, I'll be with you, we—"

"No, we could bring your ward—how old did you say she is? Maude, wasn't it?"

And her heart stopped beating.

She could not have heard that correctly. That wasn't right—she was dreaming. Perhaps she had fallen asleep in church, listening to the vicar's long, dull sermon, and she was dreaming? Nothing else could explain this. How else could she be gazing up in the sunshine at a handsome duke who was beaming, suggesting her daughter—her Maude—

"She... she is but three years old," Alice managed to say.

"Maude."

"Excellent," said William with a contented look. "She'll give us some time to practice, before our family."

There was ringing in Alice's ears. She could not be hearing him properly—she was most definitely dreaming. She had to be.

"I . . . I am sorry, William, I think I . . ." Her voice trailed away as the bickering of his brothers continued to her left. But she had to ask, to ensure she understood precisely what he meant. "Do you mean you wish for—for Maude to—"

"She should come and live with us," said William firmly. "As you said, she is your responsibility, and now you have a home in which to welcome her. Why should a child live apart from you if you have affection for them? She'll be part of our family."

Alice let out a muffled sob, clasping a hand to her mouth to prevent anything further as her eyes sparkled with tears.

It was too much. It was better than she could have ever hoped for—greater than she could have dreamed. All her plans for sending Mrs. Seaby her pin money so Maude could be cared for properly, all the economies Alice had been prepared to make to safeguard enough . . .

It was over.

"Oh, William!"

Alice launched herself into William's arms and kissed him hard on the mouth.

"Oh, I say!"

"Dear God, maybe it's a good thing we rushed this wedding!"

"Is that even legal?"

Alice ignored the exclamations of her three new brothers-in-law and poured all her gratitude, all her affection into the kiss.

And William responded, his hands tightening on her waist, his tongue teasing along her bottom lip, shooting fiery heat through her. His breathing was heavy, his need for her dark, and Alice knew she would never—

"Outrageous behavior!" came the voice of Lady Romeril.

William broke the kiss. When Alice blinked and attempted to come to her senses, she could see why.

Lady Romeril was whacking the Duke of Cothrom with a reticule. "Put that woman down!"

"She is my wife, Lady Romeril," William pointed out wryly, his cheeks tinged pink.

"That's no cause for kissing in public!" Lady Romeril retorted. "Honestly! Young people these days—I would never have dreamed of such a thing! When I was your age . . ."

She muttered on as she stepped into a carriage, tapping the roof before it jolted away.

Alice swallowed. *Well, it was not the most auspicious start.* William offers her the only desire she her heart truly wants, and she embarrasses him in just the way she knows he hates.

"I apologize," she said stiffly, smoothing her gown with her fingers. "For making a scene, Your Grace."

She had expected William to acknowledge the apology with a curt nod, perhaps a small word of apology of his own.

What she had not expected was a wide grin to creep across William's face, even though his cheeks remained a dark pink. "With you in my arms, Alice Chance," he said quietly, "I find I just don't care."

Chapter Fourteen

WITH A HEAVY slam and a heavy sigh as accompaniment, William closed the door on the final guest.

Finally.

"Was that the last of them, Your Grace?" asked Nicholls behind him.

Just for an instant, William permitted himself a moment of exhaustion.

The last of them. Yes, the last of the well-wishers, friends, family, gawkers, interlopers, friends masquerading as family, enemies masquerading as friends. In short, the remainder of the *ton* who demanded a wedding invitation had finally departed his home to leave him in peace.

He had always considered his London townhouse to be magnificent. Not that he shouted about it. William would rather have closed it up completely and vacated it than do something as uncouth as *boast*.

But it was not insignificant. Two drawings rooms, a breakfast room, a morning room, a smoking room, a library. Not a small area for hosting.

And it had been bursting at the seams all evening, heat growing, laughter pouring into every inch of space. Even opening the large French doors into the garden hadn't taken the pressure off his heart. And the worst of it was . . .

William's jaw tightened. The worst of it was that entertaining such a mob—a crowd, that was—had separated him, all night, from the one person he actually wanted to spend such an evening with.

"Your Grace? I believe your wife is waiting for you in the blue drawing room. Shall I bring you both a light supper?"

His butler's voice interrupted William's thoughts and he straightened, pulling at his jacket to remove any imaginary creases.

"Supper?" William repeatedly blankly.

Oh God, the hall was empty. Empty of people! The crush of them, the noise, the chatter, the smoke from the gentlemen's pipes and the painfully mingled scents of the ladies. It was now nothing but emptiness and calm and quiet.

And Nicholls, peering with all the curiosity of a small boy meeting a crocodile at the Royal Menagerie for the first time.

William pulled himself together. He was still the Duke of Cothrom, even if today he'd had his hand shaken to within an inch of his life.

"No," he said directly, speaking on Alice's behalf and receiving a thrill of power up his spine at the act. "No, we do not wish to have supper."

His butler nodded. "In that case, I will instruct the footmen to—"

"No," said William again, just as directly.

He wasn't entirely sure what had got into him, but something had—and the idea had left little trickles of excitement tingling over his fingertips.

Well, it wasn't a bad idea . . .

"I—I beg your pardon?" said the butler, wide eyed. "You do not even know what I was going to—"

"Ah, there you are, Your Grace, I—oh, my apologies, Mr. Nicholls, I did not see you there," said Mrs. Ransome with a nod of her head.

William forced down a grin. Was it common for every gentleman fortunate enough to have both housekeeper and butler on his staff to see them disagree and fight and get one up over each other at every opportunity?

He watched the man bristle. "Mrs. Ransome. I believe it was quite obvious I was speaking to His—"

"Yes, I wished to speak to you, Your Grace," said Mrs. Ransome, elegantly speaking over her male counterpart with a gleam in her eye. "I was just about to tell the maids to—"

"No," said William sharply.

The thought which had first been only a shadow of an idea was starting to deepen, to grow in attraction. *Well, why not?* It was hardly the most scandalous thing. In fact, many people may expect it. If he'd had half a mind on planning the proceedings after the wedding vows, he might even have organized it all beforehand.

As it was . . .

"Nicholls, Mrs. Ransome," William said wearily, and winced to see his housekeeper throw a satisfied smile at his butler. *Damn.* He should probably have called him Mr. Nicholls, to keep them equal. *Ah well, nothing for it now.* "Please inform the staff that they are to take the evening off. In fact, tell them—tell them that they will all be treated to an evening at the Royal Hotel."

Clearly he had gone too far. Or . . . or not far enough?

A flicker of uncertainty curled around William's torso. He wasn't accustomed to this sort of thing—and apparently, neither were his servants.

Mrs. Ransome's mouth was opening and closing rapidly, but no sound was coming from it.

Nicholls was staring, eyes narrowed, as though attempting to decipher the mysterious message their master had given them.

William sighed and rubbed at his left temple. All he wanted was to be left alone in his own home with his wife. Was that so difficult to organize?

"Tell them the Duke of Cothrom will pay the bill—take my signet ring from the study, Mr. Nicholls," William said, emphasizing the *Mr.* and hoping that was sufficient to make amends for the earlier slight.

"And do not return until at least . . . ten o'clock tomorrow morning. Do you understand?"

"But . . . but . . . your breakfast, Your Grace," began Mrs. Ransome.

"Hang breakfast," said William without thinking.

It was perhaps one of the most uncivilized things he had ever said, and he regretted it immediately.

Well, not exactly immediately. It was rather thrilling, doing something he had never done before, saying something he had never said before. No wonder people gained such merriment from coarse language.

Still, both of his senior servants were staring as though he had gone mad.

Perhaps he had.

As William's attention meandered away from them, it fell on the gap of the ajar door of the blue drawing room. Through it, just faintly, he could make out a woman with white-blonde hair wearing a russet gown. White-blonde hair that needed to be entangled in his fingers.

"I wish to be alone with . . . with my wife," William said quietly, not taking his eyes from the slither of firelight coming through the gap into the hall.

When he turned back to his housekeeper and butler, he saw immediately he had said too much.

"Ah, yes, right, right, I see," said the butler, cheeks flushed. "Yes, we understand—"

"Yes, completely understood, yes, right," said Mrs. Ransome, evidently unsure where to look. "We'll be gone in less than five minutes, yes, absolutely, nothing easier than—"

"Thank you," said William awkwardly.

His housekeeper left immediately, muttering away to herself about things she should have expected, but his butler lingered. His expression was clear—he wanted a word.

"Yes?"

"I hope you do not think me too bold, Your Grace, if I say that I thought your brothers..." Nicholls cleared his throat. "Well, I thought they would never leave."

"Neither did I," said William ruefully. Lindow in particular did not seem to wish to depart, which was most strange. "Well, if that is all, I—"

"In fact, they seemed so reticent to leave that I accidentally mentioned a gaming hell, newly opened nearby," said his butler carefully.

William groaned.

Well, his butler wasn't to know, was he? It was his steward who countersigned many of the checks William had to make to cover the debts of his incorrigible brothers.

Still, he would have hoped for more discretion than that. After all, Nicholls had been with the Chance family for nigh on twenty years. He knew what Aylesbury and Lindow were like!

There was going to be a significant amount of damage control in the morning.

William pulled a hand through his hair as he considered what would need to be done. Paying off their debts, but that didn't even start to account for debts of honor. Pay off the newspapers. Attempt to smooth over every insult and misdeed.

"You didn't," William said heavily.

And for some reason, as maids and footmen hurried into the hall with their coats, pelisses, and small cases full of overnight things, glancing red faced at their master, his butler smirked.

"No, I didn't," the man said quietly. "I think I may actually have mistaken it for a temperance hall. I do apologize, Your Grace, it was a complete lapse and I assure you it won't happen again. Still... they'll have just as much fun there, I am sure."

There was a sparkle in the man's eye William had never seen before. He grinned as he clapped the man on the arm, something he had never done before.

"Go, be off with you," he said with a dry laugh. "And remember, I don't want to see you until—"

"Ten o'clock," said Mrs. Ransome resolutely on her own way through the hall, though she added in an undertone, "though what you'll do for breakfast, I don't know . . ."

This time, the closing of the front door behind people was even more satisfying. William stood in the hallway and knew, without a shadow of a doubt, he and Alice were alone.

Alone.

Just the two of them, all night long.

William swallowed as his manhood stirred. They had been good—well, better than he had wanted to be. Despite the great provocation, he had not taken the pleasure he so desperately wished for.

The pleasure he would be taking in just a few minutes.

Taking care to walk, not run, William opened the door to the blue drawing room and stepped inside.

And saw a picture of exquisite beauty.

There she was. Alice. Her pale hair looked golden in the candlelight, and some had already been unpinned, curls falling around her neck as though silk strands carefully covered her bare shoulders.

She was seated on the sofa, staring at her hand.

Her left hand.

William's breath caught as the rings glittered in the candlelight as Alice shifted them, her attention focused on them.

Those rings had made her his. His wife. His future.

His hopes soared, tingling anticipation mingled now with true elation. *He'd done it.* After years of saying that he would get around to it, William had finally married—married a woman who was kind and good. Had not her impeccable conduct toward her ward proved that?

And what's more, she was beautiful, and elegant.

And even more than that, there appeared to be a fire in her, a desire William could never have conceived of in a woman.

Alice Fox-Edwards—no, Alice *Chance* was the perfect woman for him. She was perfection and would now support him in making the Chance family perfect.

Perhaps the manner of their courtship, such as it was, was unusual. But there was something about her. Alice had drawn him in, inexplicably, and William had not the heart to fight it.

How could you fight something as intrinsic as . . . as love?

He stepped forward and must have made more noise than he thought, for Alice looked up and glanced over her shoulder.

The smile that slowly curved her lips made William's stomach lurch.

Fine. Something farther down.

Thinking about the Chance family had started him thinking of the family they would one day build together. Perhaps sooner rather than later.

"There you are," said Alice, her words vibrant. "I was starting to worry."

"Worry?" repeated William as he stepped around the sofa and sat beside her. "About me?"

There was a knowing look in her eyes. "You are my husband now, William Chance, Duke of Cothrom. I think you will find it is my duty to worry about you."

"I suppose it is," he said, a flutter of delight soaring through him. "Goodness. I hadn't thought of that."

"It may be unusual to admit, but I worried about you before today, actually," Alice said, her voice low as though she were admitting to some terrible secret. "I hope . . . I hope that was not wrong?"

And William was filled with such a surge of love, he was surprised he did not declare it, announce it to the world, pour kisses onto her face as he tried to show her, not tell her, just how loved she was.

Because this woman—this woman! She understood his concern for decorum, for always presenting the right face to the world. She was a worthy partner for him—a worthy woman who he would never have to concern himself with.

Not like Lindow, or Aylesbury. Or God forbid, Pernrith.

"Did I hear Mr. Nicholls talking about your brothers in the hall?" Alice said, utterly ignorant of the thoughts whirling through his mind.

William blinked. "Brothers?"

He had brothers?

"Yes, something about a gaming hell, I think," Alice said, turning in her seat so that she could face him more directly. "I do hope they aren't going to prove a problem for you."

And that was another reason why he was so pleased, wasn't he? William could never have expected to find a woman who could so easily understand the interesting dynamic he had with his brothers—that of father, really. The fact she was willing to share in his struggles to keep the family respectable—it was more than he could have wished for.

"William?"

William cleared his throat. *Enough of that nonsensical thinking.* "I think my brothers will always be a handful, to tell the truth, but I would expect nothing less from such ruffians."

"They are a marquess, an earl, and a viscount."

He snorted. "You think that a title confers respectability? It only confers nobility, which I can tell you is quite a different thing indeed."

It had not been his intention to be amusing, but William was strangely gratified to see Alice laugh.

"I suppose you are right, though I have not much experience with such things," Alice said, taking a deep breath. "I suppose there will be lots of things, now that we are married, that I have not much experience in that I will swiftly have to learn."

William's throat went dry. *It was because your mind is thinking of only one thing,* he chastised himself silently. *She didn't mean—*

"Being a duchess . . . it is more than I ever thought could happen to someone like me."

"Someone like you?" William said in wonder. "You mean someone kind, gentle, honorable?"

For some reason, his words had a marked effect on his new wife. Color splattered across her cheeks and Alice looked at her hands, wound together in her lap, as though she could no longer meet his gaze.

William's heart stirred. And she was humble, unexpecting of praise and shy when she received it.

Dear God. How had he ever deserved her?

"Don't call me that," Alice said quietly.

"Why not? It's all true," William said firmly, his pulse pattering painfully. All he wanted to do was pull her into his arms and rain kisses—but it was too soon. He needed to woo this woman, this wife of his.

He couldn't just barrel in and demand—

"I do worry about you, you know," Alice said helplessly. "I mean, I know it is expected for a wife to care for her husband, but you—you do so much, for so many people. And you bear such burdens upon yourself. You take them up for others just because you can, and that is—oh, William, I admire you so, and I worry you take on too much—"

"Alice," William exhaled.

Without saying another word, he reached for her hand and lifted it to his lips, brushing kisses onto the ends of her fingertips.

The sudden gasp, low yet most definitely there, told William just how much gratification he was giving his wife by the simple gesture. It was . . . intimate. Something he had never shared with another and was glad to now.

It was only the beginning of what this night could offer.

When William looked up, Alice's smile had not faded. "I . . . I suppose worrying about you is not the only thing I can now do without shame, now . . . now we are married."

He swallowed, trying to calm the raging need pressing against his breeches.

Alice Fox-Edwards had been an innocent, and now Alice Chance was about to discover what it was when two people cared about each other enough to share the most intimate, the most delightful—

But he would not rush her. No, that would be—

"Like being alone together," Alice continued, a knowing look in her eye. "That was what I meant, William."

He blinked. "Of—of course it was. That was what I was thinking—" His voice faded away as her laughter grew. "You are teasing me."

William had not intended to speak in such a petulant voice, and hoped beyond hope Alice did not consider it so.

A candle flickered and went out in the candelabra on the mantlepiece. It was late. And he had been patient.

"I am only teasing you a little," Alice said quietly, entangling her fingers with his own.

Heat flared along his hands and William did his best to keep them still. If this was a sign of how the night was going to be, it was going to be a great challenge indeed.

After all, what man did not begin his wedding night with hopes of . . . well, everything?

But this was not one of the women that William had, on infrequent occasions, found to satisfy the lusts of the flesh. Alice had not done this before. She may not even know, precisely, what it was that they were about to do.

Just for a moment, William cursed the idiotic way that Society treated its ladies. Why, if they only knew what bliss awaited them in the marriage bed . . .

Then again, perhaps that was why they were sheltered. He certainly had been unable to resist temptation the moment he had realized just what delights could be found in any bed.

Alice cleared her throat and William's attention was immediately pulled to her. "And . . . and of course, there are other things that we can do now that we are married. Alone, I mean."

William swallowed. He wasn't about to permit himself to be teased again if he could help it. "You mean . . . discuss the hiring of staff, and what color to repaint this room?"

"You wish to repaint this room?" Alice glanced about the place and William cursed himself for the distraction.

He did not wish to consider the merits and demerits of blue wallpaper. He wanted to make love to his wife!

Perhaps something of his thoughts was transparent on his face. At any rate, Alice glanced over and tightened her grip on his hands. "Or, I suppose, we could do the other thing you immediately thought of," she said quietly.

William's manhood stiffened. Strange, he hadn't thought it possible to be any more taut. "I . . . I don't know what you—"

"I think you do," Alice said gently, cutting across him with the utmost elegance. "Is this the time to go upstairs and . . . and truly become husband and wife?"

Chapter Fifteen

ALICE HAD KNOWN her hope for this moment was too forward—that a proper wife, a proper duchess, would likely not be capable of even thinking such a thing, let alone suggesting it.

But how could she not? The air between herself and William was thrumming with repressed desire, the need within her building for weeks, from the moment he had first kissed her against that tree she had known what she wanted.

What she needed.

What she craved.

That, surely, was the only reason she had said what she had said. Something so heathen, so scandalous she was surprised William had not pulled away. But she drew the line at discussing paint colors.

And so she spoke incautiously. "Or, I suppose, we could do the other thing you immediately thought of."

And now her husband's eyes were wide. "I . . . I don't know what you—"

It was time for action. Alice couldn't wait much longer. The ache between her legs had been growing since the door had closed behind their last guest.

Alone, at last.

"I think you do," Alice said, cutting across her husband with what she hoped wasn't too much barefaced eagerness. "Is this the time to go upstairs and . . . and truly become husband and wife?"

There. She had said it.

And it was too bold, she knew—but what woman wouldn't wish for such a thing with William Chance?

The raw animal energy of the man had never been so potent, and Alice had never been more willing to be swept away into his arms by his charm. She wanted to feel the crush of his fingers against her skin, the guttural moan in his throat as he kissed her—as he tasted her. She wanted to touch him, see his body jerk at the sudden heady pleasure. She wanted to know him, truly know him, as a wife knew a husband.

And, muttered a cruel voice at the back of her mind, *you need to make sure, don't you?*

Try as she might, Alice could not entirely banish the thought from her mind.

Yes, if she were truly to be William's wife—and remain that way for the rest of her life—they would need to consummate it. Without their joining, there was a possibility of annulment. Unlikely as it was, she could not take that risk. This marriage had to be true.

And it was. Alice looked into William's bright-blue eyes and felt the affection she had attempted to force down rise up once again. This all may have started because she needed a protector, a husband, someone to give her pin money to pay off Shenton, the man who had held terror over her for so long. But that was not how this was ending.

Alice chuckled with delight at the sudden shock in William's face as he realized what she was suggesting.

She wasn't just a duchess. She didn't just have a house. Money wasn't the greatest asset in this marriage.

She was a wife. She had a home. And she had the power to free herself, to bring Maude to her.

Everything was going to be all right.

For she loved him. Alice could almost cry out with relief. There had been no certainty, no definite knowledge that she would care for him—but William was a difficult man not to love.

"Oh, Alice," William murmured, leaning slowly forward.

And then not so slowly. Faster than Alice could have imagined, so fast she uttered a squeak of surprise, William had moved toward her and covered his body with her own, pressing her into the sofa.

If she had thoughts to speak, she could not have uttered them. Not with his lips pressed against hers, teasing them open, ravishing her mouth and causing tendrils of decadence to sweep through her body.

Anyone who could even think under such an onslaught was a better woman than she.

Alice acted instinctively, allowing herself all the freedom she had denied herself during their odd courtship. She pulled him closer. Her fingers met around the back of his neck, pulling his nape closer, welcoming him in.

The pressure of his chest against her breasts was torture, trapped as they were by her corset and stays, but she could hardly think of releasing them.

Not with servants about the place.

The sudden thought made Alice stiffen.

William ceased his kisses, pulling back with a worried expression. "Alice, I do apologize—"

"Don't you dare," Alice said darkly, a thumb stroking the back of his neck. "What on earth do you wish to apologize for?"

She blinked, trying to regain her equilibrium. *Dear God, if the man kissed like that, just what he would be like in the bedchamber was anyone's guess . . .*

"You . . . well, you seemed suddenly discomforted," said William, equally as discomforted. "I did not wish to—"

"I merely thought—the servants," admitted Alice, flushing at the very thought.

The idea that at any moment, Mrs. Ransome or Mr. Nicholls or any one of the numerous maids or footmen could enter this room and discover them—

Well. In flagrante.

But William, strangely, did not appear to be similarly abashed. To

Alice's great surprise, he grinned. "I have taken the liberty of removing all servants from the place," he said quietly, leaning to brush a kiss on her neck so light, she almost couldn't feel it.

Alice blinked. "All—all the servants?"

Was he telling her they were alone in this huge townhouse? Truly alone?

William pulled back again to look deep in her eyes, and Alice could see his affection for her as clear as day. "Alice, I want tonight to be perfect. As perfect as I can make it, I mean, perfect for you, and I thought—well, I certainly don't want to be interrupted. Or restrained. Or quiet."

A shiver rushed through Alice. *Dear God, the man was so much more complex than she had ever given him credit for.* He had sent away the servants because he didn't want them to hear their moans of passion?

"—so we are alone, for tonight," William continued. "I hope that was the right thing. I will pay for their rooms at a hotel, obviously, I didn't turn them out onto the street—"

Alice had heard enough. She had been watching the careful twists and curls of her husband's lips for what felt like several years now and had a great desire to taste them again.

She moaned as she demanded William's mouth, demanded he parted his lips—and moaned again as he so willingly gave her entrance. His passion was equal only to hers, his hands moving down her body, one of them cupping her buttocks to pull her against his hip.

Against something rather hard, and long, and urgently pressing into her.

Alice gasped in his kiss and William possessively deepened it, his tongue claiming more.

The tingling ache between her thighs was growing, starting to heat so rapidly that Alice attempted to curl a leg around his hips. She was unable to, trapped by the fabric of her skirts and she moaned, twisting against him as she tried to rub herself against him.

Her response appeared to spur him on. William's kisses became, if possible, more passionate. His teasing tongue swept across her bottom lip before he nibbled it, hard, and Alice arched her back into him, her fingers starting to scrabble against his jacket, desperate to remove it.

Desperate to feel his skin against her own.

His hunger for her was something Alice could never have expected. The restrained, calm William had gone, replaced by a man who appeared desperate to worship her—to claim her as his woman.

Alice moaned in aching hunger. *Oh, she wanted more, she wanted him now—*

And something of her eagerness seemed to shoot through William. He pulled away, panting, looking at her with concern once again in his eyes. She almost pulled him down into her arms once more. Couldn't he not just let go for more than a few minutes?

"I . . . I did not hurt you, did I?" William said anxiously, his voice jagged and his fingers frozen against her body.

It was all Alice could do not to laugh.

Of course, he thought she was a complete innocent. A woman who had never been kissed before, who was discovering all of this new and fresh with him.

It had been one of the things she had most worried about in the lead up to this day, their wedding day. How would she pretend that she was enjoying herself if William was an ineffectual lover? And more importantly, how would she pretend she had no idea what she was doing, so he would continue to believe he was the first and only one she had known?

But Alice had underestimated William—not for the first time, and if this was anything to go by, not for the last.

His concern was for her. He was not measuring her against some vague standard of feminine innocence. No, William's entire focus was whether or not she was enjoying herself.

Which boded well.

Trying to push aside the licentious thoughts pouring into Alice's mind—of William making sure, very sure, she was satisfied—she tried to reassure the man who so evidently adored her.

Even if, perhaps, he shouldn't.

"I am quite well, I assure you," Alice said, surprised at how breathless she was. "You have not injured me."

"It is just—well, I have had to be very restrained in all my contact with you, until today," said William heavily, looking pained. "I very much wished to—damn it, Alice, there's no polite way of saying this. I wanted to bed you. Badly."

Heat swept across Alice's body, and she knew her cheeks had tinged with pink.

Which was all to the good. It would hopefully convince William of her innocent surprise.

Whereas it was, in fact, delight.

To be desired . . . it had been so long.

"I . . . well," Alice said, wetting her lips and reveling in the instant reaction it caused within her new husband. William groaned, rubbing his hips against hers with evident unrestraint. "I had no idea, William, I thought—I thought you did not permit yourself to feel such things?"

"Is it possible not to feel such things while in your presence?" William muttered, lowering his head to bestow a worshipful kiss just below Alice's ear.

Perhaps it was the kiss, perhaps it was the words—she did not know. All Alice was aware of was the sudden jolt of pleasure that tugged at her core.

And apparently, William had noticed.

Pressing her deeper onto the sofa, making it impossible for her to escape him—not that she had any wish to—William lowered his voice and murmured quietly as he trailed kisses from Alice's ear, down her neck, toward her collarbone. "Alice, I have wanted to do so much to you since you agreed to be my wife—no, even before. I have wanted to kiss you here . . . and here . . ."

Alice's eyelashes fluttered shut, unable to remain open as William growled such decadent desires into her ear.

Could she ever have predicted this?

"I have wanted to lift up your skirts and trail kisses up your thighs," he continued to murmur as his lips grazed her collarbone, drifting to her décolletage. "I wanted to slowly inch my way closer to your sex, to breathe you in, place my lips upon your—"

"William," moaned Alice, unable to stop herself.

Oh God, the picture he was painting—and his fingers were tight around her buttocks, sadly through the fabric of her skirt, but his mouth was moving lower—

"And I'd nuzzle you here," William muttered, nuzzling the curve of her breast as it strained against her corset, her breathing heavy. "And as my mouth would start to worship you, drinking your sweet nectar—"

Alice whimpered. How could she do anything else? Oh, how she craved the touch he promised, how she was desperate for him to please her in the ways he had apparently also wished!

Who was this husband of hers?

"—my fingers would reach up and take your breasts—"

"William, please," moaned Alice, clutching at him.

And though he did not precisely obey, he could sense her need, feel it, perhaps scent it, as she ached for him.

Alice gasped as William dipped his head and with his teeth, moved her corset to free her breasts.

Within a heartbeat, his mouth had closed around one of her nipples, teasing it with his tongue as it swooped around it before finally nibbling it experimentally.

And Alice almost lost herself. The sensuality, the intimacy, it was too much—yet not enough.

This was everything she could have hoped for and more. Here was a man who was not only good—a good person, with good morals, and good judgment—but a bad man, too. A man who wished to delight her, please her, pleasure her. A man who knew his way around a woman's body, just as much as she knew her way around a man's. And if he were not careful—

"William!" Alice gasped.

There had been no censure in her exclamation—how could there be, when he had done something so delightful?

As his mouth continued to worship her breast, William's hand had managed to somehow slip under her skirt. His fingers trailed a path up her thigh, the exact path he had just spoken of kissing, and Alice wiggled in eagerness, tried to open her legs, make room for—

"Oh God, yes," she moaned, eyes shut as she lost herself in the twin sensations.

William's tongue curled around her nipple and his finger slowly trailing across her slit.

"Damn, you feel so good," he groaned, his mouth only free for a second as he moved from one breast to the other.

She felt good? Alice could barely think—thinking was impossible as he slipped a finger inside her, teasing her nub just as his teeth tugged at her nipple.

"Oh, William, yes," she murmured, tilting her hips to invite him deeper.

The sensation of his finger inside her wet folds, achingly close to her center yet not close enough was surely sufficient to drive most women to distraction—but Alice had the simultaneous worshipping of her breasts to contend with.

And it was getting worse—or did she mean better? She hardly knew. The ache between her legs was building, building as it had not done for years, and Alice clung onto William's shoulders as his pace quickened, his mouth and fingers matching each other in a rhythm perfectly designed to destroy her.

"Please, please, please," she moaned, unable to help herself, unable to censure herself.

And why should she? She was with William, the one man who could make her feel—

"Y-Y-Yes, oh yes!"

And Alice exploded. Her body was no longer whole, all parts flying out in all directions, as William's thumb slipped inside her and pressed, hard, twisting slightly against the very core of herself.

Bliss like she had never known undid her. The ecstasy poured through her body like lava, twisting and shaking her limbs as she lost all control over body and voice and heart.

Her heart. Oh, it had belonged to him, William had already taken it. But this placed a seal upon it, branding her as his own. His very own.

It took what felt like a small age for the quivering sensations to dissipate. When Alice finally opened her eyes, it was to see William smiling, surprise in his expression.

"I . . ." He swallowed. "I've never known a woman to be so free in her pleasure."

Alice tried to laugh. "I've never known such pleasure."

A dark delight flickered across William's face. "Good. I . . . well, I suppose you might be too tired now for—"

"Come with me," she said in a low voice, brushing past what he had been about to say. "You've readied me, William, I'm warm for you, wet for you. Don't you want to know me fully?"

Alice had never seen a man rise from a sofa so swiftly. Though in fairness, she thought wryly as she attempted to stand on legs which only moments ago had been spasming, other parts of William had risen quickly enough.

She slipped her hand in his and pulled William to the door to the hall, but they did not quite make it.

Make it through the door, at any rate.

Pushing William against the wall by the door, Alice allowed herself the freedom to express all the gratitude she felt for his selfless lovemaking. It was a rare man who ensured his wife's gratification before his own, and he had to know that—William had to know how grateful she was.

By all accounts, he knew. William's frantic fingers started pulling up her skirts, his breathing ragged, and Alice pulled away with a teasing laugh.

"You may make love to me in a bed and nowhere else," she said with a mock severity that made William's eyes flash. "I am a duchess, you know."

"And I am your duke," William growled, throwing open the door and pulling her through it. "And I will have you where I say I will have you."

Alice's pulse skipped a beat in delight. That she could have found such a man with such depth of passion—passion for her!

It took a great deal longer than she had expected to traverse the stairs. Not because the staircase itself was particularly long. Alice guessed it was about twenty steps. She didn't precisely know, because every few steps, William pressed her against the wall and kissed her so passionately, it was rather hard to think. Or see.

Try as she might, Alice could not quite rid her husband of his clothes. As his mouth trailed over her shoulder, making tingles of delight shoot through her, she tried to pull away his jacket—but his hands were not free, too busy reaching under her skirts and cupping her buttocks, fingertips searing her skin.

And then all rational thought left her, and Alice succumbed to the passionate kisses of the Duke of Cothrom.

By the time they reached the ducal bedchamber, Alice was breathless, shoddily dressed, and had lost all her hairpins. Swathes of blonde curls cascaded down her shoulders, and she saw by the gleam in William's eye that he rather liked the effect.

Well, that was something worth remembering.

"You'll have to help me," Alice said as William slammed the door behind them and advanced toward her. "My corset, the gown, I can't—"

"I want you too desperately to worry about that," said William with a grin, not taking his eyes off her as his fingers lowered and started unbuttoning his breeches. "There will be plenty of nights for slow and sensuous lovemaking, Alice, but I admit, I am rather in need of plunging myself in you and losing myself. Do you mind?"

Did she mind?

Alice did not hesitate. Instead of attempting to remove her clothes, she stepped forward, pulling William into her arms just as his breeches slipped to the floor.

"William," she whispered as she kissed him, desperate for him to know just how eager she was, how her need for him matched his own. "Take me, William."

He needed no additional invitation. Sweeping her up in his arms, William took three strides and threw Alice onto the bed.

She gasped as she bounced, the mattress accepting her, and gasped again as William covered his body with hers.

But not quite. One of his hands cupped her cheek while the other hurriedly pulled her skirts up, parting her knees—not that Alice needed the incentive. Her own hands were reaching down to the masculine hips pressed against hers, searching for—

William inhaled with a hiss. "Alice!"

Alice did not look away as her hand cradled his manhood, guiding it toward her sex. "William."

She spoke his name as he entered her, slowly, slowly, and she did not look away as her body swelled and ached and moved, allowing him in, more and more of him.

Far more, in truth, than she had expected.

Alice flexed her hips from side to side, ensuring she could take in all of him, every inch, and William's breathing became more ragged as he palpably attempted to restrain himself.

"I-I—God, I never thought it would be so hard to—"

"Don't hold back," Alice said, reaching up to place a kiss on the corner of his mouth. "Give me everything, William. I want everything."

It was, it appeared, the permission he needed. Groaning as he almost completely withdrew then plunged himself into her, William leaned against one arm and kissed her hard on the mouth as he started to build a slow yet steady rhythm.

Alice clung to him, his shoulders all she could reach, as the aching need in her started to build once more. Oh, did he know what he was doing to her? Did he have any idea the sparking throbbing he was creating?

Perhaps he did. The desperation William had spoken of was no jest—his pace quickened, and Alice could feel his need for her building, see it in the tension in his face.

And she was so close—

"Harder," she begged, unable to help herself, knowing it was unsavory for a woman to speak her need. "Harder, please, William, please—"

Her words were cut short as he obeyed, driving his manhood into her with reckless abandon, faster and faster, harder and—

"William!" Alice cried as completion overswept her.

And as her body rippled and rocked as her pleasure once again peaked, William swore loudly and jerked hard into her once, twice, thrice.

"Damn, Alice, Alice, oh—"

Their words and cries mingled, no thoughts given to loudness for they were alone, alone to lose themselves in their lovemaking.

And when, finally, the aftershocks ceased, William collapsed into Alice's arms breathing heavily.

She drew him to her, tears prickling in the corners of her eyes at what they had shared.

This was beyond what she could have hoped for, what she could have dreamed. Such a connection, such an intimacy—

"Alice?" came the muffled murmur from the man nestled into her neck.

A small smile crept across her face. "Yes?"

"I . . . well. I don't have words for—"

"Neither do I," she admitted softly, her arms tightening around him. "Oh, William."

For a moment, they were silent. Then—

"You've given me something so precious."

Alice swallowed. It was the final part of the deception, her husband thinking she had come to his bedchamber innocent—and it would only hurt him. There was no need to tell him, no need to ruin this moment.

"And I feel like . . . like I'm not alone anymore," continued William in a quiet voice, his hands on her hips, his body relaxed after so much tension. "Like . . . I don't have to fight for my brothers' status in Society anymore, I don't have to fight for my own respectability anymore. I've got you."

Alice blinked away tears and told herself the deception was over. She truly loved him, even if she could not yet say it.

"I will always fight beside you, when necessary," she said fiercely in a quiet voice.

She felt, as well as heard William's chuckle. "I know you will. You're my wife."

Chapter Sixteen

June 12, 1812

WILLIAM SKIPPED THE last step as he cheerily descended the stairs.

A week.

A whole week.

It was almost impossible to believe such a length of time had passed since Alice had become his wife—but each day had been filled with so much laughter and lovemaking that, in a way, it was a surprise it hadn't been a month.

Happiness he hadn't known was now his constant companion. Every morning when he awoke, there was that fraction of a second before he remembered.

He was married to Alice Fox-Edwards.

Then his joy renewed again.

It was still difficult to remind himself she was no longer a Fox-Edwards, but a Chance. Perhaps that would change over time. William wasn't sure.

What he was sure of was that he had never felt so . . . so content, so right with the world. The burden on his shoulders, the responsibility of single-handedly managing the unruly family that was the Chances, had been lifted.

He was no longer alone.

William's grin was broad as he stepped into the breakfast room.

There she was. Warm sunlight cascaded through the windows and fell onto a woman studiously reading that morning's newspaper while she attempted to eat a piece of toast.

Attempted, it appeared, because she was struggling to place the toast in her mouth, her eyes never wavering from the paper. There was a look of deep concentration on her face, along with a frown across her forehead.

There was still so much to learn about each other, so much they had not yet shared. It had never occurred to him, for example, that Alice had such an interest in the news of the day.

Approaching the breakfast table, Alice's expression of concentration became a light smile as William kissed her on the head.

"Well, hello, husband," she said lightly, placing her toast on her plate and folding up the newspaper with marmalade fingers.

William sighed happily as he sat at right angles to her at the table. "Hello, wife."

Wife.

It still felt strange to call her that. Such an innocent word, yet so intimate. Short, yet packed with such richness of connection.

How had he ever managed to go through life without feeling this content, this joyful, this happy with his lot? Had he been unhappy before, he wondered, or was it simply that he had not known the depths of affection one could reach with another? Either way, he had certainly been missing out. Now he had the rest of his life to explore this connection, this affection, this . . . love.

Though he still had not said the word. It had almost tumbled from William's lips a few times, but each time he had called it back. Somehow it did not feel right, not yet.

But what else could it be? This deep well of emotion he had for her, that sprang up and deepened and washed over him every time he saw Alice . . .

William looked up and met Alice's adoring look.

Dear God, it was like a dream.

So much of his life, he was only now starting to realize, had been spent in fear. In loneliness, in isolation. He had believed it impossible to relax, to truly relish life. It had always been a fight to survive, a fight to keep his brothers in line.

But this was different. This life he could have with Alice—it was completely new.

"You're smiling," Alice said quietly.

"Isn't that allowed?" William teased, reaching forward to pour himself a cup of tea.

"Of course!" giggled his wife delightedly, shaking her head at his apparent nonsense. "I meant, why are you smiling?"

His smile faded as he took a sip of tea. It was different, somehow. He was hardly a tea connoisseur, but even he could tell it was different.

"This tea," he began.

"I hope you don't mind, I asked Mrs. Ransome to follow my own personal blend," Alice said, cheeks reddening. She picked up the toast, moving it from one hand to another. "It's mostly the standard stuff, of course, but with a hint of bohea and a teaspoon of Pekoe. I find it rather refreshing."

It was more than refreshing. It was delicious—sweeter than he was accustomed to, and with more floral notes, but William could not deny that it was delightful.

Perhaps he should say so.

And this was the trouble with being married to such a perfect woman, he thought dryly. He was always attempting to match her perfection. It was starting to become a dangerous habit of his to second guess himself at every turn.

Just thank her for the tea, man!

"It's nice," he said lamely.

Nice? Nice? Surely he could conceive of a better compliment than—

"Very pleasant," William added, more to drown out the irritating voice at the back of his mind than anything else. "Thank you."

Alice shrugged as she munched her toast. "It's the least I could do. After all, you're paying for it."

The comment was not intended to be a barb, but it tore into him like one. "Alice, we're married now."

"It's your fortune," she said with a wry look. "I am not so foolish as to think—"

"Our fortune," William said. "You have given me so much, it is only fair I—"

"Given you—William, I have not given you anything," Alice said with a laugh that sounded worried. "Look at where we are!"

William looked around himself, bemused.

All he could see was the breakfast room. It was just . . . the breakfast room. It had not changed in the last few years. The place was exactly the same as it had been when his father had died and he had become the duke incumbent.

What on earth was she talking about?

His gaze returned to Alice, who was shaking her head. "You don't see it, do you?"

"What am I supposed to be seeing?" William asked before he could stop himself.

Her peals of laughter were like golden rain falling into his hands. "Honestly, you have lived in luxury too long! Really look. Look at the splendor of this place, the wealth spent. Look at the elegance, the light, the linen on this table, embroidered with silk! Really look."

And William tried. His eyes swept over the breakfast table with its linen tablecloth, the silver cutlery that shone in the sunlight. The paintings on the walls—one was a Rembrandt, if he wasn't mistaken. The little jade sculptures that sat along the mantlepiece. The longcase clock inlaid with mother of pearl.

Just for a moment, he saw it as with another's eyes. There was luxury, money, grandeur all about the place.

And he'd stopped noticing it.

When, he wasn't sure. William could hardly recall the last time he had properly seen the marble console table upon which sat the day's newspapers, or the elegantly embroidered screen which stood between them and the fire. Maybe he never had.

When he looked back at Alice, her expression was knowing, but gentle. "When I say you have given me much, I don't just mean the riches of the Cothrom estate, William. I mean . . . I mean you. Your affection, your respect, your care for me. It is more than I could have expected—certainly more than I deserve!"

William waved a hand as though he could wave away her very thoughts. "You undervalue your own contributions."

Alice grinned. "What did I bring? A few debts, a trousseau you paid for—"

"You can't know—you can never know, I don't think, what you have given me," William said, his voice choking up quite against his will.

He halted but it was already too late. Alice was staring with wide eyes, markedly shocked at the sudden emotion pouring from him.

William cleared his throat and started to pile toast, fried eggs, and some tomatoes onto his plate. "Anyway—"

"William," Alice said quietly. "What do you mean by that?"

Though he was tempted to brush past it, tell her there was nothing else to say, no more detail required, William relented. His shoulders slumped, the tension from them draining.

If he could not be open and honest with his wife, who could he be open and honest with at all?

"You don't know what my life was like before you," he said quietly.

There was a noise as Alice placed the remainder of her toast on her plate. "The life of a duke?"

"It isn't all it seems, I can assure you," William said dryly. "I have lived . . . well, a life of fear, I suppose you could call it. Fear of what could happen, always fighting what I presumed would become a disaster. It is only since knowing you, marrying you, being with you this last week that I have realized . . ."

He swallowed.

How could he explain? There did not appear to be words in the English language to express his debt to her.

A hand reached out and enclosed his. William looked up.

Alice was smiling. "What?" she whispered. "What did you realize?"

William took a deep breath. "That I haven't been living. That everything before you was just me waiting for you, though I did not know it."

It had taken much for him to be so open. He wasn't sure if he wanted to see what reaction his new wife was having to such openness—such vulnerability.

When William forced himself to look at her, she said, "Life should be so much more than that."

He nodded, squeezing her hand before retreating and picking up his cutlery. "I suppose it should be—not that I knew that before."

"And now?"

"Oh, I know it now," William said with a wry shrug. He cleared his throat. *This damned emotionality had to stop—this wasn't what breakfast was for!* He needed another topic, that was all. "So, tell me. When does your ward arrive?"

As expected, the topic was the ideal choice to distract his new wife from talk of the depths of his soul.

Alice sighed happily and picked up the last of her toast. "A few days, I think. Mrs. Seaby wrote, and her letter arrived yesterday. They'll be departing as soon as your carriage arrives."

"You are excited to see her," said William before a mouthful of runny egg.

"I most certainly am," Alice beamed. "It has been—well, too long, I think. Maude deserves a proper family, and I am most grateful that we will be offering her one."

William waved away her words with his knife. "It's nothing. You do me the honor by permitting me to help you take charge of your ward."

It was, after all, the earliest and surest sign that they were compatible. William knew few people with wards—it was not a common occurrence. And fewer still of those individuals cared much about the actual wellbeing of those in their care. It was a burden, usually, foisted upon them by the unexpected death of a relative.

But Alice? She cared deeply for the child, far more than most wards could expect.

William's chest swelled. *His was a wife to be proud of, indeed.*

"I just hope she won't be too lonely here," Alice was saying. "I am not sure what friends she has, back in—"

"Lonely?" William repeated, speaking over her in his excitement. "You—do you think you could be with child, Alice?"

The question was forward, for she flushed. "I don't know."

His hopes sank. "You don't?"

He had assumed it would be easy to tell. After all, he had bedded the woman at least twice a day every day since they had been married, and they had taken no precautions to prevent a child.

Why should they?

William's heart stirred at the thought. Himself and Alice and this Maude girl—and their own children. Boys and girls with his height and her laughter, his tenacity and her kindness. Children throughout the house. Joy and mess and delight.

"It's too early for me to know," Alice was saying, eyes cast down to her plate. "I should know in a month or so."

Try as he might, William could not help but feel a little deflated. A whole month, just to know—and the answer could be a negative. Ah, well. It wasn't like they were in any rush. His spirits perked up at that thought. Why, they had the rest of their lives together to build a family.

"In that case," he said aloud with a grin, placing his knife and fork down. "I think we should make absolutely sure we are doing our best. Why don't we go upstairs and—ah. Nicholls. What impeccable timing."

William sank back onto his chair, his manhood immediately deflating. It was too much to hope that he could get Alice squirming underneath his hands this early in the morning.

His butler bowed as he entered with a silver platter coated in letters. "Good morning, Your Grace."

Alice stifled a giggle, placing her napkin before her lips as she inclined her head. "Mr. Nicholls."

"Your letters, Your Graces," said Nicholls formally as he placed the platter on the breakfast table. "Is there anything else I can do for you this—"

"No, no, that's all, thank you," said William hastily, waving the man away. As the door closed behind him, he groaned as Alice giggled. "Where was I?"

"About to take me upstairs and ravish me, I think," said Alice with a twinkle in her eye. "But I suppose you should read your post."

William sighed. "I suppose so."

That was one of the downsides of being the Duke of Cothrom, he thought darkly as he pulled his egg-smeared knife toward him and absentmindedly used it as a letter opener. Even when one was in the throes of a happy marriage, the letters would not read themselves.

He had the misfortune of opening one from Aylesbury first. As William's eyes flickered over the hastily scrawled lines, he frowned, the tension which had only just dissipated started to creep along his shoulder blades again.

"What is it?" Alice asked curiously.

Perhaps if he had married someone else, a different kind of woman, William would have cheerfully told her she should not concern herself with such matters.

As it was, he knew Alice to be an insightful woman. Perhaps... yes, maybe it was not a bad idea, to bring her into the challenge of heading the Chance family. She would certainly have to grow accustomed to receiving letters like this.

"Dearest brother, by which I mean, the brother with the largest coffers," he read aloud dryly, raising an eyebrow at Alice. She giggled. "I suppose you are wondering why I am writing to you—"

"This is the Marquess of Aylesbury, isn't it?" Alice interjected.

Now that was impressive. "How on earth did you know that?"

"He writes like he speaks," she said, shrugging. "Go on."

William returned to the godawful letter. "I suppose you are wondering why I am writing to you, and I think you will be shocked to discover I am not in any trouble. Or rather, I should more accurately say it is not I who is in trouble."

He sighed. *What, was he to be given a few days only to enjoy his life before the calls on his time were to be restored?*

"The Earl of Lindow, then?" Alice guessed.

William nodded. "I am sorry to inform you, brother dear, that old Lindow has managed to get himself into rather a scrape with a young lady, a Miss—I shouldn't tell you who, Alice—whose father is most insistent... yes, a whole paragraph about what the man will do to Lindow if he does not marry her."

He sighed as his gaze skimmed over the lines. Absolutely typical of Lindow. The man had no self-control—and no desire to learn it, either.

In a family like the Chances, it was astonishing to have a black sheep of the family when they were *all* so troublesome, yet Lindow managed it.

"And it ends—listen to this—I inform you only, dearest brother of mine, so that you have advance warning of the protestations to expect from both the father and our brother. Also, I owe Lady Romeril one hundred pounds. Please send her the money immediately or she has threatened to cut off my thumbs. I remain yours, ever, etc. etc., Aylesbury."

William dropped the letter to the table with a heavy sigh.

Alice grinned. "Your brothers are a bit of a handful, aren't they?"

"You have no idea," he said meaningfully.

"I think I'm starting to get an inkling."

"The trouble is, they are too much of a handful," William said. "Far too much of a handful. I've been fighting their natures for—"

"You know, you don't have to," Alice pointed out quietly.

He looked up. She had spoken gently, yes, but out of ignorance. She did not know Aylesbury or Lindow or Pernrith like he did. Besides, she didn't know . . .

William tried to smile, but his lips were too tight. "I do have to. I . . . I made a promise. To my father. Our father. When he lay dying, he asked me to take care of them."

It was a hard thing to admit. Not hard to admit that he had agreed—of course he had. But only in this moment did William realize just how tightly wound his own identity, his purpose, was tied to being the family's protector.

Admitting he only did it because of a promise to his father somehow lessened that nobility. Lessened himself.

"I mean, obviously I would help them no matter what," he added quickly, hoping Alice did not think any less of him due to his admission. "They are my brothers, they are Chances, and I would always—"

"I know," Alice said quietly. "I understand."

William stared. "You do?"

It was unfathomable. There were surely few people in the world who could even comprehend the level of responsibility William had shouldered the instant he had made that promise.

Who else had three brothers with more money than sense—or now, rather more accurately, no money and no sense—who went around Society as though there were no consequences for their actions?

"I . . . well," William said awkwardly to the woman who seemed to be challenging him at every turn. "I always thought a lady would believe my strict adherence to the rules, to respectability, my desire to keep my brothers in check . . . silly. No, silly isn't the right word—"

"I said I know what you mean, and I meant it," Alice said quietly, interjecting with a sort of elegance that only she seemed to have. William had seen it in no other. "And if it matters to you, then it matters to me."

It took a moment for the depth of her words to sink in. When they did, William broke into a smile of relief. "I cannot believe how fortunate I am to have you. Thank God I didn't manage to fight you off when you threw yourself into my arms, eh?"

And Alice laughed, and all the tension and the darkness in the room melted away. "You were unable to resist me!"

William knew no matter what faced them, whatever he had to contend with, he would always have the certainty of a genteel Alice by his side. "I suppose that's true. Now, what do you say we continue this conversation in our bedchamber?"

Chapter Seventeen

June 15, 1812

ALICE HAD NEVER known so much nervous energy in her body.

It was today. She'd woken up and known it, deep within herself, deep within her soul. Her heart had fluttered the moment that she'd opened her eyes, knowing that after waiting so long, after risking everything, she had done it.

And today . . .

She rose from the window seat, peering closer to the glass as though that would give her a clearer view down the street. The angle made it impossible, but that did not prevent Alice from performing the same action twice again in the following five minutes. Each time she sat, disappointment transformed back into excitement as she leaned close to the window, pulse hammering.

It's today.

"Now then, Your Grace, you'll do yourself an injury, bobbing up and down like that," came the gentle yet slightly reproving tone of Nicholls.

Alice glanced over her shoulder and shot a grin at the butler. "I know. I can't help it."

"Hmmm," came the reply as she turned back to the window, hands pressed together in her lap.

It was difficult to believe the day had finally come—but all reports had suggested the roads were clear. There was no reason to suppose they would be delayed. That *she* would be delayed.

Maude Shenton. Her daughter.

Alice tried to calm the shivering nerves that rustled up her spine.

Never in her wildest dreams could she have imagined this perfect family that she was about to have. The man she loved, who adored her, who was everything she could have wanted and knew she didn't deserve . . . and her daughter. Together.

She stood up again, pressing her nose against the glass as though that would aid her in looking around the stubbornly unmoving corner.

There was a chuckle behind her. Alice did not look around as the sound of a newspaper being shaken and a page being turned echoed in the drawing room.

"Alice, my dear," said William genially. "You're not going to make her appear any sooner by almost breaking the glass."

Alice smiled, despite the slight flush tinging her cheeks. "I know that."

"She'll get here when she gets here," said her husband calmly. "You know, it does you great credit, being so concerned about a ward. There is many a person who would benefit from your—"

"It's here!" yelped Alice, entirely ignoring William's words and almost falling over her feet as she launched herself forward.

Heart hammering, fingers tingling with anticipation so much she could hard wield them, Alice rushed forward, pushed aside Nicholls's offering hand of assistance, and wrenched the door to the hall open.

"William, she's here!"

"Yes, I rather gathered that," came the dry voice from the drawing room. "Finally. I thought you'd never be put out of your misery."

He might have said something else—Alice was not sure. She was too far beyond the reach of his voice. Squeezing around two maids carrying a rug outside for beating, barreling by a footman attempting to be polite and open the door for her, Alice ran past them all.

Sweet summer sunshine poured onto the drive as a carriage with the Cothrom livery painted on the side, the same russet as her wedding gown, pulled in. The horses were shaking their heads, exhausted, and the driver looked just as worn out.

"Ah, Your Grace," he said, calling out as the carriage slowed. "I am honored by—"

Whatever he was honored by, Alice was not quite sure. She had little time for the words of a man she had never met, though she would never have phrased it that way.

Put simply, she needed to get to the carriage.

Mrs. Seaby descended from the other side, muttering about exhaustion and the direction of the servants' hall.

The other door handle slipped under Alice's fingers, and she almost laughed for joy at the ridiculousness of it all. *Her daughter, out of her reach because of a silly little door!*

Eventually her fingers were able to find purchase, and the door was open—

"Mama!" cried the little blonde girl who threw herself into Alice's arms.

And she almost wept. In that moment, when only she and her daughter existed, Alice could have wept. Tears were surely the only right response to having all one's dreams fulfilled, the soft downy blonde hair under her fingertips, the tiny little body of her child.

The baby that had come from her, in pain and in sadness, had become this tiny little thing that smiled and babbled, and now walked and talked—and she was here. Her baby. Alice's arms wrapped about the little one and they stood there, in the door of the carriage, for she did not know how long. The relief that swept over her was so tangible, she could almost taste it in her mouth.

She'd done it. She had her daughter back. Mr. Shenton was gone, no longer a part of her life.

And she had William.

Everything was going to be all right.

It was only the footsteps on the gravel behind her that prompted

Alice, brushing aside a few errant tears, to release her daughter.

"Remember, I am Alice here," she whispered into the tiny shell-pink ear of her child.

Maude nodded seriously and glanced over her mother's shoulder. "Who's that?"

Taking her daughter's hand in hers, Alice helped the little one from the carriage then turned, bursting with pride, to introduce the two people who mattered most to her in the world to each other.

What a life they would have! A family, finally—and if everything went as they hoped, soon brothers and sisters for little Maude to play with. William would—

William was staring.

He had not come close. In fact, as far as Alice could see, William had only taken a few steps out of the house before he had halted, his mouth open, hands hanging at his sides.

And his face—his expression was most peculiar. As though he had seen a ghost.

Alice surreptitiously looked behind her but could see nothing that would have prompted such a reaction. Perhaps one of his brothers had arrived at the same time, and had ducked behind the coach as a jest?

"I . . . you . . ." William said hoarsely.

Perhaps he was overcome with the sudden arrival of a child to care for. *Yes, that would be it,* Alice told herself firmly as she stepped forward, gravel crunching under her feet as she approached William.

It was a great deal to take in, after all.

"Your Grace, William Chance, Duke of Cothrom," Alice said formally, though with a joyful lilt. "May I introduce you to my ward, Maude. Maudy, this is William."

Her daughter looked up at the tall man with the open curiosity only a child could have.

Something happy twirled in Alice's stomach. She'd remind Maude of this in years gone by, of how the two of them met as though they were strangers. Perhaps her daughter would be unable to believe that. If she grew as close to William as Alice hoped—

"Hello," said Maude shyly, taking a step into Alice's skirts and reaching up to grasp her leg.

Alice beamed down at the child, then looked at William.

By now, there were certain characteristics of the man she knew she could depend on. He would always be polite, of course, and merry when there was something that pleased her. William was the sort to be slightly stiff upon a first meeting, but his acquaintance once gained was warm and welcoming.

The strange thing was, she seemed to be utterly mistaken in this description now.

Alice stared, confusion rising as all the color drained from William's face. Where there should have been warmth and welcome, there was nothing but . . . it could not be horror, but it looked very like it. It did not make any sense.

"William?" Alice prompted.

Perhaps this was too sudden—perhaps she should not have accepted his offer to bring Maude into their lives so quickly. But the idea of waiting, knowing her daughter was miles away—

"Ah," said William. Then he took a deep breath and appeared to regain a little equilibrium. "Miss Fox-Edwards. I trust your journey was not too discomforting?"

"I was in the carriage a long time," Maude said solemnly. "And one time, when we stopped, the horsey at the front did a big—"

"Mrs. Ransome?" William said swiftly.

The housekeeper, a woman with a sharp temperament and an even sharper look, poked her head through the door. "Y'Grace?"

"Would you please take this . . . this child inside and . . . feed her, I suppose," William said vaguely, not taking his focus from Maude.

Alice's shoulders relaxed, the tension that had been building in them at William's strange reaction melting away. Well, perhaps

William was not the most instinctive parent, but one could not demand that of a man who had never had a child before.

Or seen one, apparently. *He trusted her journey was not too discomforting?*

"Yes, we'll all go in and eat," said Alice, stepping forward. "I want to show you—"

"Mrs. Ransome, take the child," William said, reaching out and taking Alice's arm, halting her progress. "The duchess and I have a small matter discuss out here. Alone."

Alice frowned, eyes wide as she attempted to discern quite what William could mean. After all, they had already made love that morning, and the driveway was rather exposed. Surely he did not mean—

"A-Alice?" Maude said quietly, looking up.

Alice forced as much cheer into her voice as possible. "Go on in, my dear. I will join you in a moment."

It caused a strange pang to see Mrs. Ransome take the child's hand and lead her into the house. After so many years of depending on other people to care for her daughter, she had finally got her back. Was she truly to give her up again so quickly?

But it was only for a few minutes, Alice tried to remind herself. William wished to talk, and then they would be both inside and—

"You harpy," spat William the moment the front door shut behind Maude.

There was such vehemence, such bitter anger in the three syllables he uttered that Alice felt forced to take a step back, bewildered.

"H-Harpy?" she repeated, certain she had misheard the man. "I-I don't under—"

"I can't believe it," William said, pulling a hand through his hair and looking as though he had just received the worst sort of news. "I can't believe it."

Something had happened and Alice could not understand what.

This sudden turn, this turning on her—what on earth had precipitated such a change?

Had not Maude been careful? She had been taught not to call her "Mama" in company from an early age, and try as she might, Alice could not recall a mistake they had made in the few minutes that they had stood in William's company. So what—

"You really thought you could fool me?" William said, looking her directly in the eyes.

Alice's heart sank. Swifter than a stone, it plummeted down her body and entered the earth, taking with it all hope, all expectation.

How on earth could he have known? How was it possible? She had been so careful.

Well, there was only one thing for it. She would have to lie.

"I-I don't know what you mean," Alice stammered, hating that her voice betrayed her in such a moment.

Evidently William was far cleverer than she had hoped, for he laughed darkly and turned away for a moment, as though it was too painful to look at her.

"William, I—"

"You must think I'm an idiot," said William bitterly as he turned back to her. "I cannot believe you did not tell me!"

Alice's mind was whirling, yet try as she might, there was no clue as to how William could possibly know. Had he read one of her letters? No, she had always been careful not to write down any of the specifics in her letters. Could Mr. Shenton—no, she had bought back all the incriminating letters from him almost the moment her engagement had been announced. He had his money, and no proof now as to what had occurred. What would William notice if she were a few gowns short in her trousseau?

How could this have happened?

The world was starting to spin, but Alice made one last attempt to defuse—no, deflect. "William, I don't know what you are trying to say, but—"

"She is the spitting image of you, Alice," William bit out, glaring. "The spitting image! I don't doubt you haven't noticed it, so wrapped up in your lies, but that child is so clearly yours, it's as plain as the nose on both your faces!"

Alice's mouth fell open.

Could she really have been that stupid?

She tried to picture herself and Maude inside her mind. Yes, they had the same white-blonde hair, the same gray eyes—there were probably a few mannerisms that were similar, now she came to think about it. But were they truly so alike that—

"You don't even see it, do you?" William's voice cracked, his pain so prominent. "Dear God, you really had me believing—I suppose there is no wild cousin in your family, is there? It was you, all along, all the rumors and gossip that you had me believe were because of someone else. It was you!"

Alice's breathing was short, darkness creeping into the corners of her eyes, and she was trapped. Unable to move, unable to run, unable to hide.

William knew now. He knew—not everything, but enough to know she had brought shame upon herself, her family, and now . . .

And now his. His name, the one thing he would do anything to protect.

She had ruined it.

Alice swallowed and for the first time in a long time, told the truth. "Not . . . not all of gossip was true."

William swore under his breath.

"It wasn't like—I never planned to—"

"I can't believe I have finally managed to do the one thing I have been working so hard to prevent my brothers from doing!" William spoke with such a pained laugh, it broke Alice's heart in two. "I've ruined the family name. I'm ruined!"

"No—no, you're not," Alice said hurriedly, stepping forward with her hands out, desperate to hold him.

If she could just touch him—if she could find, once again, the connection they had—

William stepped back, his dark glare not leaving her face. "You ruined me, Alice."

"No, it's not that, we can lie, we can tell the world—"

"I am not a liar," he said quietly.

Alice felt the unspoken reprimand shimmering in the air between them, like a heat haze of silent condemnation.

Because she was.

"I know you're not," she said helplessly. "I know you're not, but truly, I don't think it is as bad as you—"

"I don't think you quite understand the severity of what has happened," William said, not bothering to keep his voice down.

And why should he, Alice thought wretchedly. There were no servants about. The gardeners were in the rose garden, the coachman had taken the horses around to the stables. There was no one here to eavesdrop on this conversation.

But that wouldn't stop the gossip going around the whole of London before the day was out. If William had noticed the similarity between her and Maude . . . it would not be long.

Alice swallowed. "I'm sorry—I didn't know what to do. I was being extorted—"

William's sardonic laugh cut her short, and each syllable he spoke was a dagger in her gut. "Oh, excellent! Is that supposed to make me feel better, that my wife was being extorted about an illegitimate child?"

And fire surged. "Maude is not illegitimate."

He waved away her words with little care, as though she had not just handed him her soul. "We may be married now, but she could never be mine, you must see that. I mean, dear God, Alice. The new Duchess of Cothrom has an illegitimate daughter!"

And the fire burned, and Alice looked William straight in the eye and knew that, no matter what, this was where she would stand her ground. "My daughter is not illegitimate."

But it appeared her husband had no interest in her words. His mind had already departed this conversation, hastening forward into the future where he was certain his reputation had been stained.

"After everything I've done," William was muttering, pulling a hand through his hair again as though he could not prevent himself from doing it. "All my effort, the sacrifices I have made, the times when I have been this close to giving up and just letting the Chance family destroy itself!"

Alice bit her lip and allowed all the guilt she had pushed aside through their short courtship to rush forward.

She deserved this. She'd used him, used him most ill. William would not forgive her.

"I have been fighting against scandal all my adult life," he said bitterly. "I thought Pernrith was bad enough, but at least there was a partial solution to that. Give the man a title, some sort of respectability, and hope the damned Chance brothers would do what they were told and stay in line."

"People don't like to be controlled," Alice said, before she could stop herself. "They don't want to feel used when given a chance. They don't want to feel beholden to—"

"What would you know about being beholden?" William snapped, raising a pointed finger. "You were extorted, you say? Well, it doesn't surprise me. An illegitimate child—"

"She is not—"

"—is not something most men would understand, I suppose. Who's the father?"

Alice bit her lip. One day, she had thought she might tell William this story. When they were old, and their own children were grown, and there was no possibility of hurt because it was so long ago.

But now . . .

"He died," she said stiffly. "And—"

"That would explain why you were being extorted, I suppose," William said darkly. "No protector. And here I am, picking up the scandalous pieces—"

"I love you, William," Alice interjected impulsively. *If she could just make him see—*

In the warmth of the summer day, William shook his head as he stepped away, another bitter laugh on his lips. "No, you don't."

Her pulse skipped a beat. "I am not lying—"

"I don't know if you're lying or telling the truth, and I clearly have never known. Ward," spat William. "No, you saw me as the sap I am, right from the first moment we met."

Alice swallowed. "I—"

"Oh, dear God, you were lying in wait for me, weren't you?" William said, clapping a hand to his forehead. "In the little woodland in Hyde Park—you would have demanded marriage from any fool that walked by, wouldn't you?"

The instinct to lie, to protect his feelings, to protect her own was so strong that Alice almost gave in.

But apparently the look on her face was enough.

William swore again. "And here I am, falling in love with you—or what I thought was you. With what I thought Alice Fox-Edwards—Alice Chance—was. An honorable woman. A good woman."

The dizzy feeling was returning, and Alice wished she were standing a little closer to the house so she could be in the shade.

It was all falling apart. Her plan, her life, the life she wanted with the people she loved—she had been so close, and now it was disappearing right before her eyes. Melting in the summer sun.

"I know I should have told you," Alice said quietly. "But—"

"Yes," William snapped. "You should have!"

His interruption did nothing to salve her conscience, however, and it merely prickled her irritation. Was it her fault how her life had turned out? Did William truly think she would have chosen this life if she'd had any other choice?

"You mean I should have told you," she said quietly, "so you wouldn't have had to marry me?"

For a moment, just a moment, William met her gaze. There was such adoration there, just for a moment, that Alice gasped aloud.

Everything could be mended if they just clung to each other. If they could just be honest, and open, and vulnerable. If he could see the hurt she had endured, and she could pour the balm of her affection on his wounded pride, maybe then—

"Yes," said William quietly. "That's what I mean. I wouldn't have married you."

They stood there for a moment, gazing at each other. Alice couldn't move. There was something in this moment that was fragile, a crossroads for the conversation, for them.

In one direction, she would eventually fall into his arms, and he could console her, forgive her, and she would make wild promises about never lying to him again, and William would laugh and say it wasn't Maudy's fault, and they would be a family together.

And in the other direction—

William sighed heavily. "Make preparations."

Alice blinked. Perhaps at the crossroads there had been a third path she had not considered. "Preparations?"

"Yes, preparations."

It appeared that was all she was to be told. "Preparations for what?"

William's jaw tightened. "I am sending you and your daughter to the Dower House of Stanphrey Lacey. In the country."

Each individual word made sense. Alice knew them, understood them. But when placed together, there was a deep disconnect between the words and her mind.

"You'll be well cared for there," William was saying, his words washing over her like water. "You'll be provided for."

"Provided—you are joining us, aren't you, William?" Alice said, a flicker of uncertainty tugging at her heart.

She could not leave him. Leave William? Leave the man she loved, while they still had such misunderstanding and confusion between them?

"I'm not leaving you," Alice said decidedly as William turned and started back to the house. "William—William! What about us?"

He halted, but he did not turn around. Alice found herself looking at every strand of hair, every lock, the way his collar crept up his throat, the breadth of his shoulders—every detail, memorizing them, loving them, committing them to memory because a part of her knew already that it was over.

"There is no us," he said finally, continuing on into the house. The door slammed behind him.

Chapter Eighteen

June 17, 1812

"—AND THAT," WILLIAM said wearily, "is what happened."

The silence that filled the room after his pronouncement was not a great surprise. It echoed the silence in his soul, the emptiness in him that had still somehow weighed heavy from the moment Alice—the moment *she* had left his house.

He looked up. As he had told the tale of how it had come about, the wrenching apart of his household not even two weeks after their wedding, William's head had sunk lower and lower. Eventually he could no longer see those to whom he spoke.

Now he could. William glanced over at Lindow who was standing by the empty grate in the library, then at Aylesbury who was seated, open mouthed, in the large armchair. Pernrith was pacing in complete silence.

William could hear his own breathing. Every intake, every release, the shift of his shoulders, the grinding of his muscles. He could hear his heartbeat.

It was all so deafening. Had it always been so loud, so utterly impossible to think in the cacophony of sound?

He cleared his throat, as though that would help. "Well?"

"Well," said Aylesbury quietly. "Well indeed."

William had not wished to tell them. There was something intensely humiliating about admitting that one's wife had, without blinking an eye, lied so cleverly and so concisely to him.

"When were you going to tell me about your ward?"

Yet William had only himself to blame. He had assumed innocence when his natural caution should have taken over. What had he been thinking? He'd heard of Miss Alice Fox-Edwards, had been so easily taken in when she had mentioned a cousin of a similar name who had done all the scandalous deeds he had heard of.

The very idea that it had been his Alice, his wife, who had—who had allowed another man to—

"Maude is not illegitimate."

William stood up hastily, unable to remain seated as terrible thoughts rushed through his mind.

No, it wasn't possible. And yet there had been the girl. It would take a fool not to notice the similarities. What had she been thinking?

Lindow cleared his throat. "And . . . and you are absolutely certain the girl—"

"If you had seen Maude—the child," William corrected hastily, "you would have been in the same mind. I tell you, they were identical."

"Sometimes in a particular light, any two people—"

"The same hair, the precise shade," said William, glancing at his hands as though that would help. "Identical eyes. The same nose, the same air. They even spoke alike."

"That is to be expected, if they lived together," said Aylesbury fairly. "Sometimes people think Lindow and I have similar mannerisms—"

"And you are related, are you not?" William strode over to the drinks cabinet. "I am not an idiot, Aylesbury, I can tell when a woman presents me with her daughter."

"Her ward, she said?" Pernrith said quietly, coming to a stop at the drinks cabinet and taking the bottle of whiskey from William's hands. "I think you've had enough."

William hadn't noticed his hands were shaking until he tried to pour a glass. Stepping away with a rueful smile, he said, "I haven't had any, I'm just—I'm shaken. That a woman, that anyone could look me straight in the face—"

"You never asked her if she had a child, did you?" Lindow pointed out. "Or asked much about the ward, as far as your story goes."

William turned on his brother but managed to restrain himself. It wasn't Lindow's fault. It wasn't anyone's fault but his own. "No. I assumed—"

"Yes, so we can see," said Aylesbury quietly. "And now the truth is out. And she's gone."

William bit his lip as he returned to his seat and collapsed once again on the sofa. "Gone. For good. For all the good it can do."

Which wasn't much. Try as he might, he had been unable to sleep properly since his carriage had taken both Alice and Maude to the Dower House in the country. He wouldn't have believed how the lack of Alice could take a toll on him. They had been married a matter of days, and now the place felt empty without her.

Lonely.

It was a miracle the news had not got out. William had been fairly sure it would, what with the Duchess of Cothrom's sudden absence from the *ton*, right after her wedding.

There would be talk. There was always talk.

His lungs constricted, every movement a challenge as William tried desperately to think how he could manage such a scandal.

The gossip would be everywhere eventually. Perhaps he should drop a short note to Lady Romeril, ask discreetly just how bad the dishonor was—

"I am sorry, William."

William looked up in surprise. None of the Chance brothers used first names, they hadn't for years. They went by titles, as so many other gentlemen in their acquaintance did.

But Pernrith was examining him with genuine pity, empathy he had not expected from any of his brothers—let alone the half a Chance.

"Truly sorry," Pernrith added quietly. "I feel for you. You are in a difficult position. I do not suppose you could . . . annul the marriage? Escape it somehow, lack of consummation, that sort of thing."

William's cheeks burned. "Not . . . not exactly accurate, unfortunately."

He glared up at Pernrith, and over at Aylesbury and Lindow for good measure, but none of his brothers appeared in the mood for ribbing him. That was concerning in itself.

He couldn't continue moping like this. He'd had long enough—days—to rid Alice from his system. Everything of hers had been sent to the Dower House, and William was determined to live the remainder of his life as best he could.

Alone. Lonely.

But with his head held high.

"I suppose I should be grateful I have so many brothers," William jested, his voice taut. "Aylesbury, you'll have to marry soon."

Aylesbury looked astonished. "Dear God, why?"

"Well, for the family," said William, frowning at the obvious answer to such a ridiculous question. "Next generation, that sort of thing."

Clearly the second eldest Chance brother had not considered such a thing, for the Marquess of Aylesbury looked genuinely horrified. "You cannot be serious."

"No legitimate sons coming from my line," William said, wincing at the awkwardness of saying such a thing with Pernrith in the room. "Ah. Erm . . . no offense meant, of course."

Pernrith shrugged, his face impassive. "None taken."

"So it's down to you, now," William continued, looking back at Aylesbury. "You'll need to marry, have sons—at least three, I think, is probably best if Lindow doesn't—"

"You cannot be serious," Lindow interrupted, echoing Aylesbury, maybe just as unwilling to marry as his brother. But when he continued, William realized he was mistaken. "You are not going to take Alice back?"

The idea was repugnant to him. William actually felt his stomach turn in response to the suggestion.

Take Alice back? Pretend none of this ever happened? Pretend she had not lied, that she was not bringing her child by another man into his family? Act as though nothing had gone wrong, as though it was perfectly natural to hide a scandal from a man so utterly terrified of such a stain?

William's mind whirled so painfully, it took a moment to collect his thoughts sufficiently for speech. "You—you cannot think I would—are you out of your mind?"

"She made a mistake," Lindow said expansively, throwing his hands out as though it were not an utter betrayal. "She had fun. Can you blame her?"

Jaw tightening, William snapped, "What, you think that just because you want to have affairs left right and center, everyone else should—"

"We are harsh on the fairer sex, as a society," Lindow said, sounding far more like one of those women who demanded the right to vote and other such things than the brother William knew. "What, you never tumbled someone before you wed Alice?"

"I—it's not the same—that is not the point," William said hotly.

He'd invited his brothers here to be informed of what had occurred to the head of their family, not to be criticized!

And besides, it *was* different. Whenever he had taken a woman to his bed, it had been to satisfy an urge, scratch an itch. To overcome a physical distraction.

It had never been—not like with Alice. They had shared something primal, yes, but also something deeply intimate. Something William had thought they had shared, for the first time, together.

How could he ever look at her without picturing her with another man?

"This was years ago, long before she met you," said Aylesbury. William's head shot up. "I mean, yes, it's not ideal—"

"Not ideal!"

"—but it's not as though it was a personal betrayal. She was not unfaithful to you," Aylesbury said with a shrug.

A flicker of rage curled around William's mind, but he did his best to ignore it, dousing it in the cold water of bitter logic. "She betrayed me by not telling me the truth! She betrayed my trust!"

They did not understand—but how could they? William had been a fool to think he could gain a little sympathy from three men who cast caution to the wind, did whatever they wanted, and never cared how it would look, what stigma it would bring on the family name!

Well. Now he came to think about it, Pernrith wasn't like that, not in his conduct. His very existence was an awkward fact, however, that William had attempted to mediate in the public eye as best he could.

But Aylesbury and Lindow? How could they know what it was to love someone, truly love someone, then realize you had been used?

"She betrayed my trust," William repeated, his voice dull.

"And did you earn it?"

He glared at Aylesbury. "And what is that supposed to mean?"

Silence fell in the library as fury shot through his veins. It was no longer possible to hold back his irritation and, though William knew it stemmed from Alice's treachery, not anything his brothers had truly done, it was impossible to stem the tide.

He continued to glare at Aylesbury, but his features softened as he watched the second oldest Chance brother exchange a glance with the third.

William transferred his glare over to Lindow. *What on earth did that private silent exchange mean?*

Lindow smiled briefly, but it disappeared almost immediately. "Well, Cothrom... you want the truth? You are not the most forgiving man."

William's glare deepened as he felt a throb in his temple. *Oh, that was the last thing he needed—a headache.* "And what, precisely, does that mean?"

"Don't feign ignorance with us," Lindow shot back, not cowed by William's dark tone. "You are the first to critique others, Cothrom, but you fail to accept that you too could make a mistake."

"That is because I don't make them!" William argued, feeling the heat of his rage trickle down into his fingers.

The absolute cheek! How dare they say such—

"Criticizing us doesn't make us more likely to tell you the truth," Aylesbury said quietly. "It doesn't encourage spilling one's secrets. I can understand why Alice did not wish to—"

"If I am always critiquing, it is because I am always the one clearing up after your messes!" William said hotly.

It was painful to hear such words, but even more painful still was the suggestion that they were right.

He had spent his life—hours and hours, weeks, agonizing over how best to lead this family. Worrying about disrepute, wondering how he could best take care of them all. There wasn't a moment in William's life which hadn't been colored, since he had inherited the ducal title, by commanding a fighting chance for the family.

And this was to be how they repaid him? By condemning him in turn for actually caring!

"The messes, as you call them, are of our making," said Lindow softly. "Did you ever wonder if we should be left to clear them up on our own?"

William opened his mouth, ready for a swift retort... and found there wasn't one.

Clear them up on their own? Lindow and Aylesbury hadn't extricated themselves from a debt of a pound without his assistance, not since the three of them went to Cambridge!

Or Eton, truth be told. William's shoulders sagged as he closed his mouth, desperately attempting to recall a time when he had just left his brothers to sort out their own disasters.

And not one single occurrence came to mind.

No, that—that wasn't right. That was impossible.

William swallowed, his mind racing. Even before their father had died, he'd been the one protecting them, ensuring their mischief never came to the ears of their parents.

When had he decided to take on that burden for himself? That had been years before his father had requested his promise to cover for them in every eventuality.

"Keep them safe, William."

And now he came to think of it, that was all his father had asked of him. To keep them safe.

Not remedy their every mistake, pay off every debt, and ensure no whisper of gossip ever reached the scandal sheets. When had he conflated keeping his brothers safe to wrapping them up in lambswool and never permitting them to do . . . anything?

William swallowed. *Oh hell.* It was a nasty realization to have, and even worse, it was potentially too late.

Then a memory surfaced in his mind—a memory of child with white-blonde hair who had looked up at him with curiosity, holding close to her mother's leg.

William hardened his heart. "I cannot ignore the fact of the child."

"An illegitimate child," Pernrith said quietly.

With a lurch of his stomach, William nodded. "Alice insisted the child was not illegitimate, but that is impossible."

"Improbable, perhaps," nodded Aylesbury. "But as you have said yourself, it appears you did not know Miss Alice Fox-Edwards as well as you thought."

It was a startling consideration, and one William filed away for another day. A day when he did not have three argumentative brothers before him and a headache brewing.

"Here."

William blinked. Pernrith had stepped across the room and was now pressing a glass of something into his hand.

He looked down. It was the whiskey he'd almost had earlier.

"I think you need this now," said his youngest brother quietly.

With a dry laugh, William nodded and knocked back the entire glass. "I think I needed it a long time ago."

How could he have got this all so wrong? How could he have constructed a life that was doomed to fail—fail not only himself, but the very people he had thought he had been helping?

"The child," William said quietly. "I could never have that child in my house, knowing it was not quite—"

"Not quite family," said Pernrith, and his voice was stronger now, his jaw set. "But take it from me, Your Grace, a child knows when they are not wanted. For a child not truly of the family to be forced to dwell within it, that is perhaps the crueler choice. If you cannot at least welcome the child as a living creature that deserves to be loved, perhaps your reconciliation with its mother should be . . . postponed."

William's heart squeezed painfully.

They never talked about it. They'd never discussed it as children, and they had avoided the topic like the plague as adults.

But when Pernrith—when little Frederick had been dropped off with a note at the age of three, not much different from Maude . . . Here was a child born not long after Lindow, and despite that, he had been taken in. Cared for. Clothed, fed, educated.

Not the same as his brothers, naturally. Hand me down clothes instead of bespoke fittings. He had eaten with the servants, not the family. Educated at the local school, not at Eton.

William shifted uncomfortably in his seat. They had not been his decisions to make, and he had not made them. His father—their father—had. But Pernrith had to live with the consequences of those decisions in a way that he, William, did not.

Lindow was glowering silently, obviously unhappy with the direction the conversation had turned, but it appeared Pernrith was not finished.

"But if," he said gently, "if you can look at the child and see nothing more than that—a child, one who has done nothing wrong but exist—then perhaps you can be with the woman you so evidently love."

William cleared his throat awkwardly. "I don't know what you—"

"Do not attempt to lie to us, it does not suit you, Cothrom," said Aylesbury, his face stern. His mockery vanished quickly. "In all seriousness, do not lie to yourself. You know precisely what Pernrith means. You love her."

Glancing at the empty glass in his hands, William wished he hadn't been so hasty in drinking it. Having another sip of whiskey would be a pleasant distraction round about now.

"I don't know about that," he said awkwardly.

"Oh, really?" said Lindow with a laugh. "Did you, or did you not, tie yourself in proverbial knots just trying to decide what waistcoat to wear to your wedding?"

William scowled. "That doesn't mean—"

"And did you or did you not send away all your servants on your wedding night?" said Aylesbury with more of an admiring grin than William had ever seen on his brother in their conversations. "Damn good idea, I must say. Was it—"

"And the very fact you are having this conversation with us," said Pernrith rapidly, speaking over the undoubtedly licentious question that was about to asked. "The fact you so obviously want to talk about her, the fact we have been talking here for hours—"

"You're right, it is time for a drink," said Lindow vaguely. "Aylesbury?"

"Don't mind if I do—"

"—tells us one clear truth," Pernrith persevered over the chatter of the other two. "William. You love her."

It was on the tip of his tongue to deny it. To tell his interfering brothers that, try as they might, they couldn't convince him of such a nonsense.

And he would have said it, too.

If it weren't a lie.

William sighed, placed the empty glass on the console table beside him, and glared up at his three tormentors. *Brothers. Same thing.* "Fine. Fine! I love her!"

"Excellent, so it's all solved," said Lindow cheerfully. "Whiskey or brandy?"

"It is not solved," snapped William, dropping his head into his hands as the weight of the mistake he made settled onto his shoulders. "I have a wife who lies to me and a child who . . ."

He swallowed. The child. Maude, she had looked at him like—like she had trusted him. Maude, at least, was an innocent in all this, and what had he done? He'd been cruel. He'd been unnecessarily harsh. He'd been exactly the lout he had instructed his brothers not to be.

William swallowed in the silence. "I suppose I could . . . could have dealt with things differently. Better."

"What, you, make an error?" Lindow's eyes were wide. "I've never heard of such a thing!"

But William barely heard his brother. Now that he was beginning to look back at his actions with a measure of clarity inspired—against all odds—by his brothers, he could see how poorly he had acted. Alice . . . it was true that she had not been open with him, but it was all just to protect an innocent child.

And what had he done? Punished her for it.

His voice cracked when he finally spoke. "I have ruined everything. I had the best woman in the world as my wife, and I've wrecked it all!"

The pain was exquisite, the regret absolute. What had he done? How would Alice ever forgive him—how could they move past this? Would she ever trust him again?

Did he have any right to her trust?

There was a heavy sensation on his shoulder. William looked up to see Aylesbury, who had clearly risen just to place his hand on his shoulder.

"Welcome to the club," he said brightly.

"What club?"

"The 'oh damn, I've made a terrible mistake and I don't know how to fix it' club," Aylesbury said with a wink. "As a long-time member, may I offer you some advice?"

"Please," said William helplessly. *Dear God, was this what he'd come to? Asking advice from his brothers, of all people?*

"Don't go down without a fight," said Aylesbury, a little of the levity in his tone disappearing. "And do what I do."

"Which is—"

"Ask your brothers for help."

William just stared. Then slowly, as the words sank in, a slow smile crept across his face. "You absolute blackguard. You will?"

"Not for love nor money," said Aylesbury firmly. "Neither will Lindow, we are absolutely foolish men with no good sense and no good advice. But Pernrith, on the other hand . . ."

Chapter Nineteen

June 22, 1812

Try as she might, Alice never quite managed to wipe away the tears. There was always another to take the place of the one before.

The last tear, she thought furiously as she dashed aside one that threatened to trickle down her cheek. *Last tear!*

When would the last tear ever come, when she felt this wretched?

The sky was heavy. A dark gray and full of blustery clouds, it seemed to press upon the Dower House with a weight Alice could actually feel. It pressed upon the roof of the house with a ferocity that she had never felt before.

Or was that merely her guilt?

"Look Mama, look!"

Alice brushed aside another traitorous tear, forced an expression of calm, and turned away from the window. "Lovely, darling."

Maude was sitting in the middle of the drawing room rug, holding up two of the toy soldiers she had found in the nursery just yesterday. Try as she might, Alice had been unable to remove the toys from her daughter's hands. Tears and tantrums had followed, and so despite her misgivings, she had permitted Maude to keep them.

A lump rose in Alice's throat. They could be William's from a long time ago. The toys he would have played with when he came to visit his grandmother, perhaps.

The mere thought of William wrenched her heart. Alice forced herself to look away, back to the window.

It was a pleasant spot. Though she presumed there was a manor house somewhere in the large grounds they had come to days ago, she had not seen it. Alice had been given no instructions to stay within the environs of the Dower House, but it felt . . . sacrilegious, somehow, to depart from it.

Not exactly imprisoned, but not free to wander, either.

Oak trees surrounded the Dower House, a beautiful redbrick Tudor home of five bedchambers. It was more than Alice had ever hoped for, except for the lack of a certain gentleman.

Alice swallowed. "This is precisely what you wanted," she murmured to herself, lifting a finger and running it down the lead-lined glass.

A home, a chance to be with her child. No worries about money, bills paid, invoices dealt with, no concern over debts. Protection. Income for life.

"William—William! What about us?"

"There is no us."

Was this not everything she had striven for when she had gone to London? When she'd decided to free herself from Mr. Shenton? When Alice had known that if she did not do something soon, she would waste the rest of her life in fear?

"Tea, m'lady."

Alice turned and flushed at the words of the maid who had stepped almost silently into the room. It had been an awkward conversation with Mrs. Colfer when she had arrived. The housekeeper of the Dower House had heard the news of her master's marriage, of course, and had been delighted to meet the new duchess . . . and had looked over Alice's shoulder at the carriage, expecting the duke himself to descend.

Though she had hoped William had written a letter to explain things to the good woman, it had been down to Alice to elucidate instead.

A most awkward conversation indeed.

Clearly the maids had been instructed not to call her "Your Grace"—not that Alice minded. It was their embarrassment which caused her own cheeks to burn.

Thank goodness her own lady's maid, Jane, had been permitted to come with them. Without her constant and consistent presence, Alice wasn't sure how she would get through each day.

The maid deposited the tea tray on the console table just to the left of the fireplace, and carefully not meeting Alice's eye, bobbed a curtsy and left the room, shutting the door with a snap behind her.

Alice sighed, her shoulders dropping. Her lot was better than that of most fallen women, she supposed.

What must they think of her?

She pushed the thought aside as best she could and stepped across the room to pour herself a cup of steaming tea. The beverage had once been a comfort, but the realization that William had sent on her individual blend of tea had rocked her a few days ago.

Had he kept nothing in the townhouse that reminded him of her?

I should not complain, Alice thought as she sagged onto the armchair beside the console table that held the tea. Plenty of men would have thrown her out onto the street rather than admit they had been duped.

Duped was a strong word, but it was nothing to some of the insults Alice had thrown at herself in the middle of the night, lying in a cold, empty bed.

And William had been as good as his word. Better. The Dower House was beautiful, far more than she had ever hoped for, and the servants had clearly been instructed to treat her well, even if there was a certain coldness from some of them.

They had everything they could possibly need. Everything. Except . . .

Alice sipped her tea and winced at the scalding liquid.

Except William. She leaned back in the armchair and wished to goodness he was here so she could explain. How precisely she would explain, she did not know. She had practiced paragraphs which would hopefully clear up the matter in minutes, when they had been journeying here in the carriage, but they never seemed to be enough.

"You see, William, it's quite simple. When I was younger..."

"It's not difficult: I have a daughter, and when my brother-in-law—no, not your brothers..."

"I would do anything, anything for my child. And you were happy, weren't you? Weren't you, William?"

Alice swallowed, tasting the bitterness of her thoughts on her tongue.

Yes, they had been happy. But not for long. Within a fortnight, the truth had escaped and there had been nothing she could do to prevent it. A pang in her chest made Alice lift a hand to her breast, though she felt foolish for doing so.

What, did she think she had a broken heart? Was she truly so pathetic as to believe true love could be found in such circumstances? That mere weeks were sufficient to know the man she had left behind was the only man she could ever truly love?

Alice swallowed. The ache only grew with each passing day.

She did love him. Even now, after everything, she loved William Chance.

"M'lady?"

Alice looked up. It truly was a well-oiled door, for half the time she did not even notice when someone came in. This time it was a footman. He looked abashed, but stepped into the room nonetheless.

"Yes?" Alice said, sipping her tea again. *Ah, the perfect temperature. That was all she needed. Tea. Tea and rest.*

In time, probably, she would forget about William, and...

The rebellion within her was instinctive.

She would never forget him. She never could. He would represent the epitome of character and have all her affection for the rest of her life.

Then why didn't you fight for him, a voice at the back of her mind asked.

Because, Alice told it, *I will not fight a battle I know I will lose.*

"M'lady?"

Alice blinked. The footman was still standing in the doorway. "I beg your pardon?"

"I said, may I come in to lay the fire for this evening?" asked the blushing footman.

"Please," she said, gesturing with her hand.

Bobbing a bow, the footman entered the room and stepped carefully around Maude's rug to ensure he did not knock over any of her toy soldiers.

Well, if there was one way to her heart . . .

"Thank you," Alice murmured. "We had a tantrum the last time the tenth infantry was knocked over by my skirts."

The footman gave her a nervous grin. "I have a brother much the same age. Don't worry, m'lady, I'll be careful of the troops."

Warmth gathered in her chest—though that could be the tea.

"Your daughter is very like you, isn't she?" said the footman as he began to lay the fire. "I knew she was yours the moment I saw her."

Alice frowned. "You did?"

She glanced over at her daughter. Were they truly that similar?

"She is the spitting image of you, Alice. The spitting image! I don't doubt you haven't noticed it, so wrapped up in your lies, but that child is so clearly yours, it's as plain as the nose on both your faces!"

William had certainly thought so. Alice had never much thought about it, but now she examined her child carefully, attempting to do so as an outside observer.

And saw . . .

Herself. She could just about remember peering into her mother's looking glass when she was about five years of age, and the image that had presented itself was playing with toy soldiers on the rug before her.

The realization was so visceral that Alice's hand shook, tea almost spilling from her cup.

"Y-Yes," she managed to say. "Yes, I suppose we are similar."

They were not similar. They were identical.

How had she been so foolish as to attempt to tell William that Maudy was her ward? Oh, she was idiotic indeed.

"There."

Alice started. "There?"

"Fire's all ready for this evening," said the footman, rising to his feet and bobbing another bow. "M'lady."

He was gone before Alice could say another word—not that she knew precisely what she would have said. Her mind had already drifted again.

How she regretted so much of what she had done, had said to him, but it was not as though she could take any of it back. The lies to William, the half-truths, the avoidance of the facts. The launching herself into his arms in the copse in Hyde Park. The ball at the Earl of Chester's where she had hidden her identity so carefully.

But despite all the pain, regret, guilt, Alice could not help but consider the memories wistfully. When times had been good. When William had looked at her with something which verged on affection. He had never said as much, but—

"Do we live here now?" asked Maude conversationally.

The sudden noise pulled Alice from her reverie, but it took her a few moments to truly take in what her daughter had asked.

The child was still playing with the soldiers, marching them up and down the rug in an orderly line, seemingly uncaring about their circumstances.

Alice could not help but smile, though tears once again prickled at the corners of her eyes. Oh, to live like that—with not a care in the world. Had she been like that, once? She could hardly remember. If so, it was a great deal of time ago, before Mark, before balls and Society and keeping to the rules.

She looked lovingly at the white-blonde curls of her child. She would do anything—anything—to keep Maude from feeling as she did. From suffering as she had. From making the choices, the mistakes that she had.

Alice's stomach tightened. *But could she?*

"Mama," said Maude patiently. "Do we live here now?"

She forced herself to speak. "Y-Yes, Maudy. This is where we live now."

The three-year-old pondered this for a moment, considering it from all angles, then nodded. "Good."

Alice breathed a laugh. "Good?"

"It's pretty here, and I have a big room," Maude said carefully, as though those were the most important factors at play. "But that man is not here."

Alice's pulse skipped a beat.

She had assumed one single meeting of less than five minutes had been insufficient for William to impact on Maude's memory—but perhaps not.

"*That man.*"

The man she loved. The man she had married. The man she had lost.

How did one explain such things to a child?

"Will he come to live with us, Mama?" Maude's soldiers reached the end of the rug and carefully turned around to process across it once more.

Swallowing hard and hoping to goodness she could do this explanation justice, Alice said hesitantly, "No. No, the man isn't going to live with us. It's just us."

Maude glanced up at her mother. "Why are you sad?"

Slowly, Alice closed her eyes. Just for a moment. Just in an attempt to collect herself.

It could not be that difficult, could it? To calm her lungs, to slow her sense of self down, to center herself so the panicked cry that the world was over and she had lost one of the most important things in it did not escape from her lips.

She couldn't. She wouldn't burden Maudy with that.

"I'm tired," Alice said, opening her eyes and settling on a truth that was not quite an answer. "You know how crotchety you get when you're tired."

"I'm not tired," Maude said automatically, hugging her toy soldiers to her as though they would be plucked from her hand before being made to go to bed. "I'm not—"

"I know you are not, but I am," said Alice wearily, avoiding the argument as best she could. "Would you like a biscuit?"

It was the act of a desperate woman, but she would defy any mother to state they had never bribed a child with a biscuit and still be telling the truth.

Maude jumped up. "Yes!"

"Yes please," Alice corrected automatically.

Her daughter nodded seriously, as though this was a negotiation matter worthy of napoleon. "Yes please biscuit."

Well, she couldn't exactly argue with that.

Alice offered her the plate, and Maude took an inordinate amount of time deciding between two different shapes of shortbread. Her choice made, she scampered back to the rug as though it were "home" in a game of tag, and began munching the biscuit happily. Crumbs flew in all directions.

Try as she might, Alice couldn't stop noticing the mess. The footman who cleaned this room of the Dower House was not going to be endeared by Maude's eating habits.

Perhaps they would write to William, saying the pair of them were a nuisance. Perhaps it would get so bad he would come here—Alice's hopes rose—and talk to her about it, and she could—

No.

Alice forced the thought away. It was a dream, that was all. There was not a chance William would ever come to see her again. They'd had the conversation—or at least, William had had his say and prevented her from truly explaining—and there was no possibility of him wanting to repeat that scene.

Even the letter she had written him had been returned, unanswered. For all she knew, unread.

Just as the thought passed through her mind, the door to the hall opened once more, and the glowering figure of Mrs. Colfer appeared.

"M'lady," she grunted, stepping into the drawing room.

Instinctively, though knowing it was ridiculous of her to do so, Alice rose to her feet and curtsied. "Mrs. Colfer. How nice to—"

"Letter for you," said the older woman with a glare, thrusting it into her hands and immediately returning to the hall. "And keep that child under control."

The door slammed behind her.

Alice looked at her daughter. Maude had crumbs all round her mouth, true, but she was seated on the rug playing with the soldiers in almost complete silence.

Under control, indeed!

Sinking back into the armchair, Alice looked at the letter she had been given. It was not thick, nor large. Perhaps a small piece of paper folded inward and pressed with a red seal. The blob of wax had clearly been firmed down when it was molten, for it had spread out so wide, it almost covered the entirety of that side of the letter.

The emblem within the seal was difficult to spot. An A, perhaps? An L? It could almost be a P, if one turned it the other way.

Alice turned it around again, holding it up to the light. Honestly, it was so dark in here it was probably time she rang for a light. A few candles and she may be able to make it out.

Her hand had actually reached the bellpull by the fireplace when her mind caught up with her.

She hesitated. Would the servants of the Dower House wish to wait on her hand and foot? Perhaps it would be better if she just did what she could in the light she had.

Alice broke the seal. The wax broke into little pieces in her lap, making it impossible to decipher any further. But what did it matter? No one of any real importance would be writing to her. It was probably just a note from Mrs. Ransome at the house in London. Perhaps they found a trunk of hers and wished to inform her it had been sent on.

Yes, that would be it. It would be short and plain and matter of fact. There was no point in getting her hopes up, she thought.

And that was why, when Alice opened up the small piece of paper, she was astonished to find it was not a practical note from Mrs. Ransome or even Mr. Nicholls. It was something else.

For a wild heartbeat, she hoped it was from William.

An apology. An explanation. A love note. A question, even, an attempt to discover more about her, more about Maude.

But the instant her eyes fell across the few short lines, Alice could see it was not from him.

Alice,

I was sorry to hear of the break between you and my brother. Fight for what you want. Fight for what you know is right. I'd keep a look out if I were you. The fight may just be coming to you.

Chance

Alice's eyes widened as she tried to take in the rather vague lines.

That it was from one of the Chance brothers, that much was clear. It was signed Chance, and mentioned a brother who was undoubtedly William.

But which Chance brother had written it, Alice could not tell.

There was no clue in the writing, short as it was, and the seal was destroyed.

She bit her lip as she looked at the remnants of the wax in her lap. *Bother.* That would have been rather useful, in hindsight.

What were the letters she had thought it could be? They had been such passing thoughts, she'd barely paid any attention to them. A? P? D, perhaps? There was an Aylesbury and a Pernrith in the family, but no D—or had she misremembered that?

"Mama, look!"

"Yes, lovely, dear," said Alice vaguely, not looking up from the letter. It was perhaps not the best mothering in the world, but it had been a long day. A long few months. She could be forgiven—

"A carriage!"

"Just be careful with it, dear," Alice said, still examining the letter. "All the toys you play with are borrowed from someone else."

Just like she'd been doing. She had borrowed a snippet of someone else's life, it seemed. The life of a duchess. But it wasn't hers, and she'd had to give it back, just like Maudy would eventually have to give back the toy soldiers.

It wasn't their life. It wasn't theirs to keep.

Alice frowned as she reread the letter.

Fight for what you want. Fight for what you know is right. I'd keep a look out if I were you. The fight may just be coming to you.

Now what on earth did that mean? There was no sense to it, no sense at all. If her brother-in-law, whichever one he was, truly wished to help her, why did he not make his meaning as clear as possible?

Alice gave a slow laugh as she considered the final words.

The fight may just be coming to you.

That would suggest that William would be coming here—but that was impossible. The man had made it quite clear he had absolutely no desire to see her again. Why would he waste his precious time traveling all this way just to see her?

"*There is no us.*"

Alice leaned back in the armchair, the soft cushions welcoming her in as she attempted to understand what the point of this short letter was.

The door to the hall opened.

"She is under control, Mrs. Colfer," said Alice testily without looking up.

"So I see," said a quiet voice that was most definitely not Mrs. Colfer.

Alice rose so rapidly that the letter and all the wax pieces of the seal dropped to the floor. She didn't give them a second glance. How could she when her lungs were tight, her heart beating fast, and before her was—

William. Standing in the doorway. Top hat in his hands.

Chapter Twenty

THE DRIVE HAD been long, and William had been given plenty of time to consider how he would approach this first meeting after such an explosive last meeting, but he hadn't expected this.

Alice had risen swiftly, astonishment in her eyes, and William thought she was going to rush across the room and throw herself into his arms. His whole body had tingled at the expectation.

Oh, to touch Alice again. To have her in his arms, breathe her in, know they were together again—that no matter what, they would find a way through their differences and back to each other.

And Alice had run across the room. But not toward him.

With a pang in his chest that was violent in its grief, William watched as Alice immediately hastened to her daughter, pulling the child behind her as though he would—

The very thought of harming anyone, let alone harming a child, was repellant to him, and William's shoulders drooped as he watched Alice stare back at him defiantly. Had he truly reacted so terribly when the girl—Maude, wasn't it?—had been introduced to him? Did Alice honestly believe he was some sort of danger to her daughter?

Dear God, he had a great deal more ground to cover than he thought.

"Alice," William said, surprised to discover his voice was hoarse. "I . . ."

The speech he had almost perfected melted from his mind. All the words he had carefully chosen, organized in a straight line to make the perfect sentence, they all vanished, leaving him adrift in a sea of words and thoughts and emotions he could barely understand.

A coherent sentence would be wonderful about now, he thought darkly. But looking at her, seeing Alice—she was even more beautiful than he remembered. While his mouth hung open, desperately hoping it would be filled with the speech he had prepared, he just stared, unable to look away.

Every inch of her was Alice. The freckle by her left eye, the way her hair was pinned back yet looked as though at any moment it would cascade once more past her shoulders. The glare in her expression, the pursed lips, the way her hands clung to her daughter.

Hands which had once slipped into his own. Hands which had accepted his ring. Hands which he had considered just as vital as his own, once.

He still did.

William swallowed. All his righteous words, the way he was going to explain himself, make it clear that he was not completely in the wrong, that she had injured him just as he had injured her—it all disappeared.

He had not understood. But he did now.

All he had to do was somehow put all of that understanding into words.

Words, William. Say something, for God's sake!

"Words," William said helplessly at the same time as Alice said, "What are you—"

They both fell silent, the tension and awkwardness in the air so palpable, for a moment he wondered whether that was what was keeping him from Alice's side. Was it even possible to walk through it, push past it, reach her?

It appeared Alice was thinking the same thing—or at least, something similar. She glanced at her daughter, who was blinking owlishly up at him.

William's stomach twisted as he remembered Pernrith's words.

"A child knows when they are not wanted. For a child not truly of the

family to be forced to dwell within it, that is perhaps the crueler choice."

How had he managed to blame an innocent child for this? Maude did not deserve to be pushed aside merely because the circumstances of her birth were not precisely what he had expected. What sort of a man was he, to blame a child for something beyond their control?

Something he would have to discuss with Pernrith at some point. And Aylesbury. And Lindow. *Particularly Lindow.*

"It's the man," Maude said in a loud whisper.

William watched color tinge Alice's cheeks, watched her kneel beside the child with her back to him. As though she could not bear to look at him. As though he were nothing. As though he were not even there.

"It is," said Alice firmly. "He's come to visit his house, and then he'll be going home."

William's heart skipped a painful beat.

Though she had not necessarily spoken the words as an indictment, they certainly felt like one. Come to visit his house, then he'll be going home? Did Alice not know—but then he had been so awful to her the last time they had spoken, she surely did not realize *she* was his home. Her, and nothing else, no one else.

He could not be happy in that townhouse. Rattling around in those rooms, wondering how he'd been such a fool as to lose her—did she honestly think William could keep away?

Maude was peering up over her mother's shoulder. "Why does he have two homes? Does he want us to leave? He's got lots of room, Mama."

William swallowed, hating the truth that spilled from the child's mouth. There was nothing like an inquisitive child to pull you right back to earth.

"Hullo, Maude," he said quietly.

Alice glanced over her shoulder with a glare which could have melted a mountain. "Maude," she said quietly, turning back to her child. "His Grace will be gone in a moment. He obviously came into this room by accident, and—"

"No, I didn't," William said hoarsely.

Damn his voice, why couldn't it speak with any sort of strength?

Alice did not bother to turn around. "He'll be gone, and we will continue to live here, Maudy. This is our home, now, and . . . and we are grateful."

Grateful.

He almost groaned aloud to hear such a word. Dear God, did she think herself beholden to him? How had he managed to destroy what had been between them so utterly?

A scent that had wafted into the hall and was starting to drift into the drawing room gained his attention. And an idea, a foolish idea but one he could not ignore, came to mind.

And this time William did not do what he always did. He did not consider, did not weigh up the pros and cons. He did not consider it from all angles, wondering what damage it could do to the family, to him, to their name. He just acted.

"Maude," he said quietly. The child perked up and met his eyes. "I think Cook is doing some baking in the kitchen. Some gingerbread, by the smell of it. Why don't I ask a maid to take you there so you can try some?"

It had been an innocent suggestion, but clearly there was more distrust between himself and Alice than William had thought.

Alice straightened up, standing tall and keeping her hands on her daughter's shoulders. "I don't think that is a good idea."

There was such panic, such fear on her face, and William could not understand why. It was the kitchen. Surely they had been in there, met Cook, knew everywhere here by now? It was hardly far away.

His confusion was clearly visible, for Alice said stiffly, "It has been made clear to us that we are not to go wandering about. We keep to the dining room and our bedchambers and here. We . . . we don't wish to be in the way."

A flash of anger seared across William, but he did his best to hide it. It was, after all, not their fault.

Had he not left instructions that they were to be well cared for—to feel at home, to be given every luxury which should be afforded to a lady of the family? He would have to have a conversation with Mrs. Colfer before he left.

Though of course the nature of that conversation would depend very much on the one he was about to have with Alice. That he wished to have with Alice.

"I will make it clear that both you and the child are welcome anywhere in this house," William said gruffly. "Anywhere. This is—you should not worry about... Would you like some gingerbread, Maude?"

Apparently he had made another mistake. Alice's face flushed as she muttered, "You don't just offer...."

William swallowed. *This was all going so wrong.*

In his imagination, as he had traveled rapidly from London to the ducal estates, the scene had been quite different. He would storm into the room, Alice would burst into ecstatic tears of happiness, step into his arms, and press her lips to his with muttered delight that he had returned for her.

In truth, Maude hadn't even been in his imagined picture.

Instead...

"No harm will come to her," he said stiffly. "And I would speak with you, Alice."

Alice's glance met his, though clearly reluctantly. Her fingers tightened, just for a moment, on her daughter's shoulders.

Difficult though it was, William forced himself to hold her gaze. He wasn't going to look away any longer, he wasn't going to be the sort of man who could just ignore a problem or try to fix it immediately.

Not that Alice was a problem.

Dear God, he needed to get his words untangled.

"Fine," said Alice, though there was a lack of grace in her tone. "Maude, we will find a maid who can accompany—"

"Mrs. Colfer!" William yelled, turning into the hall.

It was a mark of the housekeeper's skill that she was by his side within seconds—though now he came to think of it, it was probably more likely that she was listening at the door. *Blast.*

"You called, Your Grace?" Mrs. Colfer said, curtsying low.

William nodded. "The child is to be escorted to the kitchen where she can eat anything she—"

"William!"

"Where she is to eat a normal amount of food, not too much, obviously," William hastily corrected, his ears burning at Alice's sharp remonstrance.

Well, what was he to know? How much did a child need to eat—more than an adult? Less? His own youth seemed so long ago, he could barely recall. His plate had always been full, that was all he knew.

Another pang echoed through him. *Had Pernrith known the same?*

"I see," said Mrs. Colfer with pursed lips. "Well. Come on then, child."

Maude skipped forward. Out of the corner of his eye, William thought he spotted Alice's fingers leaving her daughter's shoulder at the very last moment.

What was it like, to have a part of yourself wandering about the place, fearing all the time that they would come to harm? If it was half the depth of concern he felt for Alice . . .

With the child happily chattering away and Mrs. Colfer shepherding her toward the servants' corridor, William finally did what he had intended to do the moment he had seen Alice.

He stepped fully into the drawing room. And then he shut the door.

Alice spoke at once. "You did not have to come here—I would have been perfectly happy to provide a written report of our occupancy, if you had required it."

And William deflated. "You . . . you don't want to see me?"

The thought hadn't even occurred to him. His desperation to see Alice had been so potent, the idea that she might not wish to see him had never crossed his mind.

A dark flush had tinged her cheeks. "Of—of course, but—"

"I wanted to see you," William said quietly, stepping closer into the room.

It was a good sign, he thought, that Alice did not immediately rush away. Or was it? She was a woman who stood her ground. It was one of the things he admired about her. One of the many things.

There was a scrap of paper and what appeared to be red . . . red something on the floor where she had been sitting. Just for a flickering moment, he wondered what it was.

"What do you want?"

William's attention was immediately pulled back to Alice, who had folded her hands before her, fingers twisting together.

How was one supposed to melt away all this pain, this anger, this regret?

Try as he might, no matter how many different scenarios he considered in his exhausted mind, William could not conceive of a way to do it.

He could try to understand—but it had been his brothers of all people who had helped him to a better understanding of the woman he purported to love.

He could try to explain—though how he would explain, and what precisely he would say was a mystery. How did one excuse poor conduct? How did a gentleman reveal he had been wrong, that everything he had attempted to do had backfired so spectacularly?

He could try to apologize. That perhaps was the safest way to begin, but William wasn't entirely sure if he would be able to stop apologizing once he started.

I am sorry for throwing you out of my home.

I am sorry for not welcoming your child.

I am sorry for not listening to you, not believing you, not loving you as I should . . .

"What do you want, William?" Alice repeated her question in clipped tones, her frown sharp.

And William replied in the only way he knew how. "You."

A flush tinged her cheeks, creeping down her neck toward her décolletage, which William was most determinedly not looking at. Much. "I think you have made it perfectly clear that you do not. Why else would I be here?"

The clarity and accuracy of her words was painful, but William allowed himself to feel the pain. He deserved to feel this—this guilt, this remorse, it was good. It showed him he was learning . . . didn't it?

"I was wrong to speak so rashly," he said quietly. "It is one of the parts—one of the many parts—of myself that I am always trying to hide. To push away."

Alice's flush darkened, and William wondered whether she was thinking the same thing he was. That the other part of him that he had revealed to her that he so often wished to hide was his desire. For her.

Well, she had not stormed from the room, called him a brute, or cried. That was something, wasn't it?

"I was wrong," said William quietly, taking a hesitant step forward, "to judge you."

It wasn't enough, but it was a start—and it may be all he'd be able to say, as Alice launched into, "You judged me poorly, and you did not even let me explain—"

"I know, and I am sorry," he began, seeing a ray of light. If they could just apologize to each other . . . "I should never have—"

"Have you really come all this way to speak over me?" Alice snapped.

William opened his mouth to retort, to defend . . . then let the excuses fade away.

She was right. Perhaps his brothers were even more right than they had known. Perhaps he was so good at speaking over people, deciding their fates for them, fighting for their chance to be something they did not want, he had almost forgotten how to have a conversation.

It was a worrying thought.

"Please," William said, spreading his arms out in a gesture of goodwill. "Tell me, then. I . . . I want to know."

The truth about Maude, about why Alice had been blackmailed, he needed to know. Even if it hurt. Especially then, for it was a hurt that she had carried all alone.

For a moment, Alice was clearly astonished she was going to have her own say. In a heartbeat, however, she had collected herself. "I told you, that . . . that day that Maude arrived. I told you she was not illegitimate."

William's jaw tightened. *He did not like being lied to.* "Yes, but I do not—"

"I was married," Alice said quietly. "Before you, I mean."

It was a good thing there was a sofa just to his left, for upon hearing such words, he was rather in need of a sit down.

Half sitting, half falling, William dropped onto the sofa without taking his eyes from Alice. "Married."

"Married," Alice repeated softly.

Married. It had not even occurred to him. Married? Alice?

So Maude . . . she was not illegitimate, then? Just as Alice had protested. But why lie—why keep this a secret?

Alice cleared her throat. "There is not much to tell. I thought he loved me, and I certainly believed myself in love. It was an infatuation. I see that now."

Her gray eyes met his and William's heart stuttered. Did she know that now because of what they had—because of what she felt for him?

"By the time I realized that I was just a tup, I was with child." Alice spoke with a calm finality that suggested little love had truly been lost between them. "He offered—he agreed, I suppose I should say—to marry me. We were married. He died a week later."

William's eyes widened. "He died—"

"A hunting accident," Alice said quietly. "I hardly knew whether I was coming or going, the pregnancy . . . I don't know what the family did with the marriage certificate. They wouldn't give it to me, none of Mark's estate came to me. It was easiest for them, you see, if his younger brother inherited without any . . . complications."

Complications. "Like if you had a son."

"Perhaps if they had known it was a Maude, and not a Matthew, they would not have acted so callously." Alice spoke with a finality that was painful to William's ear. *How long had she suffered? Been alone, faced the stigma of illegitimacy without the true cause?* "A year ago, that brother, Mr. Shenton, found me. He . . . he blackmailed me. Extorted me, I suppose. Said he required money, that I could buy back the marriage certificate and certain letters which, if released, would make it seem . . . He threatened to take Maudy away from me, to make her part of his family, to tear my very heart from my chest! And I thought . . . I thought . . ."

William sank back into the sofa.

It was all so clear now. She thought that if she could buy back her marriage certificate, she could prove her marriage—prove that her child was legitimate.

"But you didn't have any money," he said quietly.

It was obvious, with the beauty of hindsight and a few additional facts.

Alice's smile was pained. "I needed money, and I would not consider—marriage was my only option. I arrived in London with a month's worth of coin and a determination to find a husband before he—"

"What did he want? Other than money, I mean, and Maudy," William asked sharply.

She met his gaze. The answer was apparent, even in the silence.

William swore under his breath.

"I never intended to lie to you," Alice said, taking hurried steps toward him and sitting unexpectedly beside him. "I just . . . I avoided the truth as best I could. I never thought—"

"I would see that letter."

It was difficult to concentrate now she was seated so close to him. Just a few inches separated them, and Alice's presence had always been a mild intoxicant, even when he was furious with her.

Right now, he was furious with himself.

Alice had never asked him for money. She must have planned to use her pin money to pay off this Shenton blackguard, then to support the child. Her child. Maude.

And he'd had to go and shout at her, berate her for something completely beyond her control. And send her away.

"Well, you're a Chance now," he said stiffly. "No one can hurt you."

"I paid Mr. Shenton off the day after we were married," Alice said softly. "You gave me five pounds for a bonnet. Five pounds! Riches, riches I could never—but anyway. I bought a bonnet for fifteen shillings and sent the rest to Mr. Shenton. My final payment. His letter arrived the day before Maude did."

William's hopes sank. "And?"

"He never had the marriage certificate, of course. Or any letters. I don't know why I hadn't thought of it sooner. I was a fool, I was afraid—"

"Well, he can't hurt you now," William said, reaching out and taking her hand. She did not pull away. "And when we're back in London—"

She pulled her hand away. "Back in . . . why would you take me back to London?"

William steeled himself to say what he knew he must. It was hard to be so open, so vulnerable. But she was worth it. They both were.

"Alice," he said quietly. "I . . . I have been so blind, so wrong. I was so worried about fighting off Society's expectations that I forgot what I wanted. What was worth fighting for, what was worth loving."

He heard Alice's sudden gasp, but he could not heed it, could not slow down. The words were spilling out from him, and they were not the careful, prepared speech he had curated so elegantly. They were just the truth, pouring from him.

"And I am in love with you, and I'm lost without you," William said with a cracked smile. "I never thought I would—I don't know what to do without you. And I'm sorry, and I want to learn, I want to be a better husband to you . . . and a father to Maude, if you'll let me."

Alice's face was a picture of astonishment, and William could not tell if that was in wonder and joy or disgust and rejection.

"Please. Please, come back with me."

She swallowed, glanced at their hands, entwined, and murmured, "You . . . you really want me?"

And that was when William lost all self-control.

Perhaps it was the fact that they were talking on a sofa, just as they had been when they had first started to make love. Perhaps it was being so close to her, breathing her in, feeling her soft fingers in his. Perhaps it was just sheer nervous exhaustion.

Whatever it was, William leaned forward and kissed Alice hard on the mouth.

His longing for her was unbidden, unrestrained, but it was her response that made William moan with relief.

Her response was just as ardent as his own. Alice pulled him closer, her lips nibbling along his own before she parted them with her tongue, and her whimper of delight shot eager hunger through William's body as he had never known before.

When the kiss finally ended, they were both panting, Alice's hair was half undone, and William had a rather uncomfortable pressure in his breeches.

"Well," Alice said with a laugh, her fingers trailing through his hair before cupping his face. "I suppose I cannot argue with that."

Epilogue

July 1, 1812

A LICE KNEW THE lump was going to come to her throat the moment she glanced up. But it came, nonetheless.

"Look, Mama, look!"

Her daughter. Her beautiful, passionate, eager daughter. Her child. Happy and safe and dancing in the sunshine in a gown that actually fit.

Alice clapped. "Well done, my darling!"

The lawns of Stanphrey Lacey were extensive, and so was the great number of large oak and beech trees which had clearly been planted by some Duke of Cothrom long ago. Their branches stretched out to the sky, creating some much-needed shade for Maude to play in.

At the moment, her preferred game was dancing for whatever audience she could find.

Alice suppressed a grin.

"Look, Mama!"

"I'm looking," said Alice hastily, picking an apple from the picnic basket and biting into it as the little girl with blonde curls so like her own danced about. "In the shade, please, Maude."

Maude danced along the edge of the shade, keeping just to the line but suggesting that at any moment she could slip into the sun.

Alice's smile broadened. *They were definitely two of a kind.*

As her daughter continued to chatter away to herself, dancing all the while, Alice glanced over her shoulder at the beautiful manor house which was now their home. He had promised he would join them as soon as possible. Surely his business for the estate could not take long.

"Mama!"

"Yes, yes, I'm looking," Alice said hastily, looking back.

No matter how important his business was, she knew William would be with them as soon as he could. He was the doting father Maude deserved—deserved and had never known.

It was strange to think, in the gentle quiet of this English garden, birds singing, and a gardener in the distance carefully cutting roses for the vases of the many rooms, that just a few months ago her life had been dominated by loneliness and fear.

Alice's smile did not falter. She could think about it now which calm and equanimity.

Because she had done it—gone from harlot to widow to unwed mother to duchess. And she had managed to do so with the love of a man who was incomparable, giving her everything that she could have ever wanted.

And more.

Happiness. Peace. A sense she had finally found her place in the world.

And all that remained was to tell him—

"There you are," said a cheerful, deep voice. "Ah, Maudy, excellent dancing!"

And Alice's heart soared.

What had she done to deserve such happiness? Every particle of her being rejoiced as she saw William stride across the lawn, jacket gone, shirt sleeves rolled up, a grin across his face as he beheld her and her daughter.

She did not deserve him. They did not deserve him.

And despite all that, here they were. Blissfully happy. About to be happier.

"Goodness, I thought reviewing those ledgers would never end," said William with a groan, dropping down onto the blanket which Alice had placed near the trunk of the old beech. "I honestly thought Nicholls was going to keep me there for the rest of my days."

Alice giggled and offered him the basket. "You know, I do like to hear you exaggerate. It's good practice."

"Practice?" repeated William, a frown curving across his brow. "Practice for what?"

"For an extravagant career on the stage," Alice said solemnly, then burst into laughter again at her husband's expression. "For life, of course! You think I like to see you all tied in knots over propriety or the right way to do everything?"

William chuckled, shaking his head as he leaned back on an elbow and looked up with frank admiration. "You do know I'm besotted with you, don't you?"

Alice's stomach lurched, and she placed a hand on it. "Yes. Yes, I do."

And that was just one of the things that didn't make any sense. Here she was, a liar, a woman who had allowed herself to be seduced, a mother of a child stained with false illegitimacy, a charmer, a schemer...

And he loved her. William Chance, Duke of Cothrom, loved her.

Alice swallowed. *She was not going to cry. Probably.* "You said, at breakfast, you had something to discuss." That was it. Conversation. Calm, rational conversation.

William's eyes lit up. "Yes! Yes, I do."

He stuffed his hand into a waistcoat pocket and pulled out what appeared to be a letter, which Alice peered at curiously. When her husband unfolded it, however, he snorted with distaste.

"William?"

"Wrong letter," he muttered, shoving it back in his pocket.

"Who was it—"

"Aylesbury," William said darkly. "I've given that man too many second chances."

Alice hesitated. Never having had a brother, nor any sibling, William's relationship with his three brothers was something she was still learning about. "What has he done this time?"

Her husband sighed. "It's more what he hasn't done—or rather, how much money he has lost. It's that he never learns, that's the rub!"

There was tension in the man's voice Alice only ever heard when her husband was speaking of one of his brothers. Any of them, to tell the truth. They were as bad as each other. Except for Pernrith, of course, who couldn't help how he'd been born.

"That's it. He's cut off, I can't keep bailing him out."

Alice bit her lip. It was probably too early, far too early in their marriage for her to say such a thing, but . . . "Second chances can be powerful. If you could just—"

"He's had enough of them, trust me," William said bitterly, rummaging in his other pocket. "Ah, here we are. There."

He said the last word as though he were presenting her with a diamond.

As far as Alice could see, it wasn't a diamond. It was another letter. "For me?"

"To me, for you to read," William said, and there was a hint of excitement edging every word. "Go on. Read it."

Not entirely sure what to expect from the anticipation on William's face, Alice placed the apple core down and took the letter from him.

It was folded several times, and when she had unfolded it, it was to see a bold, large hand which had written a few short paragraphs.

Your Grace,

The process itself is simple, and I have taken the liberty of beginning to arrange the necessaries from here, in London.

As the guardian is likely to give permission, we do not believe the process will be an overly long one. In fact, by the time you receive this letter, I think it would be appropriate for the girl to be titled Lady Maude Chance at your earliest convenience.

All particulars and a few documents to sign will be couriered to you by one of our men before the end of the summer.

I remain yours respectfully,
Parker, Bells, and Hamble

Alice had to read it again, her pulse thundering in her ears.

In fact, by the time you receive this letter, I think it would be appropriate for the girl to be titled Lady Maude Chance at your earliest convenience.

Lady Maude Chance.

"You . . . you haven't . . ."

"I told you, when we were wed, that I would honor you and love you and respect you," William said quietly, gazing up from where he was leaning on the blanket. "Maude . . . she's a part of you. A part of your life."

"A part of my past," Alice said fiercely, trying desperately to hold back tears. "My mistakes, my—"

"Without her existence, we would not be together now," William said softly. "Would we?"

Alice blinked back the tears still threatening to fall as her lungs tightened with suppressed emotion.

No, she supposed not. It was only the need to protect Maude, to ensure she had a future, that had driven her to London in search of a husband. It was because of Maude that she had made that desperate attempt to gain access to the Earl of Chester's ball. Because of Maude that she had been so relieved, so delighted, to have caught a duke's eye.

She had wanted to give her child a fighting chance for a future. Now Maude had one. One Alice could never have dreamt of.

"You would give my child your name?" Alice murmured, astonishment dripping from every syllable.

William nodded slowly. "My name, everything. She'll have a dowry when she needs it, the best education when she's older... Alice, she'll be my daughter. She is mine, if... if you will consent to it."

Alice almost laughed, though it came out as a splutter. "If I—you have already—I don't know what to—"

"I know I probably rushed into things a bit, getting Parker, Bells, and Hamble to start the adoption paperwork," William said hastily.

A tear finally fell. Alice brushed it away. "We are rather in the habit of rushing, aren't we?"

"Miss Fox-Edwards, will you marry me?"

"You don't know anything about me."

William's expression warmed Alice in a way nothing else ever could. "Perhaps. But I know what I want, Alice, and it's you. You and Maude. In my life."

Alice swallowed, glancing over at her daughter. Their daughter.

Miss McCall had come out of the house and was shepherding her charge away for her afternoon nap. A habit Maude would soon grow out of. She would grow into this place, into Stanphrey Lacey. This would be her home. She would probably recall nothing else.

And she had a name that would protect her for the rest of her life.

"It's... you are everything I could ever have wanted," Alice breathed, turning back to the man she loved. "And more. You... you did not have to—"

"Yes, I did," William said fiercely. "And not because it was the right thing to do, even though it was."

Alice smiled through her tears and reached out her hand. William took it, squeezed her fingers, brushed her palm with his thumb.

It was the sort of man he was. A principled man, an honorable one. She had seen this in him from the start, though she had not understood him as much when they'd first met as she did now. And she presumed she would continue to deepen this knowledge, this affection for him, over the years.

Years. Years and years with this man she adored.

"But even if it wasn't the correct thing to do, I would have wanted to do it," William was saying determinedly. "She's . . . she's a part of you. In just the last few weeks I have grown to love Maude, love her like she was my very own. And now she will be."

Alice swallowed back all the questions that rose in her mind. Questions probably best left unasked.

As it turned out, William could just as easily read his wife's mind as she could read his.

"She won't be any different to any other Chances," William said quietly. "I mean, any of our future children. If . . . if we have any, of course. I suppose we cannot assume—"

He kept talking. Alice was certain he did, but a rush of noise in her ears prevented her from hearing his words.

Was this the time?

It felt right. There was no one else around, no one to spoil or interrupt their happiness. All other secrets were out in the open, there was nothing else to hold back. No reason not to be completely open.

"—and . . . Alice, are you listening?"

Alice blinked. "Yes. No, sorry."

William snorted with laughter. "Well, that's honest, I suppose."

"I wasn't listening," Alice said hesitantly, "because . . . because of something you just said."

A frown creased his brow. "What did I say?"

"About . . ." *Come on now, this was ridiculous, she had no reason to hold back.* "About future children."

William stared for a moment, then his face became serious as he sat up, still holding her hand. "My love—look, if we are not blessed in that quarter, goodness knows I would never blame . . . Maude is more than enough, if we have her—"

"I don't think that's going to be the problem," said Alice quietly.

For an instant, it appeared William did not quite understand what she was saying. "Not . . . not the problem?"

Hoping to goodness she was about to receive the reaction she hoped for, Alice shook her head. "No. No, in fact . . . in fact I would say that we have quite the opposite situation. Right . . . right now."

William's eyes widened, and his gaze dropped to her stomach. "Right now?"

His voice was barely a whisper.

Alice nodded.

And then she was being crushed, pulled into an embrace of laughter that was mirrored by the adoring touch of William's hands around her waist. And they were falling, tangled together on the blanket, Alice's squeals and William's laughter mingling in the hot summer air, and there was nothing better.

Nothing else like this.

Alice propped herself up on William's chest and grinned. "Surprise."

"Surprise indeed!" he said with a laugh. "Oh, Alice—truly? You are sure, you are with child?"

"As certain as I can be," she confided, smiling almost bashfully as she spoke so openly. "My flux has not come since we . . . well. I shall have to ask for a doctor to—"

She could not continue. William's lips had met hers in a reverential kiss that swiftly became very irreverent indeed.

"I do love you, you know," Alice said as the kiss ended, through William's nuzzling of her neck, sparks of pleasure starting to soar through her, down to her thighs, building an ache between them that was most scandalous. "But William, we can't, not here—"

"Why not?" William growled, his fingers already pulling her skirts up from her ankles. "This is my house, my garden, why shouldn't I ravish my wife here?"

And a thrill of dark delight soared through Alice. "You know, for all your talk about trying to give your family a fighting chance because of your brothers' bad behavior, I think you're the wild one."

"Perhaps," said William with a wicked grin. "Why don't you let me prove it?"

And she did.

A short letter from the author

Hello! Thank you so much for reading *A Fighting Chance,* the first novel in my Chances series. I truly hope you enjoyed it and fell in love with William and Alice just as much as I did.

I've always wanted to write a series of brothers, but I could never 'meet' the characters that were quite right. After waiting years to meet them myself, I have had a lot of fun writing the four Chance brothers—and I think Aylesbury, Lindow, and Pernrith's stories are going to be just as much fun.

Being an author can be a lonely business but knowing that there are readers from all over the world who are going to adore my stories makes it all worthwhile. Thank you for your support, and I hope you love reading more of my books!

Happy reading,
Emily

About Emily E K Murdoch

If you love falling in love, then you've come to the right place.

I am a historian and writer and have a varied career to date: from examining medieval manuscripts to designing museum exhibitions, to working as a researcher for the BBC to working for the National Trust.

My books range from England 1050 to Texas 1848, and I can't wait for you to fall in love with my heroes and heroines!

Follow me on twitter and instagram @emilyekmurdoch, find me on facebook at facebook.com/theemilyekmurdoch, and read my blog at www.emilyekmurdoch.com.

Made in the USA
Middletown, DE
21 July 2024